ANCIENT MAGIC

LUNA PIERCE

Ancient Magic

HARPER SHADOW ACADEMY: BOOK FOUR

LUNA PIERCE

Alt Book Cover Design by EmCat Designs
Book Cover Design by Mibl Art
Editing by https://studioenp.com
Editing by Cruel Ink Editing
Proofing by Tiffany Hernandez
Formatted by EmCat Designs
First Edition 2020
ISBN 978-1-7332322-6-5 (paperback)
ISBN 978-1-957238-15-9 (alt paperback)
ASIN B08HPRBS1X (ebook)

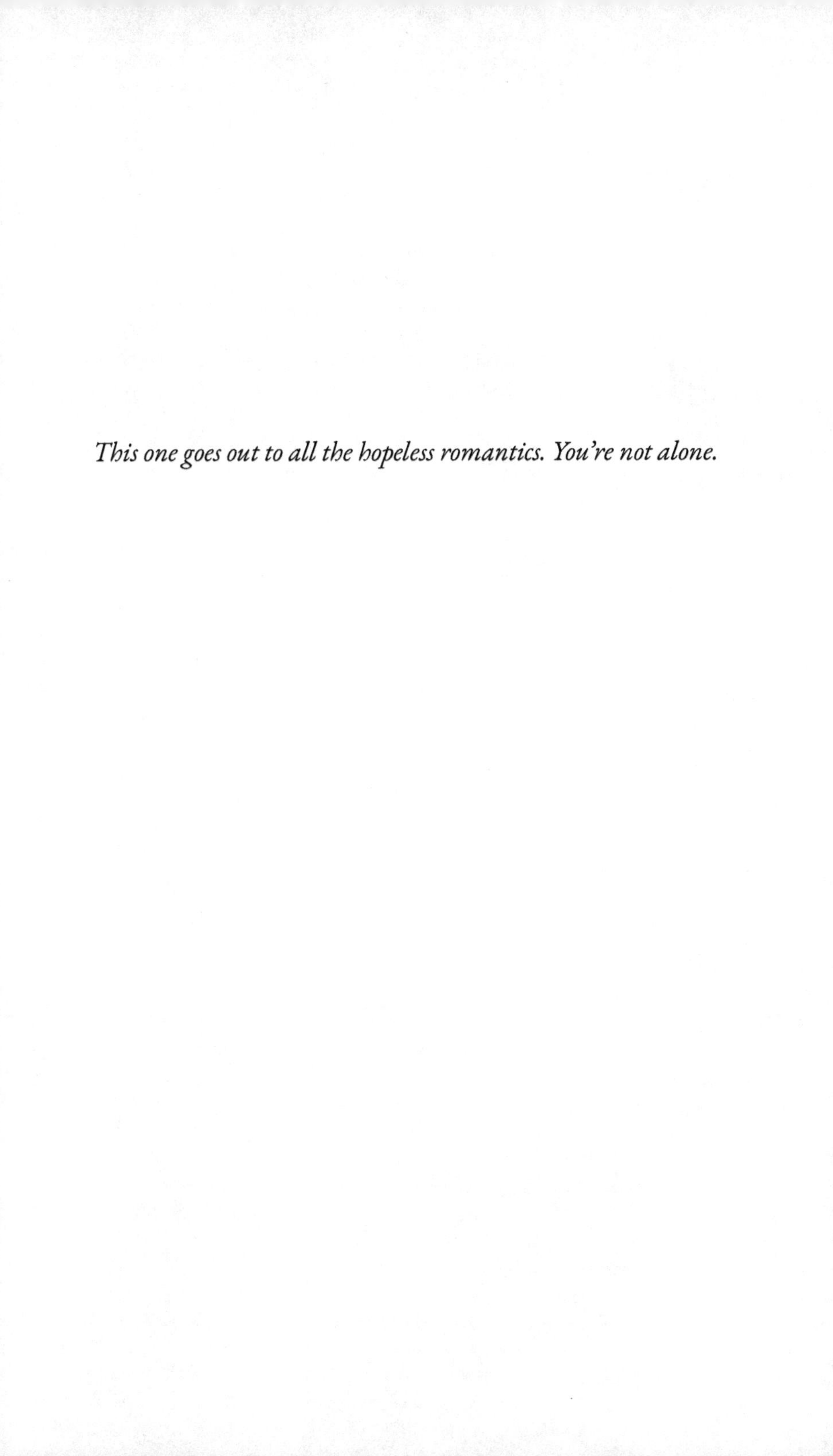

This one goes out to all the hopeless romantics. You're not alone.

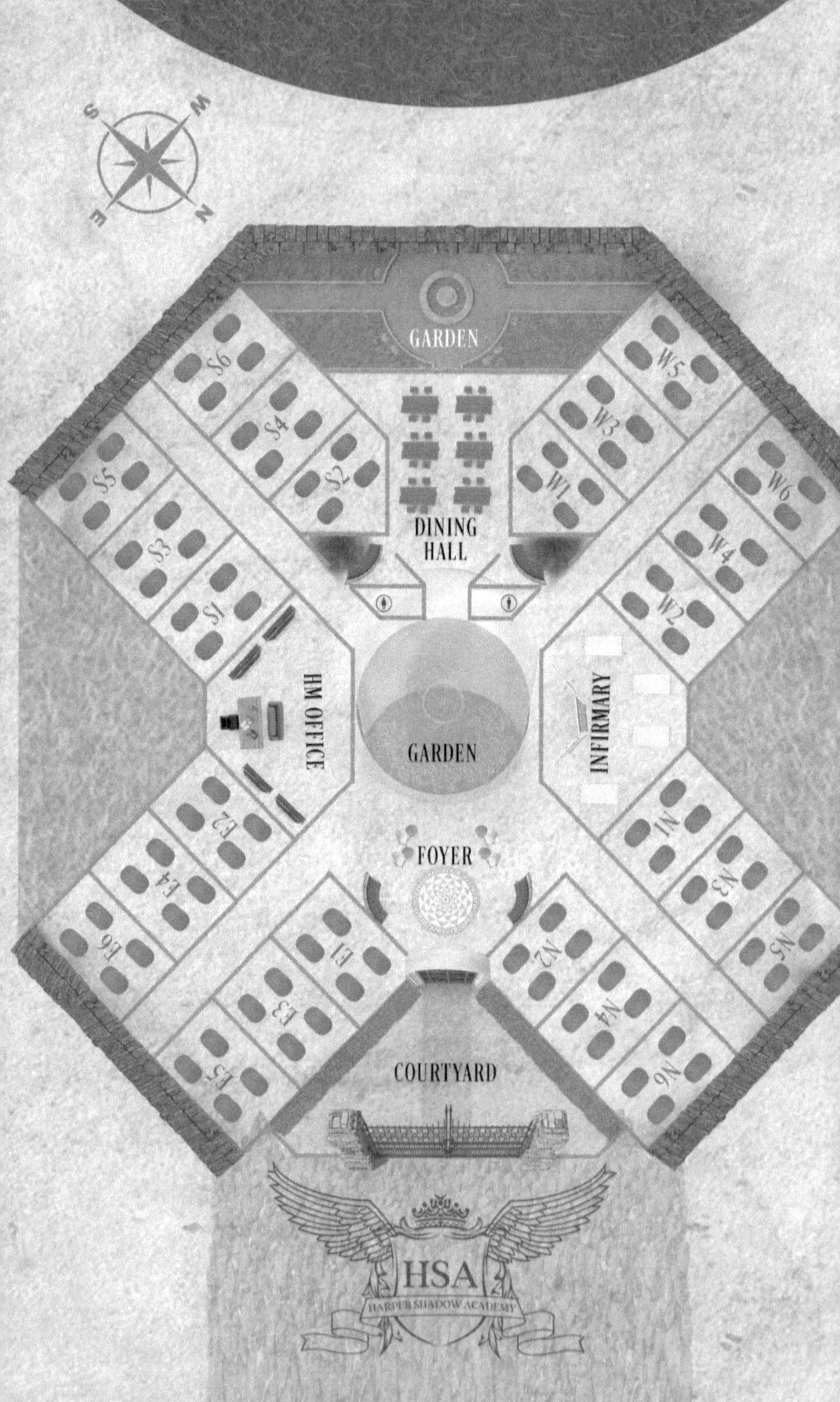

GARDEN
S6
S4
S2
S5
S3
S1
W5
W3
W1
W6
W4
W2
DINING HALL
HM OFFICE
GARDEN
INFIRMARY
N1
N3
N5
E2
E4
E6
FOYER
E1
E3
E5
N2
N4
N6
COURTYARD
HSA
HARPER SHADOW ACADEMY
S
W
E
N

BASEMENT/ LIBRARY

PROLOGUE

I am drowning in a sea of despair.
Sadness.
Agony.
Utter pain.
The ultimate suffering.

Heartache.

I am lost with no hope of return.
There is no time here, just an endless loop of aching in my chest. In my soul.

. . . .

"Willow, it's Mom...can you hear me?"

I think I nod, but I can't really be sure.

"Honey, I'll try again tomorrow." Footsteps pitter-patter across the creaky floorboards before a door slowly closes.

"Princess." Deghan smooths my hair out of my face. "I'm right here if you need me."

"She needs to eat," Cameron whispers.

I have no strength to get up, to tell them I'm okay, that I'm not hungry. Although, I'd be lying about one of the two. So instead, I lie here, waiting for the dull ache in my heart to subside.

Another set of murmurs tell me that my friends believe they're out of reach.

"He broke up with her? You mean he just left? What a fucking prick..."

"It's more complicated than that," Cam confirms.

"Is she okay?" Remi asks. "Shouldn't we like, do something?"

"She just needs some time." Cameron's energy flutters over to me—helpless.

Burning, melting flesh. Flames ripping and cascading over my arms, licking their way across my body. I hover on the hard, dirty ground, unwilling to go on. The nightmare plays on repeat but never gets any easier to experience.

Sometimes, I wake to the sound of crying, only to realize the hysterical sobs are coming from within. My emotions are a mess. I am ruined. I am terrified of the shell of a human I have become. I no longer recognize myself, and I no longer care to try.

· · ·

"Honey, it's Mom. I thought maybe we could talk...about what happened. What you did for our family. Your dad...he's home. He'd love to meet you, whenever you're ready."

My eyes stay glued shut, my legs still pulled into the fetal position. The blanket tucked neatly in place, cocooning me. I don't dare move. I don't dare face the world.

"Maybe tomorrow."

But she doesn't come the next day. That was her last visit. Because she understands what it's like to lose the man you'd die for. The one whose core is intertwined with your own. Sudden and abrupt and earth-shattering.

I relive the moment over and over. Such sweet relief, opening my eyes to see that stupid bitch of a demonic witch gone, followed by something almost impossible to explain. Imagine something that is a part of your life, that is connected so deeply to your soul, vanishing along with the person you were so quick to eradicate from the world. Like losing your vision or your ability to walk. Something so rooted in your being, that without it, living is possible but unbearable.

I lost him. And with that, the tether linking our souls is severed.

I try and try and try and try to find him. Desperately searching every inch of this world for a trace of him. But there's nothing.

He is gone.

And without him, I am no more.

CHAPTER 1

I may have lied about knowing what to do.

Silas is gone. And I have no fucking clue how to bring him back.

I can't wrap my head around what happened, let alone the intricate details of his return—if that's even possible.

The more I process the events, the stronger the realization is: I may be holding on to false hope. A future that doesn't exist.

That alone kills me over and over again.

How can I live in a world without Silas?

The words he uttered not too long ago, about not being able to go on without me, cling to my very core and push my mind into a deeper darkness that consumes me from within.

He, an immortal being who is meant to live infinitely, was

ready to end his life in order to never live a moment without me. And here I am, stuck in a world I never imagined without him.

It shouldn't have happened this way.

Silas was supposed to always be here. To be by my side and protect and love and cherish me for the rest of time. He was going to continue to let me break down his walls and love him despite how much he hated himself at times. Even Cameron and Deghan made progress with getting Silas to warm up to them.

And Sydney.

Watching the way they interacted at first, I never would have imagined the two of them ever coming together for anything, but somehow, they put their differences aside, time and time again, to do what was best for our little group.

And now he's gone.

Not just dead, but literally fucking *poof*, disappeared straight into thin air.

My mind flashes to that moment the angels guided me. The beautiful creature had assured me that I was doing the right thing, and that those responsible would meet a fate worse than the end.

A fiery inferno blipped across my vision, and I followed along with their every request.

And with that, I lost Silas.

The one thing that ever truly made sense.

The other half of my broken soul.

I would trade anything to have him back.

I'd give up all the magic in the world to see him once more.

But that isn't an option and it never will be. He's gone, and I have to come to terms with the fact that I made the biggest sacrifice of my life when I broke the Oliver curse. I freed my bloodline, and now I'm left with this empty pit in my chest where Silas used to be.

I ache. My entire body hurts, and it feels like I've been hit by a truck. My heart constricts at times and makes me think it's quite literally breaking. I can barely eat. I have had no appetite. No will to live. Breathing doesn't even seem worth the effort anymore. If I had to pick one word to describe how I feel, I'd choose broken.

Utterly, irreparably broken.

And with that, I can't help but be ashamed of my reaction.

I have friends who need me and schoolwork that screams to be completed. There are three guys who would simply do anything to erase even a tiny bit of my pain.

It's even difficult to be happy about the return of my mother and the incredible realness of having an actual father. One who was run out of town a long, long time ago, only to return once I rid us of the curse that plagued our family.

I might have completely lost my mind had it not been for my mom bursting through the door to my college dorm. Granted, I didn't exactly hold it together very well when I collapsed into her arms.

A knock rattles my door, which creaks open.

My attempt at pretending to be asleep fails miserably.

Lillian peeks her head inside, and we make eye contact.

"Can I come in?" she asks shyly but doesn't wait for a response.

I sit up and scoot back against the headboard.

"I brought you a muffin." Lills holds out a brown paper sack and sets it on my nightstand next to the other two identical untouched bags. "And a coffee." This time, she hands the item directly to me.

So what if I'm basically living off of caffeine and the occasional peer-pressured meal?

I pop the plastic tab and inhale the bitter roast. Sydney must have opted for espresso today.

"It's been two weeks. I promised myself I would give you fourteen days to grieve, and then I was going to intervene. I'm not saying you have to be okay, but Willow...you can't just forfeit your life because Silas left." Her words are meant to be kind but end up slicing my heart in two.

Because of the *strange* situation, the girls are under the

impression that Silas decided to leave. On his own. They think I'm over here being all distraught because my boyfriend broke up with me.

Little do they know, he was *taken* from this world abruptly with no chance to say goodbye. Every day I'm wrecked with the memory of opening my eyes and not finding him standing in that circle with us. A crater opened up inside me and continues to grow with each passing moment of his absence. It's infinite and debilitating, and I don't think I'll ever be able to truly make anyone comprehend how *empty* I am without him.

It's not normal.

I would have been thrilled to have Silas choose to leave and break up with me instead of the very unbelievable reality I'm forced to face.

At least then I would have some type of closure and finality other than him vanishing from my life altogether.

I could have told him bye. I could have begged him for one last embrace to ease the pain of a life without him.

But instead, I'm stuck with this haunting ghost of him that reminds me of how fucking cruel this world is and how *nothing* will ever be the same.

"Wills, are you listening to me?" Lillian nudges my shoulder gently. "Come on." She takes hold of my hand. "Let's start with a shower. Anything to get you out of this bed."

She crinkles her nose at the well-worn sheets.

Another thing I haven't been able to make myself do—wash them.

With the scent of Silas still lingering, the thought of rinsing that out of my life seems an impossible task. I hold on to every last scrap of him left in this world out of fear that once all these little things are no more, then he really will be, too.

Despite damn well knowing the excruciating truth.

Silas is already gone.

"I thought we could dive back into your coursework. Get you caught up. No sense in having to repeat the term and fall any further behind. Everyone has agreed to do their part in helping you get back on track." She hesitates, and it doesn't take much to figure out why.

I share each of my classes with at least one of the guys or girls.

All of which can be accounted for—except speech. That was the one class I had with Silas.

Such a little declaration and acknowledgment nearly takes the breath from my chest. It's everything I can do to maintain my composure in front of Lillian. I dig my fingernails into the palm of my hand to ground myself and disallow the sadness from bubbling up on the outside.

It's enough that she thinks I'm crazy over a boy who disappeared, I don't need to further prove her right.

If only she knew the truth. But that's not something I'm permitted to do.

I'm already disallowed from telling any non-supernatural student about the shadow realm or the supernatural world, so telling my best friend that my vampire boyfriend was sucked into the abyss by an ancient magic taught to me by an angel who helped me break a forever-long curse on my family—who happens to be full of powerful witches—isn't exactly permissible either.

And that really, really sucks.

I lean against the counter in the bathroom with my arms folded across my chest. Getting out of bed is nowhere close to what I want to be doing, but I really could use a shower. I'm not sure how long it's actually been. Was it yesterday? The day prior? A week ago? I've lost control over the concept of time in my period of utter sorrow.

The door to my room opens and closes, and a second later, Deghan pops his head into the bathroom. His kind, warm eyes meet mine.

My heart constricts, and I find myself drawn to his comfort.

"Hey, little one." He waltzes in without asking permission. Not that he needs it anyway.

I let myself melt into his embrace.

"Think you can coax this one into getting in?" Lillian reaches in to test the temperature of the running water and looks at Deghan.

He rubs circles on my back and holds me tight. "I can handle that."

"I'll be back in an hour. I want her showered, fed, and ready to tackle some statistics," Lills barks off her demands and heads to the door. "I'm serious."

Despite being so consumed with my sadness, having her in my life when I had once thought I'd lost her forever is nothing shy of wonderful. To watch her be concerned about me is a welcome reminder of what I have left in this life. Her friendship is absolutely irreplaceable.

She pulls the latch to the bathroom shut, leaving me and Deghan behind.

"All right, you heard the woman." Deghan gently breaks his body away from mine. He grips my face between his hands and glides his thumbs along my cheeks before pressing a soft kiss to my forehead.

My arms dangle limply at my sides. I catch a glimpse of my pathetic reflection in the mirror. Dark bags under my eyes from the insomnia, unruly hair from the constant tossing and turning, sunken cheeks from the rather rapid weight loss due to being unable to stomach any amount of food.

All the while, a different and powerful magic courses through my veins, and it's everything I can do to keep it contained. It's like I'm bursting at the seams.

And I want nothing to do with it. I couldn't care less about magic in a world without Silas. Call me foolish, but being the reason one of the people you love the most in this world is gone forever isn't something that exactly makes you very proud of what you are. Especially when using my abilities is what took him from me in the first place. If I had never come to this stupid school, I wouldn't have found out I was a witch and Silas would be here, safe and sound.

Sure, I might never have met him, but that's a sacrifice I would make to bring him back.

"Can I help you?" Deghan tucks a strand of hair behind my ear.

I nod and let him lift my shirt over my head.

A moment and a few articles of clothing later, he guides me into the shower.

I stand there without moving, letting the almost too-warm water pummel me. It's pathetic that the simple task of taking a shower can be so difficult.

"Will?" Deghan speaks from outside the curtain.

I turn to him with tears filling my eyes. My lip quivers, and I bite the inside of my cheek to try to stop myself from losing it.

Deghan's face hardens and softens all at once.

I don't mean to put this on all of them. I feel horrible about showing my emotions, but I don't know how else to handle the all-consuming agony slicing me apart. It's not like I can block them out completely. None of them would allow that to happen. Although I wouldn't blame them for closing me out when I've clearly shut down myself.

CHAPTER 2

"What do you think about going to class tomorrow?" Lillian stares at me from over her *Intro to Management* book. Her gaze penetrates me while she waits for my response.

I shrug. "I should probably retake the term. I'm already super behind. There's no way I can dig myself out of statistics." A chill snakes its way over my body at the memory of my sadistic teacher.

No one knows where he went, but he didn't vanish into thin air like Sydney's parents and Silas. Tremont fled. He ran. Fast and far and using some kind of magical abilities to help him flee the wolves that were hot on his trail. From what I was told, he eventually jumped into a body of water where his scent was completely erased, disallowing the few that were hunting him to find their target.

Headmaster Walker has reassured me that Tremont will never be able to step foot onto the school's grounds ever again. He even went so far as to extend the barrier to a twelve-mile radius around the campus, which happens to barely include my mom's house and Sydney's parents' estate. The town of Harper is vulnerable though, considering his protection spell could only be so powerful and extend so far.

And somehow, that's supposed to make me feel okay.

Tremont can't come within a dozen miles. Sydney's parents got erased off the face of the planet. And my sweet, poor Silas evaporated with them.

I've prayed to the angels, begged them to come and talk to me and help me figure out this mess. But all I get in return is silence. I've channeled every ounce of this newfound magic source of mine but come up empty-handed every time.

They're gone. The LeBlancs, Silas, and the angels.

I've lost the connection to all of them.

"Can we at least try?" Lillian gently closes the text and sets it beside her. "I've spoken to Walker; he said he won't penalize you if you get failing scores. This is an opportunity to get back on the horse with no strings attached. If you bomb, no harm. You'll take the term again, and he won't put the grades on your transcript. But there's a possibility you'll pull it off and won't have wasted any time and can continue on the same graduation track with us. I don't know of many situations where someone is given such lenience for a breakup."

I scan her face and glimpse her pleading eyes. This really does mean a lot to her, and how could I withhold that from someone so kind and pure?

I sigh heavily. "Okay. But don't expect too much out of me. I'm kind of a mess."

A small smile spreads across her dainty face.

Maybe this will be a good thing, despite all of the terrible realities. This could help me pull myself up off the ground and begin the processing of everything that has happened.

The grief and sorrow from losing Silas has overtaken me to the point I haven't even fully comprehended that my father is back in my life. And, I'm aware that I should be over the moon about that. It's a difficult task when swallowing the fact that I single-handedly erased Silas from this world.

Regardless of being lost in my own thoughts, I notice the uncomfortable fluctuation in Lillian's energy. A strange rush of uncertainty and fear consumes her. Her brow furrows slightly, but when we make eye contact, she forces a smile.

This snaps me out of my self-loathing in an instant. "What's wrong, Lills?"

She shakes her head. "It's nothing. Don't worry about me. You have enough going on."

I narrow my gaze. "Come on, let me focus on something other than myself for a change. Humor me. What's going on with you? Is it Ethan?"

Lillian bites at her lip, something very uncharacteristic of her. "No. He's great. Perfectly wonderful, actually. It's only...I haven't really been feeling myself lately. I'm sure that sounds crazy out loud." Her attention floats to the closed book to her right.

She and Ethan better be *safe* during their time together. Getting pregnant during the first year of college is a surefire way to throw things off course. Along with finding out you're a cursed witch and inadvertently killing your boyfriend while breaking the said curse.

"Are you sick?" I tiptoe around the question I'd rather ask.

"No. Not like that. I have been more tired than usual lately, and hungry..."

Oh shit.

"You promise you won't judge me?"

How could I ever? She's pretty much a saint and one of the best people I've met. People have babies at an early age, we can work through this together. A hiccup for sure, but nothing we can't overcome.

"Never, Lills. You can trust me with anything." I hold out my pinky to her.

She locks hers with mine, and a strange bit of static electricity crackles between us. She takes in a breath. "I think I've been seeing things…"

My heart seems to nearly thud out of my chest. "What do you mean?"

"You totally think I'm losing it. Oh god. What if I am? I can't believe I'm even telling you this."

I reach out and grab her shoulder to calm her down. A weird pulsing energy meets my hand. I nearly wrench away but stop myself. I don't want to freak her out any more than she already is.

"You can talk to me." I force my most serious expression and tone. "What do you see?"

She looks away. "It's hard to explain."

"Start from the beginning." I gently try to coax the confession out of her.

Her mouth opens to form words, but she's interrupted by the door to my dorm barreling open.

Deghan, Cameron, and Ethan come in with various food assortments. Compliments of Chef Cam, I presume.

I shift my focus back on Lillian, but with her evading gaze, I come to terms with the fact that this conversation will not be continuing right now.

Cameron strolls over and kisses the top of my head. "I heard you've been studying away in here. Thought you could use some brain food."

The cool and beachy scent from his body wash wafts by, accompanied by a chocolatey aroma. Without looking in the bags, I'd bet anything that he baked me brownies.

"Thanks, Cam." I flit my gaze to the door. "Where's Syd?" I ache for the sensation of Silas being near. His absence has left nothing but an aching hole.

"He's coming. Had to finish up a few things he was working on in the library."

Ethan slips his arms under Lillian and hugs her tightly. "I missed you," he whispers into her ear.

Her cheeks blush. "It's been, like, an hour."

He pulls back and grips her face. "That's sixty minutes too long." Ethan grins and plants a few kisses on Lillian's forehead and cheek and nose.

The two of them together seem so...fluid. Lills is shy, and Ethan is more outgoing. They balance each other out well in this department. They have a lot of chemistry, despite Lillian avoiding the PDA at times. I wouldn't be surprised if she secretly welcomed it, though. She deserves to be smothered in love, especially by someone she's mutually crazy about.

Speaking of that word—I need to get her alone and figure out what the heck she meant when she said she was seeing things.

Could what I'm thinking even be possible? And the more important question: how?

Deghan steals my attention when he places a plate in front of me. "Here you go, cutie."

I glance down at the chicken tenders and fries. "Thanks, guys."

"Cam tweaked his breading recipe. It's stupid good." Deghan claims the spot next to me on my small bed and wastes no time devouring his food. A moment passes, and he looks like he's seen a ghost. "Shit, I forgot your drink."

I smile at him and put my hand on his arm to stop him from getting up. "I'm not helpless, Degs."

"I can grab it," Ethan offers. He points his finger at me. "Sweet or unsweet?"

"Unsweet," I say in unison with Deghan and Cam. They know me well. "Thank you."

Ethan shakes his head and smiles. He goes to the small table where they set up the food and pours two glasses of tea. He hands one to me and then places one on the nightstand next to Lillian.

What a gentleman.

I manage to choke down a piece of chicken and a few French

fries. My appetite still hasn't returned, despite the food being absolutely delicious as expected.

Sydney finally arrives when everyone is nearly finishing up. His dark hair topples over his forehead in an unkempt kind of way. Those notorious emerald-green eyes glisten with a beauty from out of this world. He winks at me from across the room.

Sydney is the least likely of my guys to flirt, but man, when he does, he does it well. A simple wink, and my heart picks up its pace.

With his entry, I sense Lillian's energy fluctuating again. A spike in her anxiety laced with fear.

I immediately focus on her, studying her every move.

Her body is tense, and Ethan seems to pick up on that, too.

He wraps his arm around her shoulder.

Ethan speaks quietly, and I strain to hear.

"You having another one of those *episodes?*" He rubs her arm in an attempt to comfort her. If only he had the same calming effect that I do.

Deghan and Cameron are oblivious to Lillian's reaction to Sydney walking into the room. They both greet Syd and start discussing the food. It's not like they can talk about anything we normally do, considering Lillian and Ethan are in here.

I'm grateful Cameron was grandfathered into the whole non-supernatural sworn-to-secrecy thing. I can't imagine not being able to confide in him about that aspect of life.

I muffle an exhausted exhale at the situation at hand. Not only was forcing my brain to study daunting, but now I've agreed to go back to classes tomorrow, and something is clearly going on with Lillian.

I'd like to get the guys alone so we can talk freely, but first I should get Lills to herself and make sure everything is okay with her. This has to be some weird fluke.

Sydney sits at the bed across from me with his food. He takes a bite of his tender and examines my gaze.

If only we were touching, we could have a private conversation in our minds without anyone being any the wiser. Of all people I'd want to discuss what I suspect of Lillian, it would be Sydney. He's the most logical and informed. Not to mention, he was the one who helped me process the realization that I had magical abilities. And everything that followed.

Sydney will probably rationalize this and give me some reasonable explanation to put my mind at ease. Because there's no way my assumptions of the situation could be true.

"You okay?" Sydney mouths to me once he's swallowed his food.

I barely nod and flick my attention to Lillian and back.

Sydney follows my gaze and crinkles his brow. He whispers, "We'll talk," then takes another bite.

Those two words help calm my nerves. Sydney naturally has that effect on me. He's always been the one to bring me back to reality. He's reliable and someone I can continually count on. He calls me out on my shit and reminds me of my worth.

"Wills, we're going to take a nap." Lillian stands from her spot.

Ethan stacks her plate on top of his and disposes of their trash. He takes her backpack and swings it over his shoulder, then entwines his fingers with hers.

"But I'll be back this evening to go over our plan for getting caught up, okay?" She eyes me cautiously like there's some hidden meaning behind her words.

She must be letting me know that's when we can *talk* about things.

I nod in understanding. "That would be great. Thanks, Lills."

That gives me a few hours to have a conversation of my own with Sydney so he can talk me off the edge of thinking my best friend might suddenly be some kind of supernatural being.

CHAPTER 3

"Is that even possible?" Cameron whispers and shifts his focus to each one of us.

"That's what I'm saying." I look from him to Sydney.

I stare while Syd narrows his gaze to some random spot on the floor.

Deghan finds the bag filled with brownies and distributes them equally. Leave it to him to make sure we have our treats. He plops down next to me and scoots close, his warmth soaking through my long-sleeved shirt.

"Syd, you're freaking us out," Cameron says with his mouth partially full.

Sydney finally makes eye contact with me. "You said you two are going to *talk* later?"

I nod.

"Let's wait to see what she has to say before we jump to any conclusions." Sydney scratches at his chin. "You've clearly unlocked a lot of hidden power, so maybe you're able to pick up on residual magic. Think of it like magic that is floating around in the atmosphere and it happened to land on Lillian. That could explain what you felt."

"She said she *saw* things, Syd. It reminds me of when I could see the shadow realm and thought I was losing my mind. It was terrifying not knowing what the hell it was. Especially when no one aside from me seemed to notice it. Between seeing things I couldn't explain and *feeling* them, too, it was a lot. Does anyone recall me having that panic attack and getting lost in the woods when I went to get some fresh air? And then quite literally passing out..."

The memory of the first time Silas and I touched shatters my heart once more. I wanted it badly, only to go into sensory overload and faint into his arms. I'd give anything to relive that moment again. And then, fast forward a bit to the sudden realization of being able to touch him without causing him pain. There are a million things I would do differently if I could bring him back. I'd take any amount of excruciating physical pain over this heartache any day.

"There has to be some logical explanation. I think we should hear her out prior to getting Walker or Abigail involved." Sydney reaches over and places his hand on my shoulder. "We're going to figure this out, okay? All of this. I promise."

Suddenly, I don't think he's talking *only* about Lillian.

I study his face and catch sight of his drowsy eyes. He must not be sleeping well at night, but how could I blame him, considering what's happened the past few months?

Between helping me with my own issues, and then finding out the truth about his parents, and his own past, I'm sure he's struggling mentally with everything.

We haven't even discussed the fact that he's descended from the angels and what that could possibly mean.

There are a million things that I need to figure out, and being consumed with this growing despair is doing nothing to help that cause. The least I could do is be a productive sad person. So, I'll do exactly that. I'll put my happy face on enough that I can get out of bed in the morning, get my schoolwork done, fulfill my student obligations, and figure out what the hell is going on around me.

And for now, I'm going to start small. Assess the Lillian situation.

Then maybe I'll be ready for bigger things, like rationalizing this new father figure in my life and piecing together whatever story my mom has for running off and disappearing the way she did.

With that, perhaps the passing days will ease the aching wound in my soul and help me come to terms with the fact that Silas is gone forever. But until then, I will continue to be a blubbering mess without him.

"Man, why couldn't I randomly have some magical ability?" Cameron kicks at some invisible dirt on the floor.

"Don't wish that on yourself, Cam." Deghan sighs and takes my hand in his. "All it'll bring you is heartache."

I sense Deghan's sorrow and do my best to push calming energy into him to ease his pain.

He's never totally told me what happened to his parents, but it's safe to say he's had his share of heartache and loss, too. We all have, actually.

Maybe that's why we've all bonded the way that we have, because we get it. We're like-minded people who care deeply and want to feel understood. Each one of us serves a purpose to the group, and we fit together like perfectly crafted pieces of a puzzle. Except now, we're missing one member.

"I don't mean to cut this short, but I have to run." Sydney stands and stretches wide. "I have a few more things I need to research, and I'd like to be done by a decent time so we can discuss whatever happens with Lillian." He leans down and kisses my forehead. A bit of PDA that he's gotten used to in his attempt to ensure that I feel loved. "I'll be in the library if you need me."

"What are you working on?" I ask him.

He automatically gets weird. "Nothing. I mean, nothing major. Not a big deal."

"Um. Okay." I watch him walk across the room and nearly bump into the door. "See you later?"

He smiles and awkwardly waves.

"That was strange," I mutter.

"It's Sydney, what do you expect?" Deghan drags his legs onto the bed and lies back. He extends his arm and pats the perfect spot for my head. "Who's ready for a nap?"

"That's all you ever do. Nap and eat." Cameron strolls over to the wall with the light switch and flips it. He nudges one of the beds into the other where Deghan is located.

I climb into the middle between them and let their breathing lull me into the in-between.

I dart in and out of dreams, a few of them neutral, on the verge of being scary, but a sweet relief from the nightmares that plague me.

Often, I'm burning alive. Sweat ripples down my body from the intense heat. Ruthless flames nip at my face and taunt me. Everything is dark except the reddish-orange glow. I frantically scan the area for an exit, coming to the realization that there is nowhere to escape.

Screaming—familiar aches of despair that can only be one person.

I run through the inferno to the cries for help but manage to come up short every time. I reach a mangled and bloody, tattoo-covered arm reaching through a fiery pit in what appears to be a wall of the cave-like structure. The hand slips away from my grasp and into the abyss, leaving me sobbing while my own skin is being melted off.

Somehow, I'm oblivious to the deadly pain, it comes second to the loss of Silas I replay over and over in my head.

I curl into a ball, letting the flames consume me while I silently cry, each tear being swallowed up by the lethal heat. With no access to my magic here, there is nothing to do other than wait until I burn completely away.

I've replayed this nightmare countless times. Silas's screams always coming from a different direction, a new section I haven't yet explored. It's like my mind is playing it on a loop but giving me no chance to actually save him from this hell. A brutal reminder that there is nothing I can do to bring him back. I fall for it every time. The second the flicker crosses my line of sight, I become *awake* in my dream, desperate to gain control enough to rescue him.

It fails, though. I'm always too late. Silas is never mine.

And it kills me every time.

"Willow..." Deghan's voice pulls me from the depths. He wipes at my tear-streaked cheek. "Another bad one?" His body inches closer, and he wraps me tighter into his arms.

With Deghan pressing me into his side, Cameron comes closer from behind me, rubbing circles on the small of my back.

"You're safe here," Cam whispers.

But it's not me I'm worried about.

My mind has been a warning of sorts for things in the past. And with the whole, no one really knowing what happens when you die, the fate of a vampire is anyone's guess.

I've never been religious, so Heaven and Hell weren't something I put much faith into, but considering angels and devils are apparently a very real thing, I have no idea what to consider of the afterlife.

Because of what he is, could it be true that Silas is damned to an eternity of hellfire?

Did I doom him to that?

"What time did Lillian say she would be back?" Cameron glances up from our shared statistics book.

It heavily gives me the creeps to even consider going back to that classroom, but Cam assures me the new teacher is wonderful to work with and not going to be double-crossing us.

How he's so sure, I'll never understand.

Cam is too kind. He's sweet and naïve and gives his all to everyone. I worry he could be taken advantage of because of his generous heart. Like what his brother has done to him. He's treated Cam poorly and pushed this unnecessary situation on him and basically made him fend for himself. I'd hate to see what would have happened if we hadn't coaxed Cam into doing the bake sale and raising money to help cover his expenses. He may have dropped out of college and potentially followed in his brother's poor footsteps.

Cameron deserves the best. Not some future he's forced into because of circumstance.

At least he can count on the rest of us to help make sure that crappy reality never happens. His potential to succeed is immense, and I'm confident he's going to continue becoming a renowned chef.

"I think she said *later*." That could mean anything. I focus my mind to recall her words. Am I supposed to meet her there? Is she coming here? Maybe I should check on her. But if she's with Ethan, I don't want to intrude. I'm sure it's hard for them to get any privacy having multiple roommates to balance, so if she's finally stolen some one-on-one time, I don't want to ruin that.

I glance at the clock and sigh at my growing impatience. I'd rather be focusing on Lillian than this silly math homework I'll never be able to wrap my head around.

"Could she have backed out? Got nervous? You said she seemed embarrassed?" Cam's ocean-blue eyes study my face while he helps me figure out Lillian's unusual tardiness.

"When was the last time you spoke to Ethan?" I ask him.

Cameron bites at his lip, clearly lost in thought. He points into the air in front of him when the memory is recalled. "I think I saw him on my way over here. He was alone. Heading to his dorm. Yeah, I'm almost positive that was today. Or maybe it was yesterday. Shit. I'm no help." His frown deepens with every word.

He could be remembering correctly, though. Which means Lillian could potentially be alone, too. Or in the sense of not having a private intimate time with her man. I don't mind breaking up a girl talk if she's just with Remi and Kyra.

"I can't wait anymore." I hop up from the spot on the bed where I was attempting to study. "Will you head to Ethan's and verify she's not with him while I poke my head into the girls' room?"

Cam smiles, and it brightens his face. "I'd love to be of assistance."

"Thanks." I lean into his open arms for a hug.

He tilts my head up to meet my gaze. "It's nice to see you up and moving around, Will." Cameron plants the softest kiss on my cheek, an inch away from my mouth. "We've all been so worried about you."

I rest my head against his and savor the embrace. I force my thoughts away from the *reasoning* behind his words and concentrate only on the concern in them.

"I'm sorry." My voice is barely a whisper.

He squeezes me tight. "There is nothing you need to apologize for."

Except wiping Silas off the face of the planet and essentially ruining everyone's lives I come into contact with.

It's hard to not feel like a burden to those around you when you are exactly that.

CHAPTER 4

I walk at a brisk pace down the hallway of the west wing, heading toward the human girls' dorms. I avoid looking at the see-through top to the first-floor garden despite it unsettling me like it always does. I round the corner, and a not-so-private conversation catches my attention.

"She basically ran him out of town. I don't blame him for leaving her. Although, I'll never be able to wrap my head around why he was with her in the first place." Allie lets out an annoying sigh.

I slow my step to try to hear more of what they're saying.

"I heard she was mean to him," Paige adds.

Mean?

"Doesn't surprise me. What does she have going for her anyway? She's not even *that* pretty. Don't get me started on how boring she is. And utterly self-absorbed. Who does she think she is, dating so many guys at once?"

Paige chuckles slightly. "Right? Leave some for the rest of us."

I peek inside the partially closed door on my way by.

Allie shifts her weight onto one hip and folds her arms across her chest. "She knew I was into Silas and went after him anyway."

A laugh attempts to bubble its way up my chest, but I suppress it. Sure, call me unattractive and boring, but it would be impossible for Allie to share the same bond I did with Silas. She will never understand the very intricate complexities of the relationship I have with each of my guys. She can be jealous and petty all she wants—it only makes her look like more of a brat.

Of course, her accusations hurt my feelings, I just don't have time to focus on her trivial bullshit. There is no rationalizing with someone like Allie, so it would be a pointless effort to ever try, and I have far more important things going on than her drama.

I close the gap between me and the girls' room, pausing at their door to listen for any sign of occupants. I sense an energy within but hear nothing to go along with it.

Lightly, I tap on the door.

A moment goes by with no answer.

I turn toward the empty hallway and decide to knock again, this time a little louder.

Still nothing.

Some strange feeling unravels inside me as I grab onto the handle and poke my head into the motionless room. It takes my eyes a second to adjust to the dim lighting, and then another moment for me to scan the contents.

Finally, my gaze focuses on my target.

Lillian.

Lying soundly asleep in her bed.

I let out a breath I didn't realize I was holding with the realization that she must have been exhausted and took a longer-than-expected nap. That bit of relief doesn't last long when a sense of familiarity hits me.

I take a few cautious steps forward, carefully studying the rise and fall of her chest like a mother watching their sleeping baby. Each up-and-down motion provides a calming reassurance that they're alive and well. Except Lillian's breathing pattern is slow and sluggish, and the tense expression left on her face can only lead me to one conclusion.

I hurry over, no longer caring about intruding on her personal space.

I drop to her side, resting the palms of my hands above her body. Sure enough, my suspicions were correct.

Lillian has succumbed to a glitch.

Something that could only be possible if she were, in fact...a witch.

"Shit, shit, shit," I mutter. Taking a big breath in, I rub my hands together like defibrillator paddles and call forth the magic I have been so desperate to get rid of these past couple of weeks. I will myself to reverse the flow of power and begin the process of removing the toxins from Lillian's paralyzed body.

I glance at the door, frantic to remember if I shut it all the way or not. The last thing I need right now is for Remi or Kyra, or even Ethan, to waltz into this mess. Having my human friends find out about the supernatural aspect of the school isn't something I have time for right now, especially when Lillian is under such duress. Would I have to lock them up until I could get to Walker or Abigail or just let them wander into the shock of me performing magic and allow them to go on their way?

Walker was prepared to erase Cam's knowledge of the super-natural world. I can't fathom having to perform another memory-altering spell on the girls and risk potentially losing them again.

I urge my abilities to do their job in a hurry. The recognizable ripple of strength courses through me, and a faint pink crackles on the surface of my skin. The flow is larger than in the past, further proving that a new level of magic has unleashed itself within me with the breaking of the Oliver curse.

Summoning the contaminant out of Lillian only takes less than a minute, but each passing second is daunting all the same.

Her body relaxes and regains control with the removal, and what seems like an eternity later, her eyes blink open.

"Will?" Lillian's voice shakes.

"I'm here. I've got you." My hands still remain above her body in what must be a completely strange sight for her.

"Wh-what are you doing?" Lillian darts her attention from my face back to the task I'm trying to complete.

I bite at my lip. Where do I even begin? Do I start with the most obvious answer? That I'm removing something that is only paralytic to her, because she's a witch, and I'm able to do so because I'm a witch, an incredibly powerful one who has the ability to do more harm than good?

"Ugh. Can you just trust me to get back to you on that one?" I continue to pull the crud out of her and process it into my own body.

It's irrational and honestly makes no sense, but to be fair, none of this does. If only Sydney were here to help me figure out how to approach this situation.

Lillian's brow creases. "I was really tired. Like more than I ever have been in my entire life. And then it became more than that. An utter weakness. A strange inability to function. And then I...I think I passed out. Literally." She sits up on her elbows once enough of her strength has returned.

I nod. "Yes. That sounds about right."

"But. How? What? Why? None of this...I don't understand what's happening." Her body exudes a radiating fear at the endless questions forming in her mind.

Not too long ago I dealt with the same uncertainties.

Once I'm sure I've gotten to a safe place to stop, I rest my hand on top of hers, pushing a bit of calming energy into her anxious body. "Hey. You're going to be okay. I promise you'll have the answers you need soon enough, but I need help with how to approach this. Okay?"

Her fearful gaze meets mine. "You're freaking me out. Is there something wrong with me?"

I shake my head. The calming energy must be diluted by the processing of her glitch in my system. I give her another dose and try again. "No. You're perfect, Lills." I stare into her eyes. "Do you trust me?"

She swallows and tilts her head forward. "Yes."

"Okay. Come with me." I stand from her bedside and extend my hand. "Let's figure this out together."

She examines my request suspiciously. "Where are we going?"

"To the one person who will know what to do." I leave my arm dangling in the air between us. Uncertainty creeps its way into my being with the unknown of how she will respond.

The sensation of her fingers resting along mine is enough to give me the hope I need.

I help her to her feet and lead the way from her dorm, ignoring the continued conversation of the stuck-up snobs next door.

Locked together as one, I take her into the hallway of the supernatural guys' dorms.

The second she crosses the threshold, her body tenses. A normal response to the shift in energy, at least for someone who has no idea what they're experiencing.

Not even bothering to knock, I stroll right into Sydney's unoccupied and messy room. I was hoping he would have already been back from his study session in the library, but it seems I misjudged how long he would be there. He must be focused on something important if it's consuming this much of his time.

"You wanted to take me to Sydney's?" Lillian releases my hand and crosses her arms defensively.

"Okay. I know this is weird. But trust me. Sydney is going to help us. All this stuff you're going through right now, Sydney is the one who helped when it happened to me. You're not alone. This is all so new to me I want to make sure I do it right. So please, take a seat and let me go get him." I point toward an empty bed. "Actually, you should lie down."

"You had the same thing happen?" She eyes me suspiciously.

"Yes. And I understand how overwhelmed you are right now." I drag my hands along my head to get the silver hair out of my face while I scan the shelf of crystals Sydney keeps in his room. I grab onto the sort of large and memorable one. It's cold and hard to the touch.

"What is that for?" Lillian asks curiously.

I hold it out for her. "It won't hurt you. I promise. It will help you feel better. And here..." I snatch a bag of trail mix from his desk. "You should eat something, too. It's all silly, but it'll assist your recovery."

Am I forgetting anything? Suction the glitch out of the victim—check. Magical white stone—check. Food—check. Rest—check. Having no idea how my best friend became a witch all of sudden—check.

With the snack tucked under my arm, I pilot her over to the mattress and nudge her onto it.

She stares at the rock and then at me. "What am I supposed to do with this?"

"It's best if you lie back and put it on your chest. I don't really know why. But that's what we've done in the past, and it's worked." I hate how incredibly insane all of this sounds out loud. Soon enough, though, she will have the truth.

A truth that she will never be able to escape from.

That the fairy tales she was told as a child are more true than false.

Witches and vampires and werewolves and devils and angels and demons are all very real. Even fairies, too. And it's safe to say several other things.

The biggest shock of all, the reality that she's one of those creatures and some of her closest friends are, too. Plus, the very school she attends is actually a covert academy for those supernaturals.

Life as she knows it is about to change permanently, and there is no turning back.

But, if she's lucky, it won't be anything like my first few months of being a witch. No curses or fates or pressure to live up to some powerful heritage she had no knowledge of until recently.

For Lillian, I hope the biggest hurdle she'll have to face is overcoming the initial shock wave of trying to wrap her head around all of this actually being real.

If I have any control over it, her transition into the shadow world will be much smoother than mine. Although, the longer I keep her waiting, the worse I make that for her.

"Please eat some of that." I shove the plastic bag toward her. "I'm going to get Sydney. Wait here. I promise I'll have answers for you soon. We're going to get through this together." I walk away from her, holding my arms out to keep her in place.

CHAPTER 5

I rush out of the room in a frantic hurry to get to Sydney. My emotions and thoughts are all over the place, and I can't recall a time when I've been *this* wired.

The reality of Silas threw me into a great depression.

The situation with my parents gave me hope and a mountain of questions.

But this and all of it combined...*what the fuck is happening?*

I jog down the stairs, across the vast expanse of the main floor, catching sight of the abundant and miraculous garden in my peripheral. That is another thing I'll never make sense of. Between the architecture and the ecosystem, that's a mystery I've yet to uncover.

I avoid the awkward glances from passing students at the silver-haired girl being weird yet again. To be honest, I'm unsure how all of my past antics have flown so well under the radar. It's like Walker and Abigail do damage control to keep the supernatural side of things under wraps. How else could one explain the lack of people freaking out about the magic happenings of the academy?

Gripping the chilly stone wall, I swing around and catapult myself down into the basement, taking the steps quickly with just enough caution that I don't fall like I had done not too long ago. Without Cam here to catch me, I have to remember how accident prone I can be. At least this time I'm not cursed with bad luck. Or, well, maybe this is just my normal crappy life.

A brown-haired boy and bright-blue-eyed girl start when I appear abruptly in the fluorescently lit-up space. They reposition into their seats and pretend to study, like I hadn't interrupted some moment between them.

I blush at the memory of Cameron and I being caught by Deghan in this very space.

Offering them a shy smile, I continue my journey along the winding hallway, disappearing from their line of sight and venturing into the supernatural side of the library.

Luckily, there are wards put into place that deter the human students from wandering into this part of the school. To them, it's merely some boring historical section of text that doesn't apply to anything they would ever want to look into. And even if for some reason one of them decided to check out the selection, there is a faux area blocking the entrance to the actual off-limits part. Unless they had some magical ability to bypass the precautions, they would never see the seemingly endless enchanted library with hallway after hallway of rooms full of ancient transcripts.

I make a beeline straight to where I assume Sydney is studying. I allow my internal compass to guide me, and the moment I poke my head into the room, Sydney slams a book shut and pulls it under the table.

"What are you doing here?" His tone is more accusatory than it should be.

"Why are you being weird?" I shake my head to rid myself of that train of thought. "Never mind, listen. Something is *seriously* going on with Lillian. I need your help."

His face and energy shift at the same time. Nervousness to curiosity. "What happened?"

"We'll walk and talk. She needs us, *now*." I rush around the side of the desk and latch on to his arm, practically dragging him from his seat. I try to catch a glance at the text in his lap, but he does a good job keeping it from my line of sight.

That's a mystery for another day, I suppose.

"I'm coming, I'm coming. Fill me in." He weaves his warm fingers around mine on our way out. "Is she okay?" Concern lines his brow in anticipation of my response.

"Sort of. Syd, she...when I found her...she had succumbed to her glitch." I spit out the words, not understanding how it's even possible that this could be true.

Sydney stops and grabs on to my shoulders, stopping me in place. "Are you sure?" His radiant green eyes bore into mine.

I swallow down the intensity of his stare. "Yes. I removed it."

Sydney mutters, "What the fuck?" and looks to the floor. A second later, he latches on to my hand and takes off again. "Poor girl. This makes no sense."

I match Sydney's pace and dart past the jumpy couple pretending to study in the library.

"Do you know what it is?" Sydney glances at me from the corner of his eye. "Where is she?"

"Nope. Didn't get that far. I got it out of her and took her to your room. I wasn't sure what to say or do so I rushed to find you. I thought you'd be able to help me figure it out, considering, well...you were there for me during my *change*."

His hold on my hand tightens a bit. A silent reminder that he'll always be here for me.

We're across the foyer in no time and up the stairs to the supernatural boys' dorm.

A wave of relief crosses over me knowing Sydney will be by

my side to explain things to Lillian. He's been around this *life* much longer than I have, so that has to count for something in a situation like this.

But the moment we come into sight of his dorm room door, seeing it cracked open, unlike how I left it, sends a shock of uncertainty through me.

I let go of Syd and run the rest of the way, pushing into the very empty space.

"She's fucking gone." My gaze scans the room, falling upon the discarded cleansing crystal and scattered nut-and-berry mix on the bed where I left her to rest.

Wide-eyed and heart pounding, I slowly pivot to face Sydney.

"Did she mention going anywhere?" Sydney does his best to keep his exterior calm, despite his raging nerves from within.

I gradually shake my head. I drop to my knees in front of the mattress and grip the ruffled sheets between my fingers. Closing my eyes, I picture Lillian as clearly as possible. "Where are you?" I whisper to myself.

"Will." Sydney rests his hand on my shoulder, but I shrug it off.

"Give me a moment, I'll find her." I go back to concentrating on my best friend.

I've done this time and time again the past two weeks, but instead of Lillian, I've channeled myself to find Silas. Each time failing and breaking my heart worse than the last. I've never once accepted the fact that he's truly gone, but with every dreadfully long passing moment of his absence, I'm reminded of the terrible reality I'm clearly in denial of.

A blip of a tree comes into my vision. A branch with changing leaves. Golden hues of orange and red tainting the once vibrant green. The scattered remnants on the ground have a sort of light trail in the middle where someone had gone through. I focus more, zooming in on my target, and like a hidden camera appearing out of nowhere, I spot Lillian—scared and alone.

Like he can read the slightest tense in my body, Sydney speaks, "Where is she?"

I let out a long breath. "She's in the forest behind the school."

He asks the question I'm too afraid to answer. "Whose land is she on?"

"Wolf territory." Unruly memories of being attacked on multiple occasions by wolves threaten to unhinge me. "We have to go. *Now.*"

The furry beasts are sporadic and difficult to manage, so there is no telling what kind of trouble Lillian might be getting herself into.

I allow my mind to do a double take on the time of the month, becoming only somewhat relieved knowing it's not a full moon. But considering wolves can shift without the celestial event, it worries me all the same.

Lillian has no idea werewolves exist. She doesn't even know she's a witch. Letting her roam free while she's utterly terrified is a horrible idea. Not to mention she probably hasn't fully recovered from her glitch.

"Can you locate Deghan?" Sydney asks.

"No." I don't dare take my thoughts away from her in fear that I might lose track of where she is.

Lillian slumps against a familiar tree to catch her breath. She swings her focus around the eerie forest. Her chocolate-brown hair is wild and sticks up in all different directions on her petrified face. She closes her eyes and folds into herself at the base of the large oak. A faint bubble of golden magic appears around her.

She's protecting herself and doesn't even realize it.

I smile at this proud moment.

"What do you see?" Sydney opens the door to the patio and motions for me to go ahead.

"Her magic. It's beautiful." I lead the way across the area, shoving aside the memories of Silas that flitter into my head at every reminder of him.

He is everywhere I go. It is impossible to escape him. And

despite it killing me with each reminder, I typically welcome it with open arms. Only this time, I have to focus on Lillian.

In my mind, a blur of grey flashes across the sight of her.

A werewolf. And the worst one of all. The asshole who threatened Silas and me. Sure, the ferocious mutt saved us when we were attacked by Sydney's parents, but that was nothing close to redemption—not to me.

"She's not alone. We have to hurry." I tug Syd's arm and take off in a sprint in the direction my intuitive tracker leads me.

The fallen leaves scurry beneath my feet and allow no chance at arriving in a stealthy manner. I follow the crunchy path all the way to my shrunken friend. I drop to her side. "Lills, are you hurt?" I float my hands along her body in an attempt to find any sign of injury.

Lillian sluggishly tilts her head up to meet my gaze. "Willow?"

"I'm here. It's okay. Everything is going to be all right." It pains me to sense how hurt and afraid she is. I move my hand to push my calming energy into her, but her gold magic repels the touch.

She's stronger than we both realize.

She glances down at the glow coming from her skin. "What's wrong with me?" Tears litter her eyes.

Sydney kneels down with us. "Nothing, Lillian." His voice is kind and compassionate. "You're going through something right now, but I want you to know that you don't have to do this alone. Willow and I are going to help you. You're special, Lillian, and what you're experiencing—we have, too."

A rush of air swirls past us, reminding me of that ignorant wolf roaming this territory.

"We have to go, though. Once we're safe, I promise to explain what we can." Learning about the supernatural world can be incredibly exhausting—I'll have to remember to be patient and sparse with the information I give her off the bat. No sense in overwhelming her system and making this that much more difficult for her.

"Safe?" Her energy darkens, and she looks out behind me. "What's out there?"

I lower my magic and grab under her forearm. I don't want her instinctive nature to see me as a threat and block me from getting her out of harm's reach.

My efforts are wasted when her eyes grow wide and the cracking of a branch sounds in the space around us.

CHAPTER 6

I slump my shoulders and sigh. Typically, I'd be more worried about being out in werewolf land with roaming wolves, but considering my lack of giving a shit lately and my newfound powerful magic, this is an annoyance more than anything.

Leaving Lillian out here alone wasn't an option, but now that I'm here, I'm not concerned about her safety.

"Protect her," I order Sydney and turn to catch sight of the deranged wolf.

The grey-and-brown fur is a spitting image of my memory. The creature's deep and dark eyes stare at me, and its lip curls up with the snarl it lets out in our direction. Its large teeth drip with saliva and has no effect on my fear levels like the animal hopes.

Another version of Willow would be frightened, but not this one. When you've already lost so much, it's hard to remember how to react in these situations. Maybe I should be afraid. Having the sheer volume of power running through my veins that I do right now, though, this wolf is nothing more than a bothersome and persistent pest that won't go away.

I take in a breath of the crisp and earthy air, letting it fuel me more. A moment later, I permit the magic to bubble onto my skin and out into my palm.

Lillian gasps from her place safely next to Sydney.

The wolf growls again, this time taking its paw and scraping some dirt, like a sprinter does before it takes off running.

I steady my flow and wait for it to make a move.

It leaps from its spot, and like the world goes into slow motion, I move.

I run forward, tossing a ball of pink at the beast, not permitting it to get more than a few feet off the ground. I've frozen the dog in place completely.

A yelp leaves its furry muzzle.

I can't help but laugh at how pathetic the creature is.

It really thought it had a chance. And now here we are, it stuck in place, entirely helpless at my hand.

"Damn, Willow. Did that even take any effort?" Sydney asks from his spot still near the tree.

I shrug. "Not really."

I barely hold out my hand and twist it, moving the wolf at the same time. I have an absolute hold over him, and I love it. I squeeze gently and watch the pain ripple across his massive body.

I step closer, examining the thing in more detail.

Its eyes are a kaleidoscope of blue and green, tinged with honey and chocolate. On anyone or anything else, I'd consider them to be beautiful, but on this vile creature, I'd love to pluck them from its stupid skull.

The wolf whines, and panic washes over its helpless body.

I grip tighter and savor the agony I cause it.

"Willow..." Sydney gently warns from behind me. "You can't kill him." When I don't answer, he continues. "It's against the policies in place here. You'd be thrown out of school. Banned from the grounds. Basically, you'll be blacklisted in the supernatural community."

So what if some magical folks don't like me. This beast tried to kill Silas. If things would have been different maybe I could have prevented what happened. If this wolf had never attacked us in the first place, the chain of events may have been altered. Maybe if I do this now, it will somehow relieve some of the pain I carry with me like a weighted vest that's permanently affixed to my heart.

I have to do this, if not for me, for Silas. To avenge any harm that ever came to him.

A calm rage settles over me, and my fingers twitch, ready to close completely and end the life hanging in the balance in front of me.

"What about Deghan?" Sydney interrupts my thoughts.

A vision of kind brown eyes and a velvety coat of fur replace the beast, and I shake my head to get back to reality.

"And Cameron? You want Cam to be afraid of you?"

I take a step forward, closing the distance between me and this disgusting being.

"You'd lose us all." Sydney's words are a quiet plead.

Little does he know that the moment I lost Silas, they lost me, too. Now, there is only an empty shell of a woman who is barely capable of getting through each agonizing day. The hole that opened up inside me won't cease to keep expanding into a darkness that has swallowed me entirely.

But if I could prevent them from experiencing this torment, of course, I'd do that.

I swallow, and instead of crushing this wolf's heart without laying a finger on him, I mutter the word, "Turn." I grit my teeth and will it to happen.

If I can't kill this monster, I'd like to at least know who it is I'm dealing with. I will no longer roam the halls uncertain of who would like me and my partners dead.

"Change into your other form." I summon some deep dark power within me and bring my command into fruition.

Pink sparks glitter their way to the floating wolf.

The feral mutt whimpers under the magical hold as its limbs retract and take the shape of a person. First, a leg appears, then a human nose instead of the dog-like muzzle.

I focus all of my attention on finishing my task, not daring to let go of the paralytic control I have. I lower my hand and permit the naked individual to rest in a heap on the foliage-covered ground.

It's not until they glance up that I recognize who it is.

"Clayton?" Sydney gasps from his place still behind me, only this time, he's come a little closer.

Clay's once beastly eyes radiate sorrow and remorse. "I'm s-s-sorry." He tries to bring his legs up and cower, but the hold I have over him is too strong.

I grant him his mobility but summon a dome around him so he can't move outside of the barrier. A gentle relief comes at the realization of the rogue wolf not being Ruby. I had my suspicions, but it never really sat right with me to accuse her. Sure, she's a spitfire, but she's my friend and she would never do something like this.

"What the fuck is wrong with you?" The words force their way out of my thoughts and through my clenched mouth.

Just then, leaves crumble a few rows of trees down. My eyes adjust and settle on a confused and frantic Deghan.

He meets my gaze. "Are you okay? I could hear..." He trails off when he lands his sights on the unclothed man at my feet. "Shit, Clay, was that *you* calling out for help?"

"Are you *friends* with this guy?" I blurt out at Deghan.

Deghan scratches behind his ear. "Yeah. I mean no. Not really. He's, well, he's part of the pack. So, we're all like connected or whatever. I've coached him a couple times, but we don't exactly hang out on the weekends if that's what you're asking."

I shake my head in disbelief. "This asshole tried to *kill* us, and you're training him? Explain to me how that makes any sense." A wave of strange anger bubbles up inside me. I pinpoint the emotion—betrayal.

"No, Will, you've got it all wrong. He's new, so I was trying to help him get his—"

I cut Deghan off. "Whatever. I can't deal with this right now." I turn to the shivering and bug-eyed Lillian. With a flip of my wrist, the barrier around Clayton disappears. "Mark my words. If he so much as looks at me the wrong way, I don't care what kind of agreement the factions have, I will end him and not think twice about it."

"Willow," Deghan calls out.

I ignore and leave him behind, focusing on my terrified best friend. "Let's go."

Sydney and I grab each of Lillian's arms and guide her away and back to the relative safety of the building.

Lillian is quiet as she allows us to guide her back to Sydney's dorm.

Once inside, I sit her on his bed and hand her the discarded stone. "Here," I say gently, trying to erase the menacing version of myself I was only moments ago. I can be pissed off another time, but at this moment, Lillian needs me.

She hesitantly takes my offering and flits her gaze from me to Sydney.

Syd kneels in front of her and sighs. "Lillian, can you tell me how you're feeling? Physically, not emotionally."

"I, uh, I guess I'm fine." She clears her throat. "A little tired but mostly confused. I don't understand what's happening. Was... was that a werewolf?"

Sydney and I exchange a glance.

I reach out and touch his hand, allowing my mind to wander into his. *"We can't lie to her."*

"I know," is all he responds mentally.

"Are you, did you just...?" Lillian's energy shifts.

Sydney takes a deep breath. "Lillian, the information we're

about to share with you is going to seem unbelievable. It will liter-ally overwhelm your body and drain your energy, so I need you to keep me informed on how you are. We aren't going to be able to explain everything, but we can start. Okay?" He stares into her eyes and waits for some sign of approval.

When she nods, he continues.

"Yes. What you saw in the forest, you are correct. That was a werewolf."

I expect her to flinch at the admission, but she remains calm and focused. Maybe the truth really is the best thing for her. Personally, I'd rather know things than be in the dark and have to guess. The unknown is really a terrifying thing.

"Willow, she's a witch." Sydney raises his hand to his chest. "As am I." He touches her knee slightly. "And you are, too."

"How is that possible?" Lillian's fingers grip the stone tighter.

"We aren't sure," I admit. "Did Abigail wave a wand over you during admission?"

Her brows furrow while she digs up the memory. "Um, yeah. Why?"

"She was scanning us to see if we have supernatural powers." Apparently, my powers weren't the only ones hidden that day.

"I think she mentioned something about the Wi-Fi being broken."

"She told me the same thing."

"Wait, so Abigail is..." Lillian leaves the sentence dangling in the air.

"Also a witch," I finish.

"And Deghan is, too." She says it more like a statement than a question.

I quickly look at Sydney and then correct her. "He's actually a werewolf."

Her eyes widen a little, and she bobs her head up and down slowly. "Is Cameron a werewolf? He and Deghan are pretty close."

I shake my head. "No, Cameron is...well, he's just Cam." A

perfect, totally sweet and considerate, amazing chef and utter human.

Her mouth opens like she's going to ask something else, but she stops herself.

My heart breaks while sensing the path of her thoughts.

Sydney steals the direction of the conversation. "Part of the school consists of supernatural students and staff, where the rest are human. We coexist together to have the ability to blend in and go unnoticed. For the most part, we draw no attention and can go about our business without issue. Situations like this, with you, are not typical."

I side-eye Sydney. These conditions may be rare, but Lillian and I seem to share in this whole 'having no idea we were a witch' thing. And, in a limited window of time at that. From what I've gathered during my study sessions, the majority of witches grow up in a magical household and never experience a lapse in knowing whether or not they're a witch. So why all of a sudden are there two unknowledgeable witches sprouting from the universe back to back?

"But you said you've gone through this?" Lillian's deep eyes stare into mine, pleading with me to help her understand.

I nod. "I had no idea either. Not until I came here, to Harper Academy. I thought I was losing my mind. I could sense these strange vibrations in the school. It was like a generator was always running and got louder and rattled my core in certain parts of the campus. These shadows kept appearing, and I couldn't wrap my head around any of what was happening. It wasn't until Sydney and I talked that I figured it out. Usually our *kind*, we grow up with the knowledge that we have magic. It's not common to just *become* a witch."

Sydney decides to take over, and I gladly let him.

"Have your parents or anyone in your family ever mentioned anything about this?" He relaxes his body and leans it against the side of his desk. His disobedient hair tumbles onto his forehead, begging for me to run my fingers through it.

"No. I think I'd remember something like that. Can't say we've ever sat around at Christmas, talking about our magical ancestry or anything." She pauses, and nervousness washes over her. For a second, she doesn't meet my gaze. "Ethan…?"

"No. He's human." I don't hesitate to get the words out. If there is anything I can reveal to ease her mind, I'll do it gladly. "The girls, too. Actually, anyone in your dorm or Ethan's. But mine or Syd's…those are reserved for the supernaturals."

A sense of understanding cascades across her face like a light-bulb going off over her head. "That's why you switched rooms." A second later, a frown forms. "You had to go through that alone. I'm so sorry. And I even got mad at you for leaving us. That wasn't fair of me. I was selfish for acting like that."

I reach out and gently cup her hand in mine. It's refreshing that she finally knows part of the truth, at least enough to comprehend why I had to do what I did. Although the reality of the situation was that I was putting everyone I cared about in danger because, at the time, I was habitually cursed. But for now, I'll let her in on the little bits she can handle. Maybe someday I'll explain what really happened.

"I hate to bring up a touchy subject…but…was…?" Lillian bites at the corner of her cheek, almost like she's regretting what bits she's already said.

"Ask anything, and I'll do my best to answer you." I brace for what's to come.

She lets out a small breath. "Silas…was he a werewolf or a witch?"

A tremor rocks through my body that only I can sense. Heartbreak that keeps coming regardless of what I do.

Detecting Sydney is about to come to my rescue, I somehow find the courage to speak. "No, Silas…" Speaking his name rattles me that much more. "He was a vampire."

And with that, Lillian's eyes roll back as she faints.

CHAPTER 7

"I don't think we should say anything yet," Sydney whispers to me from our place near the door to his dorm. We're far enough to not wake Lillian but close enough to still keep an eye on her while she rests peacefully.

"I'm not opposed to that, but why?" I quietly respond.

His body is only inches away, and his warm breath mingles with mine while we chat.

I ache to melt into him and let the worries of the day be temporarily forgotten in his embrace. Studies show that hugs can reduce stress and lower anxiety, and right now, I could potentially use a thirty-seven-day-long hug.

"I'm not trying to be that guy, but honestly, who can we really trust? I'd like to piece this together a little bit more prior to involving anyone else."

He's not wrong, which doesn't help settle my nerves whatsoever. Around every corner is another person we shouldn't have confided in, so keeping things to our tight-knit little circle makes the most sense until we can get a better grip on whatever it is that's happening.

"Clayton probably knows. And he could have told Deghan." My blood boils at the memory of missing a chance to end that mutt's life. It's not exactly like me to want to kill someone, but desperate times call for desperate measures.

"Pretty sure you scared the shit out of that kid. I'd guess the only thing on his mind is never crossing paths with you again." Sydney trails his hand up my arm and weaves it along the side of my face, resting his palm against my cheek. "Speaking of...are you okay?"

I bite at the inside of my lip and force a quick nod.

He pulls me into him, and my head finds a perfect spot on his chest.

"We're going to get through this. All of it." He pauses and then adds, "I promise."

I close my eyes and think about those last two words. To him, they're something he thinks I want to hear. But to me, they're nothing but empty assurances that could never possibly come true. I'm aware he means well, it's just that some things I'll never be able to recover from.

Sure, we'll figure out what's going on with Lillian and help her transition into this new world. Maybe even tame my bloodlust toward the piece-of-shit wolf that threatened to kill us. And then the other stuff like handling the new dad in my life and determining whether or not my old statistics teacher will come back to try to murder me again. Dealing with one of the men I love disappearing into thin air and being gone forever? That's something not even the brilliant Sydney can help me process. And fuck do I wish he could.

I'd give anything to have some kind of answer or knowledge of how to bring Silas back. No matter what, though, there is nothing. The angels have stopped communicating with me. And even if they hadn't, the connection I had with Silas...it's dissolved. There used to be this tether tying us together, and now there's an empty, bottomless pit of despair, reminding me that the greatest thing I've ever experienced in my life is no more, never to return.

So instead of confirming his guarantees to fix things, I say nothing and let Sydney's hold on me momentarily soothe the aching wound that is my soul.

"How are we going to explain this?" I ask while staring at the still-sleeping Lillian.

Sydney scratches his chin and checks his watch. "I'll tell Ethan that you were having a rough night and Lillian came to comfort you. It turned into you two staying up too late and deciding to take a personal day together." He crosses his arms and shrugs. "What do you think?"

I kneel beside the bed where Lills is sprawled out. I quickly scan her body and come to the same conclusion I have the last few times I've checked her. She's exhausted and needs to recharge.

Learning about the shadow world has drained her and telling her that vampires exist was the nail in the coffin to send her over the edge. I was naïve for thinking she could handle the information we were throwing at her. Figuring out the delicate balance of not giving too much at once will be a learning curve.

Not too long ago, I was desperate for information, too. I wanted someone to give me all the answers to the millions of questions I had, and even now, I still don't have a fraction of the knowledge that I'd like. But coming into this world so late in life and not having a tolerance to the energy-sucking aspect of all things supernatural is something that Lillian and I will have to deal with on our journey of integrating with our kind.

I may be a few months ahead of her, but at least we get to do this together.

Part of me has felt so left behind because every gifted person close to me either grew up with their powers or already has an advanced understanding of the ins and outs of the world. And it seems like no matter how much I learn, there is always so much more left to uncover.

For instance, until recently, no one had really interacted with fairies, and here I am, getting assistance and having some unknown connection and trust with them.

Plus, the whole, one of my boyfriends is actually descended from the angels, despite being brought up to think he was a dark witch. That's an entirely new mystery on its own, considering his parents were demonic witches. His bitch of a mother had said he was an anomaly, cursed to her from the angels to ruin her plans of world domination.

Sydney leans down and plants a soft kiss on the top of my head. Meeting my gaze, he asks, "I'm gonna get you a coffee and some breakfast. Do you want anything else while I'm out?"

"What about some reading material? There's a tan bag in my room near the foot of my bed. Could you grab that for me?" My heart palpitates harder when I study the glowing green of his eyes. It's like they're mesmerizing and capable of putting a spell on me with just one glimpse.

It pains me that I ever thought Sydney could deceive me. I had looked him in those gorgeous orbs of his and told him to leave me alone. I thought he was plotting against me and using me to help the witches who cursed my bloodline. When in reality, he's one of the kindest and most considerate men I've ever met. He has his demons, but who doesn't? He's never once treated me poorly or failed to follow through with anything he's said. He's a man of his word and goes out of his way to make sure I'm taken care of. He's loving and generous and more than I will ever deserve.

All of my guys are.

And right now, one of them thinks I'm super pissed at him.

Don't get me wrong, I'm definitely not happy with Deghan, but I should have heard him out. I asked him to explain himself only to quickly shut him down and not actually give him a chance. I was acting irrationally and emotionally instead of with logic like I should have at that moment.

Deghan has never let me down either, so I can't imagine he would have helped Clayton without some sensible excuse. I can be upset with the situation and feel a way about what he did, but I should give him the opportunity to defend his reasoning.

"Hey, something else." I sigh and glance from Lillian back to Sydney. "Could you see if Deghan has time to talk before he goes to class?"

Sydney's lip turns up in one corner. "Absolutely." He leans forward and leaves the softest kiss ever on my lips.

***

I'm creepishly watching the rise and fall of Lillian's chest when Deghan quietly enters the dorm with my breakfast and bag I had requested from Sydney.

"Hey," he says shyly and sets the paper sack of food and coffee on the table.

I walk over and take my bag from him and lay it along the wall. I take his hand in mine and look up at him. I nearly crane my neck at the height difference between us.

"Deg...I'm sorry for shutting you down."

A split second later, his arms wrap around me and pull me into a huge hug. His heart is beating loudly, and the anxiety coursing through his body is on a whole new level for him. Relief slowly trickles in but not nearly quick enough.

I close my eyes and push some of my calming energy into him and he relaxes into it. "I should have given you a chance to explain."

Although he's practically smothering me, not for a second do I consider backing away. I might be upset with him, but I'm nowhere close to turning down affection from Deghan. Especially knowing that it's his love language. He needs this more than I do.

"Wills, I was so worried. I thought you hated me forever. I couldn't sleep, and believe it or not, I haven't had an appetite. And listen, it's only been like twelve hours, but that's a long time for me."

I rub circles on his back to comfort him. "You're a growing boy; you need to eat."

"I'm sorry I didn't tell you sooner. I wasn't supposed to. Pack rules and stuff. It's stupid, and I hate it. I thought I was doing the right thing. He's new to the whole werewolf thing and he's having trouble adjusting. He was turned, not born into it, so it's more difficult in certain ways to figure out how to separate the two and not let the animal nature overpower the human side."

I had no idea there was a difference in how someone became a wolf. Add that to the list of things I'm continuing to learn.

"A few of us, we've been working with him. He shouldn't have been out there last night. His *other* form keeps shifting at random times and, well, it's pretty agonizing if you don't go along with it and fuel its desires. You know, the running and feeding. It's not really fun for any of us. The transformation is stupid painful, and the nutritional aspect is gruesome if you leave enough of your human-self intact. Some wolves like to only let the animalistic nature shine through because it helps with the pain and disgusting stuff we have to do, but that's when things can go bad if someone non-wolf is around. Clay is having trouble turning his human-self back on when he's in his wolf body because he's weak. The reason I'm able to be around you in my wolf form is because I've trained myself to be fully there the whole time. It sucks a lot, but if I'm going to turn into some beast, I want to be in full control."

It's like Deghan had a reason to want to be in total power. Like either he had lost it before or risked losing it and never wanted to experience that again. I could be misreading the situation, but something tells me otherwise.

I peek around Deghan's arm at Lillian, still snoozing like Sleeping Beauty. I can't help but compare what's going on. Not too long ago, I was a newbie witch who had no idea how to use her magic. Heck, to this day I don't really know what I'm doing. I've hurt people, especially people I've cared deeply for. And now, Lillian is going through something similar, so how can I be so hypocritical of Clay and his experience? Granted, he tried to kill us on numerous occasions, it's not like he really wants that. Otherwise, he wouldn't have been so apologetic when I forced him to shift. Plus, if he really wanted us dead, he could have done it as a human. I shouldn't hold him to some unfair standard because I'm taking shit so personally.

Yeah, he's in the wrong for trying to bite our faces off, but it's not like he's in control of himself when he turns into a werewolf. I should give him a little more time to develop his skills before I decide to hate him forever. In the meantime, though, I'm going to keep my guard up and snap his ass back to reality if he pulls another stunt like he has in the past. My magic is powerful enough that I can paralyze a rogue wolf with the snap of my fingers, so if I'm around, my friends should be safe.

I'll just have to make sure everyone is aware that the wolf territory is off-limits.

"I shouldn't have gotten mad at you. You're doing the right thing," I finally say to Deghan.

"Thank the Angels." He exhales and squeezes me tighter. "Now, what the heck is going on with Lillian?"

I pull away and grab the delicious-smelling bag he brought in. I hand him one of the blueberry muffins and peel back the paper on the one for myself. "Good question." I take a bite and once I've swallowed, I continue. "I'm not sure how it's possible, but she's definitely a witch."

"Is she okay? What's wrong with her?" Deghan shoves his last bite into his mouth.

"Found her yesterday totally consumed by her glitch. Got it out of her and then went to get Syd, came back, and she was gone. Tracked her out into the woods. Fast forward to you finding us when I was going crazy on Clay. Took her back here, and the second she heard the word vampire, she passed out. I think it was an overload of info. A lot all at once. I hate that it's even a thing. Why can't we naturally accept this stuff?"

"I read something one time, that it's because we've been conditioned to look the other way about supernatural stuff, because it's not *supposed* to be real. So, once we start unlocking all these secret hidden doors in our minds, it's like a circuit overload. Even one little piece of information can set it off. It's kind of cool if you think about it, but yeah, it really blows when you have a bunch of questions or you're trying to explain something to someone." Deghan leans against the wall and crosses his arms, studying the passed-out Lillian.

"It doesn't make any sense, though, how it happened all of a sudden. Mine eventually worked itself out. My powers being hidden because of the curse. But how do we explain Lillian's? Sydney said it's rare for this kind of thing to happen, especially twice like this." I take a sip of my caramel latte, compliments of barista Sydney.

"What if it has something to do with you?" Deghan suggests.

Me? How could Lillian's magic be linked to me? "What do you mean?"

Deghan shrugs. "I don't know anything about magic. But you're right, it is weirdly timed. You find your magic, you just broke the curse, and now this? Seems like a strange coincidence."

I never thought about it that way. I assumed Lillian's newfound powers were isolated to her. What if they do have something to do with me or the curse? Or even worse, what if they're related to Sydney's parents, or the demonic witches?

What if Lillian is a demonic witch and she happens to be a part of something wicked that is yet to come?

Could it be possible that my best friend has been sent here to settle the fight between the light and dark once and for all?

Deghan blips his attention to the clock above Sydney's cluttered desk. "Shit, I've got to run to class. I'll see you when school is over, okay?" He takes my head between his palms and tilts my face toward him and kisses my forehead, then my nose, and lastly, my lips.

I savor the tingly warmth lingering over each spot. "I'll be here."

He exits the room and leaves me behind to continue staring at the girl who has left me with more questions than answers.

The biggest one of all...

Can I trust her?

CHAPTER 8

"Will you go with me?" Lillian's doe eyes bore into mine. "Please."

I swallow down the uncertainty. Of course I want to be there for my friend, but what if this is another elaborate trap laid by another demonic witch? How can I be so sure that she isn't a spy or puppet?

Sensing her energy, though, it's hard for me to assume she desires anything other than a friend to help her through this rough transition.

"You don't want to do this alone?" I ask her.

"Would you?" Lillian brings her knees up to her chest and sits against the headboard in Sydney's room.

We've been in here all day. For a while, I watched her sleep peacefully, and then around late morning, she stirred and finally woke up. She was disoriented at first until she settled her sights on me.

We chatted on and off. Mainly about the cover story we gave to everyone about why she wasn't attending classes today and the shortage of power she experienced.

I'm taking things slow with her and monitoring her energy levels closer so the same thing doesn't happen again this time.

I shake my head.

"That's what I thought. Plus, you can help me make it more believable."

The plan is to inform Lillian's parents about an ancestral project we're working on. That we need to gather family history and the student who can go back the furthest gets extra credit. Not that Lillian would ever need the additional help, but considering she's an overachiever, it seems fitting that she would want to excel.

I should take the opportunity and stop by my own house while we're in town, but facing the reality of my parents isn't something I'm equipped to do just yet. My mind is an unstable place right now, and I'm only allowing one major thing at a time; I'm afraid I might combust or revert back to the non-functioning, ultra-depressed version who doesn't leave my room for weeks.

At some point, I'm going to have to build the courage to figure out what happened. For now, I'll leave that for another day.

I recall bits and pieces of my mom coming to talk with me, her weak attempts to comfort me and explain what happened. Being the actual mother figure, though, was never her strong suit, so decoding how to handle a loose cannon of a daughter was exhausting for her. I don't blame her for giving up on me the way she did, because for as long as I can remember, I've been the one caring for her.

The important part is that she's okay. My dad is okay. I brought her love back to her.

And maybe that's part of the reason I'm not capable of seeing them yet. My heart is torn open, and the wound is too fresh to be around *that* kind of romance—the type that lasts through life-times and curses and impossibilities. It's too much of a reminder of what I lost. Breaking that curse and giving my mom her person back meant I had to lose mine.

"When do you want to go?" I take another bite of the grilled chicken salad that Cameron brought me for lunch.

She glances at the clock on the wall. "Maybe right when classes are over, that way they don't think we're skipping. Think Sydney would let us borrow his car?"

I swallow the mouthful. "You kidding? For answers, absolutely."

"Listen..." Her energy shifts. "I'm sorry about last night. I shouldn't have asked."

I hold up my hand to stop her. "Listen, I get it. You have a lot of questions. I think that's fairly normal considering our very *not-so-normal* situation."

"Can I ask one more?" She bites at her lip and twirls a piece of fuzz on Sydney's blanket.

I take a deep breath. "Sure."

"He...he didn't break up with you, did he?"

Uncontrollable tears well in my eyes. I force them to go away, but it's no use. They roll down my cheeks and refuse to stop coming.

"Oh, Wills." Lillian closes the space between us and pulls me into a hug. "I should have known something else was going on. I've been hard on you. I take it all back." She circles her hand on my back and tries to comfort the silent sobs that wreck their way out of me.

"You didn't know," I manage to blubber. And even then, it's not the whole truth. It's not just that Silas is *dead*, it's that he vanished without a trace, never to be seen again. I didn't get the chance to mourn the loss of him in the flesh. There was no closure of a funeral or being able to hold his hand and kiss him one last time, to whisper to him that I would love him forever—that he changed my life...that he made me whole.

He's just gone.

There would be no more *firsts* with him. No more stolen kisses or deep understandings or secrets murmured in the dark. I lost my best friend, my lover, my protector, the other half of my soul.

He told me he couldn't go on in a world without me, and it wasn't until I lost him that I truly understood what he meant.

Color has dulled, and food doesn't taste the same. Things I once enjoyed no longer bring me the same pleasure. Everything has changed, and nothing will ever be the way it was.

Not without him.

But with that, I realize I have friends and lovers who count on me still. So, I force what little bit I can, despite them deserving much more from me. Maybe in the future, I'll be able to give more to them, but for now, they continue to stick by my side and carry me through this suffering. For that, I will be forever grateful.

"Is there anything I can do?" Lillian breaks the silence.

That same question that keeps being asked. There is nothing anyone can do to ease this suffering unless they can do the impossible and bring Silas back.

"No, Lills, you're going through enough. Let's focus on you." If anything, all of this helps distract me from the constant agony and heartache. Staying absorbed in figuring out what the hell is going on with her is temporary, but a distraction all the same.

"I hate to change the subject, but do you think I have time to grab a shower?"

We both glance at the ticking clock.

"Good idea. I could use one, too."

Lillian and I gather our things, and I leave Sydney a note on his desk, telling him we're going to get ready and where to find me.

"Meet me in my room when you're done." I give Lillian's hand a gentle squeeze before we head our separate ways.

Maybe soon enough she'll be joining me in the supernatural girls' dorm.

Well, that is if she's not plotting against me.

———

I'm towel drying my hair when the door to my room opens. I peek my head out to find Sydney entering. I lean against the doorframe of the bathroom and smile at him.

"Hey, you." He grins back.

The towel covering my damp body attempts to come unraveled, but I snag it just in time to tuck it firmly in place.

Syd strolls over, looking sexy as hell in a light-grey hoodie and dark denim jeans. Simple but somehow massively effective. He hesitates in front of me and examines me like I'm a fragile thing about to fall apart. His hand lingers in the air next to my face.

I lean into his palm and savor his soothing touch.

He runs his thumb along my cheek and leans forward to touch his lips to my forehead. He takes his other hand and tangles his fingers around mine.

His voice appears in my head. *"I love you."*

I sigh and wrap my arms around his neck, severing our mental connection but whispering into his ear, "I love you, too."

I pull back, grazing my face down his until our mouths are barely touching.

He closes his eyes and trails his nose beside mine. Finally, he moves in for a kiss so sweet and delicate, telling a story of longing and desire with just the subtle movements.

The tenderness quickly turns into something with more passion.

I grip his face and weave my way into his hair, dragging him closer to me and pushing my body into his.

His hands find their way up and down my body, and the bulge growing in his jeans lets me know he wants the same thing I do.

Our tongues dance together, and the heat between us steams

up the already foggy bathroom. We stumble back, bumping into the counter.

I kick the door shut for privacy.

Sydney snakes his way under my towel, sending spikes of pleasure at his every touch.

I reach down and unbutton his pants without breaking the kiss. Once I have him free and in my hand, I let my covering fall to the floor and turn away from him, pivoting over the counter so he can enter me from behind.

At first, he obliges, running his length over my ready entrance, teasing me with want.

But he doesn't continue, which only drives me wild.

I back into him in a desperate attempt to get him inside.

"No." He flips me back around. "I want to kiss you."

He grinds his body firmly onto mine and clutches my face for another passionate exchange.

Grabbing the bottom of his sweatshirt, I drag it over his head. I waste no time slipping his shirt off, too. His skin is warm on my fingertips as I run my fingers down his chest and then latch on to his back to bring him closer.

In the blink of an eye, he lifts me off the floor and settles me right into place.

I slide down onto him and bite back a moan of pleasure upon his entry.

His right arm is firmly around my back, holding me in place, with his other gripping under my thigh. He backs us into the wall and tenderly thrusts himself up and down while our lips fight to communicate with one another.

It's not long until I'm nearly ready to burst, having gone weeks without a sexual release yet dating the sexiest guys I've ever met.

Sydney grows even harder inside me as our bodies become in sync with each other. His desire fueling mine.

Suddenly, I hear the door to my dorm room come open.

"Wills?" Lillian calls out. Her tone lowers and she says to herself, "She must still be in the shower."

I grin against Sydney's lips and kiss him harder.

He picks up his pace, doing exactly what I need him to do, like he knows the very things my body wants.

Seconds later, I'm muffling the uncontrollable sounds of a much-needed, blissful orgasm.

Sydney slows his movement, prolonging my satisfaction that much more.

Still throbbing and aching for his own completion, Sydney continues to twirl our tongues together. Not seeming to care about himself but only about me.

I lower myself to the floor, sliding off him and dropping to my knees. I take him into my mouth, not wanting to delay him any longer.

Sydney suppresses his groans and grips the sides of my head tighter when it's his time.

I let him guide me through until the end, only stopping my movement when I'm sure he's done.

I rise to my feet, aching between my legs for more. Bringing him his pleasure made me only want another round. Maybe later we can go for session number two.

Sydney latches on to my face and tangles his lips with mine once again.

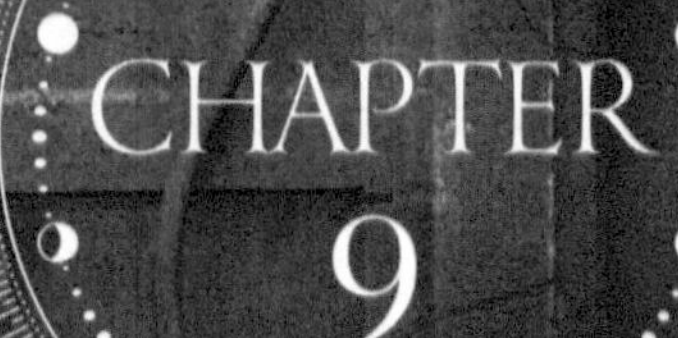

CHAPTER 9

Lillian blushes when I come walking out of the bathroom—Syd trailing behind me—with nothing but Sydney's sweatshirt on.

"Oops," she says. "I didn't mean to interrupt anything."

"You didn't." I grin.

Somehow, we were able to continue regardless of her coming in prematurely. And if we weren't pressed on time, I would have potentially kept her waiting even more. It's been so long since I've felt *anything* other than sadness; it's only natural I'd want to savor what I can while I can…

Especially considering I'm well aware it will be fleeting.

The guilt of the situation is already weaving its way through me and reminding me I shouldn't get to enjoy anything—I'm a monster.

I go to my dresser and pull out a clean pair of panties and step into them. I find a black pair of leggings and tug them on, too. My hand brushes one of Silas's shirts in my attempt to find a pair of socks, and then my mind wanders to him helping me get dressed.

The sorrow is like a heavy anchor, making sure I'm rooted in place forever.

Silas was such a caring and gentle soul, despite his hardened exterior. He was misunderstood. Broken from an early age and treated poorly. He put up wall after wall in an attempt to protect his immeasurable heart.

I was incredibly lucky that he let me in as much as he did. His love was abundant and pure and nothing that I've ever experienced. He was selfless and defensive, but in the best of ways. He believed in me and never doubted my strength. He wanted me to be the best version of myself, and he never failed to help me achieve that.

And now he's gone.

I have to keep reminding myself, otherwise, I'll stay up all night expecting my door to come flying open and Silas to swoop in and pull me into his arms.

He's never coming back, and that's a reality that I have to face head-on. One of the worst parts of all—it's all my fault. If it weren't for me, Silas would still be here. It eats me alive that I could have prevented this from happening.

From the moment his skin touched mine and it sent a crackling pain through him, I knew I had to protect him from me, but I kept being overly persistent. I was greedy. I pushed and broke the first curse, killing him in the process. It wounded me to put him in danger, and yet I continued to do exactly that. I thought I was doing the right thing but instead erased him from existence with the final spell to free my bloodline.

I should have let him keep his distance every time he tried. He thought he had to shelter me, when in reality, it was him who needed to be saved all along.

"Willow." Lillian breaks through my self-loathing. "Are you

good if Sydney comes? He said he'd drive. I don't have my license, and I'm not so sure you should be operating a motor vehicle." She quickly adds, "No offense."

I huff. "None taken. You're right." I turn to Syd. "You don't mind?"

"A chance to spend time with you girls?" He winks and opens the door, motioning for us to exit.

A frantic and terrified Ethan pops his head into the room before we can leave. "Lills," he breathes. "Are you okay?"

She gives him a shy smile and lets his hands find her shoulders to inspect her. "I'm all right."

"What happened? That's not like you to just disappear."

She must not have found him in our window of time to get ready. I'm assuming she was too caught up in the whole *finding out she's a witch* thing to bother with checking in with her boyfriend. She and Ethan spend a lot of time together, though; it's only natural for him to worry when something fluctuates in their predictable schedule. I thought Sydney's cover-up story had appeased everyone, but it seems Ethan wouldn't be satisfied until he heard it straight from the source.

"Sorry, babe. Willow needed me, and we stayed up late and decided to skip today. Mental health day or whatever." She kisses his cheek. "Everything is fine."

Little does he know, everything is not, in fact, fine.

Granted, this isn't exactly life-ending like an endless curse. It's going to take some time to figure out what the heck is going on with Lillian and why she all of a sudden has magic. Speaking of, we need to get a move on if she's going to have a chance to talk to her parents.

Walker enacted a pretty strict seven p.m. curfew now that it's getting dark earlier.

The more I learn about this school, the more the little things make sense.

Like the students having to maintain residency here. Harper Academy is one of the few colleges that require *all* students to live on campus. Some just require it for freshmen and sophomores, but here it's any pupil. Which makes things easier for keeping track of the coming and going of bodies. Especially the supernatural kind.

Wouldn't want some rando-supe to come strolling in and mess up and think it's Susan from first period coming back from her aunt's.

For the not-so-new students, the headmaster doesn't totally mind if we leave, he only prefers we check ourselves in and out. It leaves little room for surprises.

Seems reasonable.

"You had me worried," Ethan mutters into Lillian's hair. He glances around to the open door and then at me and Syd. "Are you guys going somewhere?"

I speak up to eliminate Lillian having to make up a story on the spot. "Yeah, there's this thing with my mom. Part of the reason Lills came over last night. We won't be too long, but we're running into town to meet with her and then we'll be back. Syd's driving us in."

The cover-up is complete bullshit, and somehow, Ethan buys it. "Oh, okay. Well...be careful."

Relief flashes in Lillian's features.

For a second I think he's going to invite himself—thankfully, he doesn't.

"We will." Lillian tightens her hold on him. "I'll come over when we're done."

The drive to town is quiet and full of bubbling energy.

Lillian is nervous, and Sydney is excited.

And I'm sitting here watching the trees buzz by the window as I wonder whether or not Silas enjoyed the way the leaves change their color in the fall.

There was so much more to learn about him, and it kills me that I'll never get to uncover all of his layers.

Our time together wasn't enough.

An idea strikes, and the thought of it not occurring to me before now sends chills through my body.

Silas might be gone, and while I'm yearning for more of him, his cabin in the woods near the school is still intact, full of bits and pieces of him scattered throughout.

I have to go there in an effort to be closer to him. I will cling to anything that remains of him—even if it's only a whiff of his scent or a strand of his hair. I could touch his favorite book or snoop through his fridge. Anything to momentarily bring Silas to life in my heart, the place he will stay forever.

It will tear me apart, but it will give me fragments of him I've yet to explore, and to me, that's worth any amount of suffering.

"It's that driveway up on the left, the brick house with the garage door open." Lillian points ahead from her spot in the rear seat.

The house is quaint, tucked in neatly beside other similar houses on the far end of town from where my childhood home is. It's no wonder Lillian and I never crossed paths, being that even if I had gone to public school, this is a different district than the one I went to.

Sydney slows the car and pulls into the driveway. He shifts it into park and then turns to face us. "Ladies, we have arrived."

I let out a breath. "You ready?" I study Lillian for any sign of treachery, finding only a scared little girl.

She nods. "Yep. Let's do this."

Lillian and I hop out of the car, but she pokes her head back inside.

"You can come if you want," she tells Sydney.

His cheeks turn upward, and he unbuckles and climbs out.

We approach the front door as it opens. A kind and tradi-tional-looking woman is on the other side.

"Lill!" She beams. "What are you doing here, honey?" The lady glances between all three of us. "Is everything okay?"

"Yeah, Mom," Lillian reassures her. "We have this project thing at school, and I needed to come up and see if you could help." Lills cranes her neck around to peek inside the house. "Where's Dad?"

"Oh, I was just going to grab him. He's at one of those cooking classes Mrs. Dawson puts on. Today was manicotti day. Your father is excited to try his hand at Italian." She focuses her attention on the old gold watch on her wrist. "I guess I have a few minutes to spare. Come on in, kids."

"Mom, this is Willow and Sydney, my friends from school. Will, Syd, this is my mom." Lillian motions to all of us.

Sydney holds out his hand to her mother. "Pleasure, Mrs. Fairchild."

She blushes and says, "You can call me Greta."

I watch for Sydney's reaction but don't catch one.

I extend my arm next for an introduction. "Nice to meet you."

Our skin touches, and absolutely nothing happens. No jolt of power, no fizzling energy, just a boring human shake.

Sydney seems to observe my reaction because he quickly takes hold of my hand and speaks into my mind. *"You noticed that, right?"*

"Yep...nothing."

"That's strange."

"Shame we don't get to meet the dad."

"Here, make yourself comfortable on the couch. Could I get you a glass of water?" Greta nervously flutters into the kitchen without waiting for a response.

"Thanks, Mom," Lillian calls out after her.

I gaze around the room, spotting various pictures littering the space. A nice couple with a small child in most of them. None of them dating back any further than the little girl as a toddler. A few with just the man and woman, smiling at various famous locations—Las Vegas, the Eiffel Tower, Niagara Falls.

Greta comes into the living room holding three glasses between her fingertips. She hands one to Lillian and then to me and Sydney.

I smile and thank her, not really wanting the water. I take a fake sip to be polite. It's hard to trust clear liquids, especially considering what's happened in the past. The water smells clean of alcohol, but one can never be too sure.

"So, I don't mean to rush this visit, as I'm so tickled to see you Lill—I just hate to keep your father waiting. What is it that you think I can help you with?" She sits against the armrest of a worn-in, oversized sofa.

Lillian clears her throat. "I was hoping you had records of our lineage. It's for a school assignment."

Greta suddenly becomes nervous. Suspiciously uneasy, given the context of the conversation. Why would a mother not want to share this information with their child unless they're hiding something?

"I see," is all she says.

Lillian continues with her cover-up story. "The student who can trace their family tree back the farthest gets extra credit and, well, I'm always down for an academic challenge."

Greta crosses her arms over her chest, a telltale sign of dishonesty or defensiveness.

"We lost all those records. Remember when the basement flooded. I'm sorry, sweetheart. I'm afraid I won't be of any help." She checks the time again and stands. "Was that it? I really do have to get going."

"Do you at least know where we were from? Our nationality? Anything to help me with this project?" Lillian rattles off whatever comes to mind to gain a tiny piece of information from her seemingly clueless mother.

I study the woman's face and attempt to match similarities to Lillian. Different eyes, nose, cheekbones, hair. I stand, trying to be inconspicuous about inspecting the photos in the frames a bit better.

A quick look reveals Lillian doesn't bear a resemblance to her father either.

"German maybe, a little Irish. I never looked into it, sweetheart." Greta walks toward the door, holding it open and all but shoving us outside. "Call next time, and I'll make sure your father is home. I'll have him make those pot-pies that you like." She forces a smile.

"Okay. I will." Lillian sighs and steps out the door.

Sydney and I follow her out awkwardly.

He grabs on to my hand. *"She's hiding something."*

"That's clear, but what is it?"

Lillian tells her mother goodbye.

"It was nice meeting you two," Greta says to us.

"You, too," we both say in unison.

A moment later, we're loaded into the car.

Syd and I stay quiet, waiting for Lillian to speak.

Sydney backs his Honda out of the driveway and gives Lillian's lying mother space to get her Jetta out of the garage.

He starts to go back in the direction we came, but Lillian speaks up.

"Let's make one more stop. Turn left here."

Lillian directs us to a senior center a few blocks away. The building is outdated and in need of a fresh paint job.

We step through the large automatic doors and approach the front desk. She signs in and then motions for us to follow her down a long, narrow corridor. She stops in front of a partially cracked dark-blue door and knocks lightly and then pushes it open the rest of the way.

"Hey, Grandma."

"Little Lillian, what a pleasant surprise." She looks her over. "Ah, you're growing up on me. Come over here and give your grannie a hug." The grey-haired woman's face spreads into a toothless smile.

Her dentures sit next to a can of Pepsi on the nightstand beside her.

Lillian greets her and gets right into it. "I'm doing an assignment for my history class, and we're doing a family tree kind of thing. I was hoping maybe you could help me. Do you have any record of our family lineage?"

"What good would that do ya, pumpkin?" the old senile lady says.

"It's for school, Grandma."

"You said that already." Her grandma sighs. "Your mother never told you, did she?"

"What didn't she tell me?" Lillian holds her breath.

"That you're adopted."

My eyes widen along with Lillian's.

For a second, I think Lills might pass out on me again. I rest my hands on her back to support her weight just in case.

A young nurse walks into the small bedroom and shuts off the television. "Time for your evening walk, Miss Betty. Tell your visitors goodbye."

The lady helps her grandma out of the room while the rest of us gawk in silence.

We came here for answers, but it appears we are leaving with even more questions.

CHAPTER 10

We quietly walk through the gated courtyard of the academy. Students are sprinkled sparsely around, either with a book in hand or chatting with a friend. Life to them is normal, simple, routine.

To us? It's nothing but one chaotic thing followed by the next.

I'm a newbie witch. A damn powerful one.

My family was cursed, but I somehow overcame every single obstacle thrown my way to free the magical bind suppressing our talents.

I'm dating a werewolf, a witch, a human, and my other boyfriend was sucked into oblivion.

The very school I thought would make my life a *little* more interesting ended up being a place for the supernatural.

My stats teacher was plotting against me with someone I love's parents.

My dad—who I thought abandoned me when I was an infant—is mysteriously back in my life. My mother randomly went missing for a hot minute.

Demons lurk on the other side of our realm.

My best friend is suddenly a witch.

There is a stupid wolf that has minimal control over his animalistic nature.

And honestly, I might be failing all of my classes.

"There you are," Remi calls out from her place near the entrance to the building. She wastes no time rushing over and latching on to my arm. "I heard you were up and at it. About damn time if you ask me. Anyway, I need your help."

Surprise, surprise. Something else needs my attention.

I've been such a shit friend lately, though, so I owe it to her to help with whatever it is she's about to ask. No matter how mundane it may be.

Her auburn hair falls in gentle waves over her shoulders, and a chunky braid lines her forehead. It's simple but makes her shining eyes stand out. Her pleated, navy-blue skirt falls at her mid-thigh, and I can't help but wonder if she's cold considering the chilly fall sweeping in.

"Ky-bear's birthday. It's this weekend. I want to throw a party. A little birdie told me Deghan's twentieth is coming up, too. And by that, I mean Cam. Cameron told me he wants to do something special for him." Remi rubs her hand along mine and grips it firmly. "So, you're in, right?" She turns to plant herself in front of me and stops me in place.

I smile at her. "Of course, I am."

Amid all the disorder, I never considered when everyone's birthday was.

"Perfect. We should do a surprise party." A huge grin settles onto Remi's already bubbly face. "What about you two? Will you help?" She glances at Lillian and Sydney, who until now were silently walking with us.

"I—um. I've got to go do this thing..." Lillian blurts out and takes off toward the oversized front door.

Remi lowers her voice. "What's gotten into her?"

I sigh. If only Remi knew everything that has transpired in the last twenty-four hours, maybe she wouldn't be so quick to judge Lillian's reaction.

Sydney clears his throat. "I'd be happy to lend a hand. Let me know what you need from me." He takes my free hand and pops into my mind. *"I'll go after her."*

I lock my sights onto his gorgeous green stare and attempt to wink my response.

He blushes and follows Lillian inside, leaving Remi and me alone.

"We haven't really gotten to talk, Will." Remi meets my gaze and softens her tone. "You doing better, I take it?"

Internally, I shudder. I'm nowhere close to being okay, but how do I tell her that without her thinking I'm some psycho ex-girlfriend who can't get over a breakup?

Oh, hey, yeah, I'm not really doing so great since I murdered the love of my life. You know, typical, normal teenage problems.

"Define *better*," I finally say.

"I'm glad to see you moving around. I'd call that an improvement. That guy doesn't know what he's missing." Her words rip open the aching wound that is my heart.

If I want to protect what's left of my sanity for the day, I need to get the hell away from her and this conversation.

Like a gift from the angels, Headmaster Walker calls out, "Willow, a moment, please."

"Make me a list of whatever you need so I don't forget." I let go of Remi and make my way to the guy in charge of things around here.

His salt-and-pepper hair is a bit more undone than it normally is, his droopy eyes revealing his lack of sleep. He paints a happy look on his face and motions for me to follow him into his office.

"Have a seat, Willow." Walker points to the leather couch positioned against the wall. He takes his place at the front of his desk, leaning into it like he normally does. "How are things?" His energy is genuine and sympathetic—Dad mode engaged.

Or, well, what I assume to be the caring behavior of a father figure.

I kind of wish people would stop asking me such difficult and impossible questions. How can I answer something I don't even know? It's not like I can tell them the truth. That I'm miserable, an aching shell who would rather be swept away into nothing than continue to live another day in this world but chooses to go on because there are people who are counting on me. That I feel guilty for being heartbroken to the point I haven't functioned properly the last few weeks and have let the ones I care about—the ones left—down. That I don't deserve to feel reprieve but for some reason still expect the sadness to eventually subside at least a little.

So instead, I lie. "Good."

Walker cocks his head to the side and deadpans. "Uh-huh."

I bite at the corner of my lip, begging the tears to stay at bay and not embarrass me yet again with another uncontrollable display of emotion.

"Listen, Willow, you've been through hell. Quite literally, I might add. I don't anticipate you to behave any certain way right now, but I want you to realize that your feelings are valid. You don't have to hide within the confines of yourself. There are people around here who care about you. I've mentioned this to you already, about the therapist who specializes in PTSD—the offer still stands if you want a professional to speak to. It worries me that you're bottling this all up and carrying the burden alone." He pauses and lets out a breath. "I'm not trying to overstep any boundaries here. I hope you understand that. You've experienced more in the last few months than most people do in their entire lifetime. If anything, I'm in awe at how well you're handling things."

I blink up at him. "Really?" I've felt like I've been barely holding it together, constantly on the verge of losing my damn mind at any given point. I am falling apart, and I've lost the battle of gripping the seams that keep me from unraveling.

He lets out a small poof of air, almost like an *are you kidding me?*

"Absolutely. That's why I wanted to touch base with you. Rumor has it that you'll be going back to your studies soon. While I'm pleased to hear this, I thought I'd see if there's anything I can do to be of assistance at easing this transition. I've already spoken with your teachers, as I have been throughout your... hiatus. They've all agreed to lighten your load while maintaining the required curriculum. The situation is a bit unique, and I'm doing my best to handle it properly."

The air in the room grows thick with a strange emotion.

Walker's gaze diverts to the floor and then back to me. "I feel partially responsible for what happened. I should have done a better job vetting the professors, and I assure you that I will not make that mistake again."

I cringe at the thought of that slimy asshole prolonging the injury to my hand to preserve his hold over me. Tremont deceived me, and despite my reservations about him, I was still vulnerable and susceptible to his wicked antics.

And now, weeks later, he's still on the loose. Whatever spell I created to eradicate the LeBlancs and the man I love had no effect on him. He fled that day, never to be seen or heard from again.

Although, I have a sneaking suspicion he'll eventually show his face sooner or later.

I open my mouth to speak, and the words come out crackled. "I don't blame you." The only person I fault is me. I was a fool. A stupid, oblivious girl who thought she could take on the world.

"That's kind of you, Willow, but I have a duty here and I let you and your fellow students down. For that, I will be forever regretful." Walker's blueish gaze meets mine.

Part of me wants to reach out and press my calming energy into him, to relieve him of his sorrows. The other half of me realizes I can't fix everything, and I should stop trying to play the hero. It only leads to continued heartache for myself and those around me. I have to relinquish control and stop failing at saving the day.

A light knock permeates the room.

"Come in," Walker calls out.

The dark solid-wood door creaks open, and Abigail pokes her head inside. "Am I interrupting?" Her gaze flickers between us.

"Not at all! We were just finishing up." Walker stands.

I mimic his movement, totally ready to end this conversation. It's not that I don't appreciate his attempt to console me, it's just more than I can handle right now. I've been partially secluded from the world for the last few weeks, and all of a sudden, it's like sensory overload.

"Great." She funnels into the room, a small brown bag in her hand. "I've been working on this—I thought it might help." Abigail holds the parcel out to me. "A little family recipe. I had to order some of the ingredients, that's why it's taken me a while to get to you."

I unroll the top and peek inside. "What is it?" The floral and woodsy scents tickle my nose.

"An herbal tea that's known to ease...well...a broken heart."

"Oh," I reply, unsure of what else to say. "Thanks."

She studies me for a moment. "My dad, when he passed...my mom was a wreck. This was the only thing that got her through it. I'm not trying to compare your experience to anyone else's—I just wanted to help in any way I could."

"That's kind of you," Walker chimes in. "I've read about the medicinal properties of such in my time doing earth and magical studies."

Abigail reaches toward me and places her hand inside the bag to reveal a tiny slip of paper. "I've included the suggested instructions on how to prepare it. If you need or want any help, I'd be more than happy to oblige."

I smile respectfully. "Thank you."

I did this. How can I justify something to ease the pain when I caused this to happen? I'm the reason Silas is gone, and I should have to live with the consequences and the pain that it brings.

I do the one thing I've grown good at, mentally push them and their offering of assistance away and leave the office.

I head straight to the one place that will either rip me open or continue to tear me apart. Either way, I'll be a little closer to the man I have loved and lost.

CHAPTER 11

The land behind the school is cold and damp, and leaves plaster the earth in a haphazard kind of way. Each breath is filled with a musky-sweet mix of decaying, fallen debris.

I underestimated the cold under the foliage-covered space, but I don't let that discourage me, despite it taking longer than I anticipated to find what I'm looking for.

My sights settle on the hidden gem tucked delicately in the wooded area.

I suck in a breath, having finally found this treasure.

Pausing, I stare blankly, unsure of whether or not I want to actually go through with this mission. I came all this way and yet I can't help but consider how intrusive this may be.

This is Silas's place. His home away from Harper Academy, from the world.

It's wrong of me to encroach even though my heart is screaming for me to take a gander inside. Something foreign tugs at me like a subtle nudge toward the small house. I'm inclined to go forward, almost as though gravity is calling me to enter.

An owl hoots in the distance, and I whip in its direction, suddenly fearful of being alone out here.

I take a step, willing my body to move, to do anything other than simply stand out here in a foolish manner. The two-by-two-foot wooden step creaks when I climb on top of it. My heart picks up speed the second I place my cold hand on the even colder handle. I turn to no avail. The door is locked. How silly of me to assume it would be anything else.

A breeze whisks by, sending a chill through me. I rub my shoulders to keep warm.

I look around my dark environment. Do vampires hide keys like humans do?

Standing on my tiptoes, I run my hand along the edge of the rickety roof. Nothing.

I close my eyes and let the dissatisfaction take its course.

I could break a window. But the thought of destroying something of Silas's quickly has me tossing that idea. I will cherish every last bit of him like it's all I have left, because, at the end of the day, it is.

Calling my powers forward, I focus on the lock and locating a way in. A blip of a second later, a faint buzzing directs me to a random spot on the ground near the front door. I dig my fingers into the earth, rooting around until my skin touches something hard and metal.

A freaking key.

I nearly jump with joy, fishing it out and wiping the dirt aside.

I take a deep breath and consider walking away. A little voice in my head reassures me that what I'm doing is okay. I don't quite understand who or what it was, but I allow the blind faith to slide the thing into place and unlock the door.

The second I push into the space, the scent of the forest around me is replaced by him.

Clean, crisp, a bit of something spicy, like myrrh. My senses start rapid firing, sending a flood of emotions over me. Want, desire, longing, sadness, hopelessness.

I flick the switch to my right, and a lamp in the corner illuminates the living room with a stale dim light. I slowly gaze around, soaking in every bit of Silas left behind.

Books overflow on a tiny shelf tucked in with a cozy chair. An old record player and a stack of vinyl records sit next to it. The room leads into an open dining room, kitchen, and bedroom. The only closed-off space is the bathroom in the far corner. The bed is disheveled, reminding me of our time rolling around in the sheets.

My hand finds its place on the crook of my neck where his lips once sent chills up my spine. I drift over and settle my weight on the edge, pulling the sheets up to my nose to breathe him in. Tears trickle down my cheeks. I smooth my palm across the dark-grey comforter.

Silas loved all shades of black and grey. It was rare to see him in any other color. Maybe the occasional white. But typically, he stayed well concealed in his leather jacket, black tee, and faded jeans. He had a simple sense of style, but it was sexy nonetheless. He was truly gorgeous, and quite frankly, the most attractive man I've ever laid my sights on.

I close my eyes and recall his ink-stained skin. The wisps of onyx covering his entire upper body. The elaborate rose that leads to an intricate pocket watch. So many tattoos that I never got the chance to ask him about. Like the greyscale skull with images hidden within it. Once I saw a set of hands and a bleeding heart but was too distracted by his naked body to question him. Not that I'm complaining; at times like this, though, I wish I had taken a moment to learn more.

I stand, strolling to the kitchen where he made me breakfast. I poke my head into the fridge at the carton of eggs and an expired jug of milk. A lone jar of pickles stuffed in the door brings a bittersweet smile to my face. The infamous Silas enjoys a salty treat.

A dirty cup sits in the sink. Oh, how I grow desperately jealous of the thing.

I'd give anything to have his lips pressed against me one more time. To be held in his hands and spend a fraction of a second with him.

I graze my finger along the countertop on my way to the makeshift dining room table in the middle of the space. A compact notebook catches my attention from under an outdated newspaper. It appears worn, like it had been well-used. The chocolate-brown leather binding is cracked and chipping away. I reach out to it, drawing my hand back a moment later.

What if it's his journal?

That would be an invasion of his privacy, even more so than I'm already committing.

I force myself away. I'm desperate—just not enough to violate him that much.

A stack of old letters is strewn in a chaotic pile. I glance and find one dated back to September 1954 from someone named James Dean.

My mind does a double and then a triple take.

The James Dean? The famous actor who died tragically in a car accident?

I laugh. Of course, Silas would have been friends with him.

It occurs to me that Silas lived an extensive life that I'll never get to hear about. I crave to sit around a warm fire with him, wrapped in his embrace while he tells me stories of his youth and what it was like growing up when he did. To hear about his friends and family and people who he's come into contact with. Places he's been and things he got to experience.

Had he been out of the country? Traveled to South America? Seen the Eiffel Tower?

Did he mourn the loss of loved ones passed like I do right now?

Does he have relatives I should have contacted to let know what happened?

He claims we were fated, but were there others before me? People who brought him joy and companionship. Silas was a loner—was he always that way?

What happened in his past to break him into the sad and broody man I knew him as?

I yearn to uncover each piece of him.

An ache consumes me when I realize I never will.

The man I fell so deeply enamored with is no more.

So, in an attempt to savor what is left of him, I curl up on the bed we shared a beautiful night in and close my eyes, pleading with my mind to dream of him.

I wake to the sound of screaming. Something I've grown accustomed to these past few weeks. My throat aches, and I cough unintentionally. I force away the absorbingly scary image of the skin melting off my arms in a pathetic attempt to reach Silas. I blink to clear my eyes and spot the old wooden clock on the nightstand, ticking away at half past three in the morning.

Like the night Silas and I shared, I'd much rather stay here and revel in the remnants of him, but I have to get going. The guys are probably worried, and I need to properly rest if I'm going to get up and attend my classes in a few hours.

I sigh, rolling off the incredibly comfortable mattress, and plop my feet to the hard floor.

Slipping into my shoes, I say a silent *see ya later* to the place I now hold so near and dear to my heart. If I can't have Silas, I'll hold on to these remaining bits of him while I can.

At least until someone comes to repossess the cabin or whatever the hell happens in situations like this. Does he have an electric bill that needs to be paid? I'll have to remember to come back and see if I can figure out how to maintain the property for as long as I can. The thought of losing what's left of him rips a brand-new hole in my chest. I'll do whatever I can to make sure that doesn't happen. I can't lose him again, not like this, not if I can help it.

Once I've locked the door and tucked the key into my pocket, I wander my way back through the forest, following the trail I took to this glorious treasure. The walk is cold and dark, the only light coming from the waning moon. A bright reminder that the wolves will be extra dangerous soon.

A subtle rage builds within at the memory of that ruthless wolf who didn't deserve my mercy. He'd better figure out how to control himself or I'll make him pay for his ignorance.

A translucent light-pink orb radiates around my body. Apparently my magic decided to throw a force field around me to protect me from any shadowy threat that may be lurking in these thick and eerie woods.

A fork appears between some trees, and I pause, not quite remembering which path I'm supposed to take. I suck in a breath and concentrate, pondering how to get to the school. A flicker of light appears to my left, verifying the correct direction. Small blips of energy dance along the ground and then float up around me.

I gasp when I recognize what's before my eyes. It's not my magic, it's fairies.

Two of them flutter across my line of sight, and I hold still, not wanting to startle them.

"Hello," I whisper.

One with blue wings dares to hover in my line of sight.

"Hi," I say gently.

A purple female with long, beautiful flowy lilac hair comes to meet her sky-colored friend. "Willow Oliver." Her voice is dainty and crystal clear.

"You know my name." I continue my motionless stance.

She smiles from ear-to-ear, showing her bright-white teeth. It's like she's a tiny human, just with wings and fun-colored hair and skin. She wears a skirt and matching tank top that are a few shades darker than her body. "We've known you your whole life."

Memories trickle through my mind of various moments in the garden, out in a wooded area quite like this, where there were unrecognizable flutters similar to what I'm experiencing now. I had once chalked it up to tricks my eyes were playing on me, or the sun casting strange rainbows. When in reality, it was always fairies.

"Thank you. For all of your help. For keeping me safe." I want to reach my hand out, let them have a place to land so they can rest their constantly flapping wings, but I don't want to scare them. Considering this is the first time in all my life they have taken the opportunity to talk to me, I don't exactly want it to end because I moved too quickly like an idiot.

"We will always do what we can to protect those who are worthy."

The worthy? Surely, they have their facts wrong. I've done nothing to deserve their aid. All I seem to manage is getting myself and others in trouble and hurting those I love.

I glance at the blue fairy, wondering if he is going to speak.

"What's your name?" I ask her.

"Daphne. And this is my mate, Gabriel." She points toward a hovering cluster of colors to my left. "That's Rune, Finn, and Astrid. They're a tad shy, but they mean well."

"It's lovely to meet you, all of you." I pivot at the waist to face them and offer them a kind smile and a slow head nod.

The bashful fairies drift a little closer, stopping a few feet away. I can make out the individual colors now that they're within a nearer range. Bright-orange, pale-yellow, and a glittering-red. They're all so magnificently radiant—if I weren't seeing it for myself, I'd never have believed they were real.

"You sent the bad woman away." The ruby one flows over to Daphne.

"Yes, I killed her."

The tiny creature shakes her head. "No."

Hadn't they seen it happen, since they lurk in the forest? They must have witnessed what I had done. "I did, she's dead." Along with my sweet Silas.

"She's not dead. She's *gone.*"

I huff. "Isn't that the same thing?"

A branch snaps in the distance. The fairies flicker out of my line of sight.

Shit. That's the very thing I didn't want to happen.

I open my mouth to call out, but Daphne appears beside my head.

"It's not safe here. You need to go." She motions through the trees ahead. "That's the way. You had better hurry." She fearfully shifts her attention to where the sound came from. "Now," she urges and then disappears without letting me stop her.

I don't doubt my ability to protect myself, considering how easily I subdued that wolf without any effort. I just don't really want to face whatever it is that's prowling through the forest. I skipped dinner and haven't properly rested, two big red flags for a witch, especially one running on stress and coffee.

I take one last look at the dimming colorful lights in the distance and then take off in a sprint toward the school, my thoughts running as rampant as I am through this dirt and leaf-covered ground. I don't stop running until my feet touch the gravel path lining the patio behind the academy.

CHAPTER 12

I don't fall back asleep at all.

Instead, I lie in bed, tossing and turning, rolling around the words the fairies told me over and over in an attempt to make sense of them.

Did I hear them correctly? Have I gone mad?

I imagined the whole thing. That's the only explanation.

Fairies themselves are a bit unrealistic. Maybe I was having a delusional episode. A hallucination caused by lack of food and rest and trauma. That seems more reasonable than a handful of brightly colored tiny creatures insinuating I didn't actually *kill* Sydney's mother.

If she's not dead, then what is she?

Is there something worse than dead? Now that I'm considering it, didn't the angels tell me that what happened to her would be crueler than death? And if that's the case, did I sentence Silas to the same fate?

An image of a fiery inferno dances across my vision, and I shove it away.

I can't control my nightmares, but I'll be damned if I let myself be forced to witness it in my waking life.

Damned.

"Angels," I whisper. I close my eyes tightly and attempt to summon them. "Please. What does this mean?"

Silence. Nothing. They're not here with me anymore. They've left me alone.

If they won't speak to me, maybe the fairies will. And the moment classes are finished for the day, I plan on going straight into the changing forest and staying until I find them again.

I need answers.

I take the pillow out from under my head and smash it onto my face to muffle the groan that leaves my mouth.

There is a light knock at the door. It takes my eyes a second to adjust to the dim room and focus on the beautiful blue-eyed boy tiptoeing in.

"I didn't think you'd be awake yet." Cameron comes over and sits on the edge of my bed, holding out his offering.

I breathe in the blueberry and coffee scent and smile. "Breakfast in bed? What did I do to deserve this?"

He places the bag next to my arm.

The warmth soaks into my skin. "Wait, are these *fresh*?" I open the bag and am assaulted by the straight-out-of-the-oven aroma.

"Maybe." Cameron blushes. "I wanted your first day back to school to be as good as possible." His hand twitches like he wants to reach out but doesn't.

I take the items and place them on the nightstand. A second later, I grab him and drag him under the covers with me. "You are the best."

His body presses up against mine and snuggles in comfortably. "Agree to disagree." He wraps his arms around me and reels me in close.

It's the kind of comfort I wasn't aware I needed.

About twelve seconds later, I drift away. And what feels like three moments after that, Cam is nudging me awake.

"Already? Not fair." I latch on to his hands and don't let him go.

He kisses the spot right behind my ear and then leaves a trail of smooches down my neck.

It awakens the part of me I thought I had satisfied yesterday.

"Time to get ready, pretty lady." Cameron wiggles out of my grasp and rips the blanket off me.

I do the thing. The whole *get ready and go about my day* stuff I'm supposed to do. It's all I can do to keep my mind on the task at hand when rampant thoughts of what the hell the fairies meant keep flitting into my head.

Cameron had waited for me to get decent and then escorted me to first period where the handsome Sydney was saving me a seat.

"Good morning, Willow," Abigail calls out from her spot behind the mahogany desk. "Come on in."

I glance from her to Sydney, not sure what to make of things. Last I recall, we were teamed up and training in the shadow realm with partners. But right now, Ruby is nowhere in sight.

"You doing okay?" Syd quietly asks me.

I place my backpack on the chair and nod. "How's Lillian?" I reposition my dark-grey sweater.

Sydney doesn't get a chance to respond.

"You're probably wondering how your *special* classes will go now that you've been absent for a few weeks." She puts down the stack of papers in her hand and shifts her attention to me. "Since you've been gone, Sydney has helped maintain the integrity of the shadow realm. It's held up well with all things considered. It would be beneficial if you were able to make a contribution, although we don't expect that from you."

I study her energy and pick up on nothing out of the ordinary. Just regular Abigail vibes.

What happened with Professor Tremont has me slightly cautious with giving out my trust. I'm growing persistently paranoid. Abigail has never done anything to make me question her, but I can't help the nagging insecurity of not knowing that with absolute confidence.

She continues on. "That decision is entirely up to you, and I'll be sure to let you think about it. In the meantime, I'd like to get back to regular studies."

"What about our partners?" I speak up.

"For now, we've put that on hold. I imagine you'd be more comfortable during your realm sessions with Sydney as opposed to an unfamiliar species. And right now, our goal is to reintroduce you without overwhelming you." Her gaze flickers to the door and immediately back to me.

I strongly dislike that it seems she's implying I'm weak. "You're not wrong, but I would have preferred to be with Sydney even before all of this happened."

"That's understandable. If you'd rather we change things around, I'm open to your suggestions. Whatever works best for you during this unfamiliar time."

Why is she being so...cooperative? Are they really all actually concerned about my well-being or is it something else?

"Okay. I'll let you know. Thanks." I notice Sydney staring at me when I peek out of the corner of my eye.

All of the pieces finally click in my mind. If I want them to stop handling me like I'm this fragile thing, I have to stop acting that way. I shouldn't be upset at any of them for walking on eggshells around me, despite it not being what I want. I've quite literally been a freaking mess, and their behavior is a natural reaction to that. They care. I'll have to do a better job of maintaining my composure and appearing strong, and then maybe they'll treat me normally.

"Good." Abigail wavers and then smiles. "I've prepared some assignments for us to work on today if you'd like to head over." She motions to the door.

To the entrance of the shadow realm.

A lump forms in my throat, and I have to remind myself to keep my composure.

It's *just* another dimension. One where Cameron was lured in and held hostage by a demonic entity that was trying to steal my powers, which resulted in a big-ass battle that ended in me killing Silas and annihilating the seams that held the place together.

No big deal.

Sydney merges his hand in mine, and his tender voice floats into my head. *"You don't have to do this."*

I grip him reassuringly. *"I'm fine, really."* I do everything I can to focus my thoughts and not give anything away at how I'm actually freaking out inside.

"Infito grantum modem." The words roll off my tongue in a way that would make one think I spoke this language my whole life.

A bubble of color appears and grows larger—the familiar shades of purple mix with black, resembling ink spilled and swirled around.

Still holding on to each other, we step through to the other side.

My gaze immediately scans the room to check for any inconsistencies or weaknesses in the wall keeping our world separated from the demonic land. Magic fizzles in my veins. My increased power adjusts to the difference in the terrain and then neutralizes once its content.

There are two long tables set up in the middle of the room. One of them has various crystals placed all over it, and the other is scattered with different species of flowers.

Apparently, we will be classifying plants and rocks today.

This seems like such a silly task, but this is actually a great fundamental building block that all witches—and people, in general—should learn. Both of these things have healing properties regardless of magical ability. Not to mention other positive characteristics that I'm sure we'll be learning about here.

I immediately recognize a few of the blossoms. Lavender is easily identifiable with its long stems with lilac-colored flowering shoots. I can practically smell its aromatic scent from where I stand by the entrance to the realm. Next to that, the golden-yellow blooms turn into balls of fluffy white seeds. During my younger years, I ran around the yard plucking them and making endless wishes.

My mom deep-fried the yellow flowers and made salads out of the dandelion stems.

I'd snatch the tops and rub them on my skin, staining my hands and arms with whatever thing I decided to draw on myself with the magical orangish ink that came from within.

As a child, that's all I ever really knew of magic.

"We're going to be working on identifying and studying these stones and flora. Each is crucially important to witchcraft and will aid in providing you with the tools you need to become a more knowledgeable witch." Abigail points toward the objects—an invitation to step forward.

I glance at the selection of crystals. Varying shapes and sizes, but most of them could fit comfortably in one hand. I'm called to a specific one. Smooth and green with lighter green circles and swirls, reminding me of the rings within a tree trunk.

Abigail smiles at my wondering gaze. "Malachite. I'm not surprised to see you drawn to its direction. Do you know anything about it?"

I shake my head and pull back the arm I didn't realize was extending out to touch its shiny exterior.

"Malachite has been around for thousands of years. It's a protective stone that can help guard you against negative energies and provide you with the strength to heal. People take it with them on planes to assist with jetlag and prevent accidents, others keep it near their electronics to eliminate pollutants and toxins. It's a stone of transformation and recovery, meaning that it can ease depression and anxiety." She gently takes the beautiful emerald piece off the table. "Here, I think it was meant to be yours."

The malachite is as smooth and cool as I expected. I roll it around my hand and sense its calming vibrations. "Thank you," I mutter.

"During the full moon, leave it out where it can be exposed to the natural light. Send your intentions along with it, and it will be cleansed and recharged for you by morning."

I study Abigail's features. Her skin is lightly freckled with minimal wrinkles. Her healthy red hair doesn't seem to have one strand of grey. She's stunningly beautiful, and if I had to guess, I'd say she was in her early twenties. I've never asked how old she is, and considering the mishap with Tremont, I'm suddenly very curious.

I recall the time Sydney had called her Abby, like they were long-time friends. I'll ask Syd later what her background is and settle the newly nagging curiosity I have of her.

If she really is that young, how does she have such power and authority here at the school? Abigail is almost always in cahoots with Walker and has immense knowledge of pretty much all things supernatural. She's basically the Hermione Granger of Harper Academy.

And I'm the completely clueless Harry Potter. A witch thrown into the magical world, doing their best trying to figure out what the heck is happening and how to save those we love.

"Do you recognize any of the other stones?" she asks.

I flit my gaze at Sydney and grow aware that he can probably identify and categorize every single thing on these tables. He's clearly here for moral support.

I study the selection and focus on a gorgeous purple cluster. "That's amethyst."

Abigail nods. "You are correct. What do you know about it?"

"Um...it's pretty."

She lets out a small laugh. "You are correct. Although, there is much more to it than just its looks. Its name is derived from a Greek word that actually means 'not intoxicated', which is quite interesting if you ask me." She picks it up and tilts her hand, letting the light reflect off the bumpy nuggets. "Amethyst is a versatile crystal. Known to protect from evil thoughts and expand the higher mind. It has healing properties, too. The darker pieces can aid in creativity and focus. It's great for calming and soothing and has been used by diplomats and businesspeople to help with angry people and debating."

Sydney places his palm against my lower back. His silent way of letting me know he's there if I need him.

"I could probably spend an entire session going over each one of these in detail. It's magnificent, really. The power they all hold." Abigail sets the amethyst onto the soft white plush lining the table.

My gaze flicks instinctually to the seam of the room and then back at a familiar small rough black chunk. "What's this one?"

Sydney had offered me this type of stone in the past, but it feels like an eternity ago.

"Black obsidian," he speaks up. "Protective. Healing. Truth-telling. It can shield you from negativity. This one is interesting because it is made of earth, water, and fire elements. It dates back to prehistoric times and has been mined pretty much all over the world."

Sydney's knowledge and confidence are incredibly sexy.

"Good job, Syd." Abigail breaks through my lustful concentration on the green-eyed man I'm nearly drooling over. She motions to the opposite table. "What about over here? Recognize anything?"

I examine the display, trying to decide on which thing to point out first. Clearly, the lavender caught my attention from across the room, but that's the easy choice. The rather pointy and tannish star-shaped seeds are anise—another no-brainer. The delicate white petals that remind me of snowy broccoli florets on a lengthy stem appear to be yarrow. I decide on the one with dark-green leaves that have a silver bottom covering of wooly hairs.

"Mugwort." I point at the plant.

"Correct." Abigail grins.

I choose to show off. "Anise, yarrow, chamomile, jasmine. That kind of looks like rue? Um, the orange is calendula. Lavender, obviously. Is that...rosemary?" I name every single flower and plant on the table and cross my arms over my chest in triumph. I may not know a damn thing about them, but I can tell you what they are. Flowers and I go way back.

My mother always had a garden full and made sure I knew what each one was. Not to mention the whole glowing magical petals and stuff that alerted my mom I was, in fact, a witch.

"Wow. That's impressive, Willow." Abigail glances at Sydney's proud smile. "Did you know there are forty-seven species of lavender?"

"No, I didn't."

"They mostly serve the same purpose, but it's interesting to find the small intricacies of each." She points toward the sprigs with the needle-like leaves I had questioned. "And yes, that is rosemary. An interchangeable and powerful herb. It can be used in things ranging from exorcisms, to purification, to even attracting the fae."

Her last word seems to stop my world from spinning.

I clear my throat awkwardly. "Do you, uh, mind if I took one? I'd like to examine it further."

She beams, clearly pleased with my level of participation. "Of course."

CHAPTER 13

"That went rather well," Sydney says to me on our walk to my statistics class. "Are you still feeling all right?"

We stroll down the long corridor of the north wing, disregarding the passing students as they do the same to us. That's one thing I enjoy about the people here at Harper. Unless you're causing a commotion, most of them simply ignore you in an attempt to get through their day.

Except for Allie. She pretty much gawks at me any chance she gets. If looks could kill, I'd be dead a hundred times over. And now with the faint spreading of my return to classes, I sense her glare more often than I had in the past.

Part of me thinks she was hoping I'd never come back. She's never known an Oliver, though. We're resilient as hell.

And now that I have the tiniest bit of hope coursing through me, Allie is going to have to get the fuck over whatever vendetta she has against me.

"It did, didn't it?" I finally reply to Syd.

With a newfound sense of invigoration, I'm ready to face the world.

Which, luckily for me, happened to be timed well, considering how triggering this damn classroom is, haunted with the memory of my evil teacher.

Sydney kisses my cheek. "I'll be here when you're finished, okay?"

I tilt his head and plant my lips on his. "Deal."

I bury the aching reminder of Silas walking me to and from—always there lurking in the shadows or wherever I needed him. This class is going to be difficult to get through, but it'll be nothing compared to the deafening empty seat in my third-period speech course I shared with Silas.

A beautiful Cameron greets me and leads me to our spot.

I anchor onto him and force myself to be strong. A vision of Tremont moseying in with that devious smirk on his face appears in my line of sight. He glares at me and winks, sending a chill down my spine. I blink hard and rid myself of the taunting apparition.

"Will?" Cam places his warm hand on my shoulder.

"Hi."

Just then, a very real person walks in, a small briefcase in hand, heels clicking on the floor on her way to the front of the room. She turns, facing the lot of us and scanning the group. Her gaze settles on me.

Overflowing blonde hair, cascading down in waves around her shoulders. Black-rimmed glasses covering her bright-greenish eyes. An onyx pencil skirt, showing off her sculpted frame with a matching blouse and blazer.

It's no wonder Cameron likes the replacement. She's smoking hot.

I let out the breath I was holding and smile. I lightly elbow

Cameron. "I think you failed to mention a few details about the new teacher."

"Right?" He winks at me and kisses my cheek before settling into his chair.

I push away her stupid attractiveness and focus my attention on the energy in the room, eliminating the mix of unstable testosterone coming from the guys in the class. I narrow in on her and find she's nervous, but not in a scheming kind of way like Tremont, more that she's a bit skeptical herself. Insecure even.

If only I could read minds instead of moods, I'd be able to pinpoint what it is that she's thinking right now.

"Good morning, everyone." Her voice rings out clear and angelic. She grabs a chunk of white chalk and writes *Eleanor Sanders* across the top of the board. "For those of you who are new here, I'm Eleanor. No, I don't mind if you call me by my first name, we're all adults here, and I think we should treat each other in that manner."

Those of you? Isn't it only me who's meeting her for the first time?

I block out what she's saying to scan the faces. Is there someone I hadn't noticed when I came in because I was preoccupied with myself?

That's when I spot him. Sharing an equal level of attraction that Eleanor exudes, the brown-haired tall friend of Deghan's meets my stare.

Jackson. What the hell is he doing here?

I spend the rest of the time compelling my mind to pay attention to our radiant teacher. If I intend on getting caught up and not failing this term, I need to concentrate. Especially in the most challenging course I'm taking—statistics.

Eleanor makes it easy with her captivating smile and gentle

way of teaching. But the pesky what-ifs of the reason why Jackson is here penetrate my mind no matter how hard I try.

Just when I think I have enough things to worry about, one more is added to the pile.

Will I ever catch a break?

I still have so much to do nagging at me, and each is a challenge in itself. There is an endless amount of schoolwork to complete. I still don't really know what the heck happened to my mother, and I've yet to properly meet my father. Poor Lillian is a freaking witch and less than twenty-four hours ago found out she's adopted, and I've been a shit friend at helping her process this information. Not to mention the fairies and what the hell happened with Silas. Then there's the super-ordinary stuff, like Kyra's and Deghan's birthdays.

And despite all of that, I sense some strange energy from Cameron that is hard to pinpoint.

Adding another concern to my already full plate.

I shove everything to the side and turn my attention to Cam. I'm much better at fixing other people's problems than my own, so I'll start with him.

"What's on your mind?" I ask him when we're packing our bags.

"Cake," he answers, matter-of-fact.

I narrow my eyes at him and put a hand on my hip. "Really?"

"Yeah. I'm not sure if I should go a German chocolate route or maybe something fruity?"

"You're serious." I toss my backpack over my shoulder.

"Absolutely. Which do you think Deghan would prefer?" He stares at me in a *please help me* kind of way.

"Deghan is an actual garbage disposal. He's going to be stoked with whatever you choose. Well, if he slows down long enough to taste it." I laugh and take Cameron's hand between mine, still noting how stressed he is. I let a little calming magic float through me and into him.

The power flows through one of my hands and somehow

ends up lightly caressing the other. The sensation is startling and completely foreign.

He's oblivious to my abrupt shock. "But if you *had* to pick one. Which would he like more?"

I shake off the strange sensation. "You can't go wrong with something chocolate. Deg loves it."

Sydney meets us outside the room.

I long to tell him what just happened, but if I'm being honest, I'm not really sure what that was. Maybe it has to do with the new powers I unleashed once I broke the curse?

"You still haven't told me how Lillian is," I say to him the second we're alone.

"She's okay, really. I didn't want to talk about it in front of Abigail this morning. I didn't mean to leave you hanging. I assume she's overwhelmed with everything. She's handling it well, though. I'm having her write down everything she ate or interacted with the twelve hours prior to her glitch reaction to pinpoint what she should stay away from. We're going to take all this slow and try to figure it out without involving anyone else."

"What can I do to help?" Not that I exactly have the spare time.

We walk through the foyer and past the enclosed garden. The leaves on the massive tree are changing from a dark green to a crimson-tinged orange. A few of them scatter onto the grass-covered ground.

"I've got it under control," Sydney confirms.

I pause on the opposite side of the thick glass containment. "I'm going to take a quick potty break."

I step into the girls' restroom, and the chattering stops. I walk in to find Allie and her friend standing near the sinks.

Allie is applying a thick layer of some obnoxious and tacky lipstick. The bright red against her skin-tone makes her look sick and washed out instead of giving her the appeal she thinks it does. The color is much better suited for Remi or Kyra. They're both capable of bold and sexy styles.

Our gaze meets in the mirror, and she smirks.

She twists the lid in place and then smacks her lips together to rub it in. She rotates, leaning against the basin. "Well, well, well."

I sigh, not wanting to deal with her right now. I just want to pee and go to my next class.

"I don't have the time to entertain you. If you'll excuse me, I'm going to use the bathroom." I gesture to a stall.

She stands up straight and then walks over, blocking my path. "I thought maybe we could have a little chat. Since you're here and all."

I roll my eyes. "You're acting like a child, Allie."

She tilts her head back and laughs. "Me? Are you sure? Aren't you the one who spent the last few weeks holed up in your room because you ran your boyfriend out of town?"

I grit my teeth and flare my nostrils. I will maintain my cool.

"Aw, that's cute. Did I strike a nerve?" She taunts me by taking a step closer.

"You really don't know when to shut up, do you?" Anger bubbles up inside me, and it's everything I can do to stifle it down.

"Do you think I'm scared of you, Willow? You're nothing without your friends around." She puts her hand near her face and scans the bathroom. "Nope, no one here to fight your battles today."

I bite at the corner of my lip in an attempt to ground myself from losing control.

"It's really no wonder he left you. Shame though, really. He would have been much happier with me. It won't be long until you scare them all off." She rotates her finger in a circle next to her temple and points it at me to insinuate I'm crazy.

"You don't know anything about him." My jaw clenches harder, and my voice deepens.

The lights flicker overhead, and a wind-like gust floats through.

"Um, Allie. Come on, we're going to be late to class," the other girl says.

Allie lifts her chin at her. "Go ahead, I'll meet you there."

This is not good. I can't be alone with this bitch. I'm a ticking time bomb, and my magic wants nothing more than to explode out of me and disintegrate her with the snap of my fingers. I can watch it all plain as day. The second I give it the go-ahead, a blast of power bursts out of me and snaps her neck, leaving her motionless on the cold tile floor.

A cruel reminder comes barreling at the moment I thought I had killed Silas, his body lying limp and immobile in that shadow realm classroom.

"Nothing to say?" She obnoxiously chews on a piece of gum I didn't realize she had in her mouth. She blows a bubble and snaps it right in my face. "Is it because you know I'm right? That he's *so* much better off without you?"

She's not wrong, Silas really should have stayed away from me. But not for the reasons she assumes. And the fact that she thinks she knows anything about him or our situation boils a fury within me unlike no other.

I grip my fist and stare right into her eyes. "I never want his name to touch your lips ever again."

She grins out of the side of her mouth. "What are you going to do about it?"

I imagine the breath leaving her lungs, sucking the life out of her terrifyingly and painfully. It's probably a bit dramatic, considering the circumstances, but this girl has been nothing but a complete she-devil to me since the second she discovered I existed.

Her brows furrow, and she brings her hand to her chest. Her mouth opens, and she grips at her throat like she's gasping for air. Her eyes grow bloodshot, and she stumbles back, bumping into the stall and falling onto the floor next to a toilet. The door swings and slams into her legs.

Stunned, I gawk at her flopping around like an idiot on the dirty floor.

Am I imagining all of this? Did I do that? My power must be stronger than even I realize.

I unclench my fist and watch the air return to her body.

Her chest heaves, and she sucks in thirsty lungfuls.

I kneel down to her and lift her chin despite her trying to flinch away. "You have no idea what I'm capable of." I turn and walk out, leaving her behind to swallow my words.

Sydney's facing the garden when I come out. He seems lost in thought.

I approach him and tug his arm toward my next class.

"Everything okay?" he asks.

I smirk, the overwhelming satisfaction now coursing through me. "Mm-hm."

CHAPTER 14

I should probably be a little worried about going off on Allie, but even if she tells the truth, who's going to believe her? If I hadn't been there myself, I'm not sure I would have trusted what happened. I had no idea those types of powers existed without proper spells and practice.

Allie has no clue what that was, and I don't intend on explaining it to her. My only hope is that she got the hint and leaves me the hell alone.

So, I do nothing. I don't say a word. Because I don't need to worry anyone more than I already have. I'm a loose cannon, and I need to get my shit together. My behavior was reckless and irresponsible.

I'd be lying if I said it didn't feel damn good, though.

Unleashing that anger on Allie was the best I've felt in a while, and not only does that scare me, it makes me feel more alive than I have in quite some time.

I'll use it as a forward momentum to figure out what is going on in my life.

Which leads me to this very instant, walking the path behind the school with a handful of rosemary and a mission to find the fairies.

I'm almost to the covered area when a voice calls out.

"Willow!"

I glance over my shoulder and settle my gaze on a frantic Remi waving her arms like a wild woman on the patio.

Endless alarms sound in my brain. Is something wrong? Is someone hurt? Did Allie actually tell everyone what happened? Did I screw up and break whatever oath I had signed about not telling the humans about the supernaturals? Maybe Lillian passed out or consumed her glitch again?

I sprint to her, shoving the herbs into my pocket on the way. "What's wrong?"

"It's an emergency. I have no idea what to get Kyra for her birthday."

My heart drops. "You scared the shit out of me. I thought someone died." I grasp my knees and take in a breath of chilled air.

"Around here? Yeah right. It's like cricket central. Nothing bad happens at Harper. This is real, though. I need your help." Remi presses her hands together in front of her and juts out her bottom lip. "Please. I wouldn't typically ask, but I'm desperate."

I flit my gaze toward the forest. I'll have to put that on hold for another time. Right now, Remi comes first.

"What the heck were you doing, anyway?" she asks and quickly changes the subject. "Oh, I forgot to tell you. Cam has some cake samples for us to taste. He's such a catch. That man can *cook*."

"He's talented, for sure. Professional level chef." It warms my heart that others see how gifted he is. When his partners notice, he sort of brushes it off thinking we're just telling him what he wants to hear. The immense success of the bake sale really helped with his confidence and showed him that it's not only us who think he's wonderful. He has a natural-born ability to cook and bake, and the results are out of this world.

Not to mention, he's one of the sweetest and kindest souls I've ever known. A true romantic.

"I told him to come up with something lemon. Kyra *loves* lemon." Remi threads her arm through mine and squeezes tight. "Oh, Will, I'm so glad you're back. I mean, I know you're still processing everything, and I don't expect you to be totally fine. I'm just really happy to see you functioning again."

That's what hope can do. It can light a spark under your ass and drag you from the deepest and darkest trenches. It's a dangerous thing, because it can be taken from you so easily. That's why I'm clinging to every fragment of it like it's the only thing keeping me alive. If I didn't have it and the million and one tasks keeping my mind occupied, I'm not so sure I'd be able to get through the day.

Nothing masks the aching pit of despair that has consumed my soul. But even if there's the tiniest shred of a chance, that's something worth fighting for. And I will follow every lead I can until I take my final breath.

I've mourned for long enough. I should have been on this from the start. I was pathetic to fall into the state I was in. I can no longer let my weakness control me. I will rise from the ashes and overcome this situation, like I have every other one that's knocked on my door.

My entire bloodline had an ancient curse suppressing their magic, and I broke it. I freed them. I have battled demons. I have done things that Sydney and Walker and Abigail have said shouldn't even be possible. I went inside my own mind and defeated an evil being. I shattered the entire shadow realm when I thought I had killed Silas. I have spoken directly to the angels—to fairies. My blood was capable of reversing a very permanently deadly poison. I slowly sucked the life out of a human being today because I *thought* about it.

What else could I be capable of? The possibilities are endless.

I'm a freaking Oliver witch. If I have to resurrect Silas from the dead, that's what I will do to bring him back. Nothing will stop me from seeing him again.

I switch my mind from hardcore Silas mode to helping my friends. One thing at a time to keep everyone happy.

Remi and I take turns tasting a selection of the tiny delicacies Cameron came up with. In the short period following our final class, he somehow baked a bunch of sample-sized cakes.

"How did you pull this off?" I ask him in disbelief.

Maybe Cameron's magical power is baking, has to be.

"I couldn't stop thinking of all these combinations," he admits. "It's a blessing the school is so well-stocked and had everything I needed. My biggest hurdle was Deghan. I told him the kitchen was being sanitized and cleaned so I wouldn't be making him anything. I legit had to prepare him a post-learning meal to tide him over." Cam shakes his head. "That guy can eat."

I can't help but smile. The relationship those two share is unlike no other. They have this incredible bond that is unmatched. They tease each other and are there when they need them. They're both supportive and treat one another with so much respect.

I'm truly happy they have formed an unbreakable bond.

"Which one?" Cameron's nerves bubble up.

It's adorable watching him be worked up over Deghan's birthday.

"That one for Kyra, for sure." Remi points at the yellowish square with a bite taken out of it and then at another darker piece. "What was in this?"

"Hazelnut." Cam grabs a notepad and jots something down.

"Yep. Definitely." Remi nudges me. "What do you think?"

I don't even need to give my input; she chose the best options already. Not that any of them were *bad*. "Same. Those two were perfect for them."

Remi scans the room and settles on the clock ticking away on the wall. "Shit. I have to go. I promised Ky I'd help her color her hair. You good?"

"Yep, we've got this under control," I tell her.

Cam cocks his head to the side. "We're onto frosting next."

"I think I can handle your sweetness." I pitifully wink at him.

He successfully winks back and walks over to the large commercial-sized refrigerator. Cam slides out a tray with small dishes on top. He places them on the stand next to me and grabs a taster spoon. "Try this one." He dips out a bluish portion and gently slides it into my mouth.

It's sweet. Creamy. Blueberry for sure.

"Mmm. That's good." Although, I'm not surprised.

"I thought you'd like that one." He tosses the utensil and grabs another. "It would pair well with the lemon." Taking another scoopful, he says, "And this?"

"Is that coconut?" It has a bit of a flaky texture.

"Yep." He licks the remainder off and continues on his task.

The way his tongue skims the plastic sends my body and mind into a frenzy. I can't keep my eyes off him.

Cam's blue gaze swallows me whole. He goes to get another dollop and misses, dipping the side of his hand into a chocolatey mixture.

Without skipping a beat, I gently latch on to him and lick the icing off.

He stares at me and doesn't move. His energy shifts, and his expression hardens. Cam's lips meet mine a second later, crashing into a chaotic embrace.

We're out of breath and desperate for more.

Cameron's palms envelop my cheeks, and his body grinds on mine. Our tongues dance, and he pushes into me.

I can't help but want more, more, more.

I trail my fingers on his body, down his back, under his shirt, all along his skin. The touch is warm and electric and fucking marvelous. I glide over the muscles layering his sides and abdomen, finding my place at the button of his jeans.

A quiet moan leaves his mouth and calls itself home against my lips. He mimics my movements, cascading his hands all on me.

He stops abruptly, fiddling with something. Cam holds the thing in front of my face and crinkles his brow. "Is that...rose-mary...in your pocket?"

"Maybe." I snatch it from him and toss it to the side, fully knowing there's another one still tucked in place. I slide his pants down and take him in my hand when he springs out. I wiggle my own bottoms down enough to give us ample room.

Already forgetting the random thing that was stashed in my pocket, he slides the palm of his hand over me, sending pleasure coursing through my body.

I don't want to wait any longer, so I turn around and widen my stance, pulling him forward and into me from behind.

He bends me across the cold metal counter.

I bite my lip and glance to the door. This is reckless and risky, but that seems to be how I roll lately. I grip onto the far edge and push into him once he's in place.

Cameron's wide hands grasp onto my lower half and guide me up and down.

Between the exhilaration of where we are and how badly I have been missing his body, I'm not so sure how long I'm going to last.

He reaches one hand around and gently rubs on just the right spot.

Yeah, this definitely is going to end soon.

The buildup comes, but the sound of the door swinging open in front of me has my heart wanting to thud out of my chest. Then I realize who it is.

"How many times am I going to walk in on you two?" Deghan shakes his head and grins.

I release my hold on the table and raise my finger, motioning for him to come near.

He comes across the other side of the counter, and I reel him in.

Cameron doesn't seem to protest at the new arrival. He actually somehow grows harder inside me.

I ride my body back and forth on him and take Deghan's face in my hands, kissing him deeply.

Luckily, the bench is short enough that I can reach the other side. Without taking my mouth off Deghan, I weasel one of my hands into his pants, gripping him securely and noting how firm he already is.

He groans against my lips and tugs down his sweats.

I break from him just briefly enough to spit into my hand.

It's not long until I'm the first to cascade into bliss.

Cameron thrusts through my pleasure, pulling out and finishing on my back at the same moment Deghan tenses and comes undone.

Grinning and out-of-breath, Deghan says, "Remember that time you wiped the syrup off my lip and sucked it off your thumb and I told you it was the hottest thing you've ever done? Well, I think that's officially been topped."

CHAPTER 15

The sky has darkened by the time we step foot outside. Fluffy grey clouds with slivers of oranges and pinks pave the path to twilight.

Deghan sighs. "Isn't she wonderful?"

I study him while he soaks up the sunset. I'll never grow tired of watching him love this time of day with such a fiery passion.

What I wouldn't give to have Silas here with us. I'd take his silent brooding over his absence any day.

My heart and mind are torn between venturing out into the murky night to try to find the fairies or checking on Lillian. They're fighting a battle of tug-of-war, and I can't seem to figure out which side to choose.

With Cameron and Deghan next to me, it's going to be diffi-cult to wiggle my way free and escape into the forest. Not to mention, I'd much rather go out there in the daylight than when it's dusk. I don't doubt my powers, but I can't rely on them fully when I'm not totally in control of them yet. I still have a lot to learn about regulating my magic. I shouldn't be so casual with running off on my own in such unfamiliar and potentially dangerous territory.

"I'm going to see how Lillian is doing," I finally decide.

"Okay, princess." Deghan rubs my shoulder without taking his sights off the beautiful scenery ahead. "I'm pretty sure she's with Sydney. I think I remember them saying they were going to the library."

"Thanks." I give his cheek a smooch and then plant one on Cam. "I'll see you two later."

Cameron and Deghan gravitate a little closer to each other once I've stepped away. They both stare into the distance quietly.

I cross into the dining hall and am greeted by the ooey-gooey aroma of pizza.

Today happened to be a sponsored dinner night by a local anonymous businessperson. Every so often, this random individual lets the students vote on which restaurant they want food from and covers the entire bill. Apparently, with my absence the last few weeks, I missed the selection window.

Luckily for us, though, it meant kitchen duty started much later than usual, meaning we had time to clean up the mess we made.

Walking past an open box, I snag a small slice and take a bite. The mouthful is warm and salty with a little crunch of the crispy pepperoni. Just how I like it.

I steal a napkin from another table and stroll through the room. My gaze meets with Allie's across the hall, and she immediately averts her eyes.

No one has said anything to me about what happened between us, leading me to assume she hasn't told a soul. If she knows what's good for her, she'll keep things that way.

I nibble another piece of the to-go dinner I snatched and

continue on my journey to the library. I summon my magic to my core, attempting to locate Lillian and Sydney.

A vision of Lills grazing her finger along a wall of books comes into my mind.

I blink and it's replaced by the garden in the center of the academy. The thick glass reflects a person on the stairs to my left. I whip around, disappointment consuming me the second my eyes adjust.

Just a random person.

I'm not sure why I had thought it was him, but the dissatisfaction is all the same.

Not long ago, Silas waited in the shadows, watching me, and keeping me safe. He was my protector, my guardian angel, the one person I shared a soul connection with.

And now, he's gone. The link between us is severed despite the aching pit in my chest growing with each passing moment without him.

If he ever thought for a second that what I felt for him was because of some curse, he's wrong. That thread is broken, and I love him more than ever. He had told me this wasn't fair to me, not giving me a choice in the matter, but he couldn't have been more wrong. What we shared was deeper than some stupid magical bind, and I would go to the ends of the earth to get that back.

I won't stop until I do exactly that.

Nothing will get in my way of finding him.

"Off to do some studying?" Abigail steps into my path.

I nearly choke and hold out my hand. "You startled me."

"Are you okay?"

"Yeah. I was in the zone." I clear my throat. "And yes, I have a few things I wanted to research. Is it still okay that I use the room?"

"Absolutely. It's yours for the foreseeable future. It's safe to say you have the most pressing investigative needs, it only makes sense to grant you that access." She studies my face. "Well, if you need me, you know where to find me."

"Thanks, Abigail." I walk away at a casual pace, trying not to show any type of urgency and add to any concern she may have.

Because it's suppertime, there isn't a single soul in the human section of the basement library.

I'm surprised Sydney was so bold in bringing Lillian down here since we were trying to shield her from the supernatural people. I hope he was at least a little cautious in hiding her from their prying eyes.

I let my internal compass guide me to my friends. I walk down the winding and seemingly endless hallway until I've found the correct chamber.

I frown, finding Sydney alone in the space, his head buried in a book.

I was so sure that Lillian was here. Perhaps my magic tricked my mind. That only reinforces my earlier thinking that I shouldn't put so much blind faith in my abilities.

"Hey." I position myself in front of Syd's desk. "Do you happen to know where I can find Lills?"

A sly look appears on his gorgeous face.

Something blips in my peripheral, forcing me to take a step back. My heart all but jumps out of my chest at the very near intrusion.

"Can you believe this place?" Lillian motions around the room. "It's incredible." She elbows my arm. "You've been holding out on me, Wills."

"I hope you don't mind. I let her borrow that pen Abigail had made for you. Thought it would help her if she saw all the resources we had, ya know. Obviously, I didn't want anyone to know she was down here."

"Of course." I try to calm my pounding heart. "That's a great idea." One I hadn't thought of. Leave it to Sydney to be the brains of the operation.

"No wonder you got all weird all of a sudden." Lillian returns to the texts lining the wall. "It's a lot to take in."

I climb onto an open spot on the edge of the desk and watch her explore. "How are you handling things?"

She shrugs. "Okay, I suppose. I'm not sure which I should be more concerned about." Lillian glances at me. "The being a witch thing or that I'm adopted. Both are kind of crazy. I'm pissed at my mom for not telling me, that's for sure. I hate liars. That's probably my biggest pet peeve. I prefer honesty, even if it's a shitty truth."

"That's fair," I add.

"What could have stopped her? I'm an adult. Why wouldn't she have just told me? That's the part I find most bizarre. She had the perfect opportunity to tell me and she didn't. That's messed up." She slides an old book off the shelf and holds it out. "Who are the O'Hares?"

Sydney perks up. "Coven from Louisiana. They're decent people. Mostly known for earth magic and their dealings with healing remedies. Folks travel from all over the world to buy their potions. They have a pretty solid reputation among our kind."

"Hmph. Cool." She shoves it back into the open spot and turns around. "Is there anything he doesn't know?"

Sydney rolls his eyes and scans the page he's on.

I can't help centering in on the text he's trying to hide in his lap. "What's that one?" I point to the spot.

"Nothing really. Some stuff on unlocking powers. Research for Lillian." He lies terribly.

"I mean this." I rush over and snatch at the hidden object.

He blocks me and smacks his legs off the bottom of his table. The thing falls to the floor.

Without touching it, I conjure my powers enough to take it from him. It floats over and into my hands, and I hurry out of his reach from where he sits.

"Willow, please." Sydney's eyes plead with me.

Lillian rears herself into the corner to avoid conflict.

"What are you hiding from me, Sydney? You've been acting strange. Either you tell me, or I'll figure it out myself. You're well aware I always do." The fear of Sydney hiding something bad eats away at any positive feelings I had developed. I've put myself on the line numerous times in trusting him and gotten myself in trouble in the past.

What if this time, he really is up to no good?

"I'm begging you. Give it back." Sydney stands and shifts his gaze from me to the book.

"This is your last chance," I threaten and tighten my grip.

A green ripple flows over him and throws off my concentration.

It's mesmerizing and divine. My power yearns to mix with his like it has when we've done the shadow realm repair. Our connection is otherworldly. Nothing similar to what Silas and I share, but glorious all the same.

I accidentally let my guard down, and he seizes the opportunity.

"Bronte fallus mote," he mutters with his hand swiftly outstretched.

The hold I have falters, and the text slides away from me too quickly for me to correct.

I spot the cover before it's too far, and that's more than enough proof I need.

He realizes what I saw at the same time the shock registers through my body.

I clutch at my chest in disbelief. I should have known better. If Silas were here, he never would have let me fall victim to this behavior. He would have seen it from a mile away.

Family is everything. Sydney's words ping in my mind.

Despite what his mother and father put him through and all that they did to me, and to Silas—he's never been able to get over losing them.

That explains why he's been so secretive and shut off at times.

I may have recently found out about the bad woman only being gone, but maybe he's known all along?

Why else would Sydney possibly need to research demonic portals if he weren't trying to summon one to avenge or return his parents to this realm?

Tears well, and a sickening wave crashes into me. I throw out my arm and latch on to Lillian with my powers, dragging her to my side. "Click the pen."

"Willow, what's..." she drones fearfully.

But I don't let her finish.

"Now! We're leaving."

"You don't—" Sydney speaks.

I snap my fingers and clamp his mouth shut. I turn on my heel, pulling Lillian from the room and leaving him behind.

CHAPTER 16

"Y"ou have to teach me how to do that." Lillian sits on my bed and gawks at me in awe.

I pace back and forth, unsure of what the hell to do or how to process this information.

This can't be. That couldn't have happened. Sydney couldn't possibly betray me.

Right?

Wrong. Because he did. Everything adds up to him doing the unspeakable. The ultimate wrong that can never be made right.

"I'm confused, though. What happened? What pissed you off so bad?" Lillian brings her feet up to sit cross-legged. Her dark-brown hair falls over her shoulders.

It dawns on me that she's handling this all incredibly well, especially for her first few days in this new world. She witnessed her best friend go witch-crazy on a guy, and judging her reaction, it was nothing out of the ordinary. I mean, she's amazed, but not in a *this is terrifying* kind of way.

I force myself to sit next to her. I exhale, placing my feet firmly on the floor and my palms on my knees. I will myself to chill the fuck out. "Sydney is plotting to do a terrible thing."

Confusion racks her features. "What do you mean?"

How can I explain this to her without telling her everything? If I divulge too much information, it could blow a fuse and zap her energy for the day, or maybe even longer.

"Let's just say, there are bad people out there that Sydney is trying to locate and potentially bring into this realm." I rake my fingers through my hair, surprised at how long it's grown lately.

"I think you're mistaken." Lillian's voice is as calm and pure as her energy.

"You wouldn't understand. I can't disclose the whole thing. If I did then you'd get it."

A persistent knock sounds in the room.

"Who is it?" I call out.

The banging remains. If it were Cameron or Deghan they'd have responded or come in by now. If it were Sydney, he would say his name.

I let out a huff and spring from the bed to see who it is.

Sydney is standing on the other side, his lips pressed into a firm line. He flicks his finger toward his mouth and awaits his freedom.

I snap and release him. I hadn't realized my magic would have held that long. Not that I should care about his ability to speak when he's such a traitor. I shut the door in his face.

"Willow, please. Hear me out." Sydney sounds like he's right up against the wooden entry.

I flit my gaze to Lillian and roll my eyes.

"Wills...do you trust me?" Lillian glares at me seriously.

"Yeah, why?" I cross my arms over my chest and lean against the wall. What could that possibly have to do with anything?

"Have faith in him, then. You're wrong. I promise you; you are mistaken."

I watch her intently, studying for any sign that could be a red flag.

Did he somehow brainwash Lillian in the time I've been away to go along with his plan?

That has to be my irrational paranoia speaking. I couldn't have lost two of my closest friends in a span of a few days, could I?

I was dead certain Sydney had deceived me once in the past, and boy was I ignorantly incorrect about that. What if this situation is the same?

Everything in my heart screams to me that Sydney means well. How can I shut off my mind from throwing out warning signals?

I twist the knob, leaving enough space for him to enter. "You have five minutes."

Relief washes over him, and he steps in, reaching for me and then instantly pulling away. He tugs at his hair and fiddles with his hands, avoiding eye contact and staring at the floor.

"Sydney, spit it out."

His growing anxiety is overwhelming.

He finally speaks. "What if whatever I have to say could potentially hurt you?"

My heartbeat picks up its pace. "I'm not sure there's anything that could damage me worse than I already am."

Sydney swallows loudly. "The book you saw. It's not the first one of its kind. I've been scouring them, researching about demon portals and realms."

"Is there a point you're going to reach that doesn't make me think you're in cahoots with your psychotic parents? Because I'd probably skip to that if I were you. My powers have grown, so if you intend on planning an attack against me, you better come prepared to fight." I grit my teeth and try to keep my cool.

Sydney glances over to Lillian, and she barely nods some sign of approval.

"What is this?" I call out. "You two are in this *together*. Someone had better explain to me what is happening *right* now."

"Silas," is all Sydney replies.

The single name stops me. Throws me off balance. Rocks my world and sends five billion emotions flooding through me.

Sadness. Anger. Rage. Despair. Longing. Desperation. Fear.

I stand firmly in place. "If you so much as hurt one hair on his head." The fury inside me swirls around like a violent tornado.

Sydney shakes his head. "No. I would never. Willow, don't you see? I'm doing everything I can to find him and bring him back."

I blink. Once, twice, three times. This isn't real. None of this is. I must be dreaming. This is a nightmare. A sick and cruel, torturous display meant to toy with my mind. I'm being tricked.

I stumble back, losing the control I had a moment ago. My legs give out, and I slide along the wall onto the floor.

Lillian jumps up. Sydney rushes over.

"You're lying," I manage to spit out.

Sydney's clammy hands grip my face. "I would do anything for you. Including doing everything I can to bring back the one person who hates my guts the most."

Lillian smiles with tears in her eyes. "He's telling the truth. He swore me to secrecy. You weren't supposed to find out like that. Not until he had a solid lead."

"I don't want to get your hopes up." Sydney lifts me off the cold, hard surface. "And that's why I didn't want to tell you. I've been frantically trying to find something, anything. Do you remember? There were no bodies. None. And considering what we know, the sky is not the limit on what could have happened. It didn't make sense that they were dead. But I don't have any facts. Only theories and wishful thinking. I don't care about what happened to my parents, I just want to get Silas back for you. I have spent every waking second I could, scouring every piece of text I thought might be helpful."

I clear my throat, wishing it would remove the fog from my mind, too. "I might have a tip."

"You—you do?" Sydney does a terrible job of hiding his surprise. "Here, sit down." He leads me to one of the spare beds and sits next to me.

I glimpse over at Lillian, unsure of whether she should be hearing this next bit.

"Ah, come on. I've held it together this far." She puts her hands on her hips and takes a seat opposite us. "I want to be a part of the cool kids club."

Sydney raises his shoulders. He fumbles in his pocket and pulls out a protein bar, throwing it at Lills. "Eat this, it'll help."

The moment she takes a bite, I blurt out, "Fairies."

Her eyes widen, and she continues to chew.

At least she didn't faint.

My words come out in a rush now that I'm getting the chance to confess them to someone. "In the woods. I spoke to them. Bad woman, not dead, gone."

"Wait, what? Slow down." Sydney places his hands on my shoulders. "One more time."

"I went to Silas's cabin. On the way back, I got lost and did that thing where I ask my magic for directions. Only this time, it was the fae who answered my call for help. Some of them showed themselves to me. Like up close and personal. They told me your mom was *gone, not dead*. There was a noise, and it scared them away. I wanted to try to find them again, see if I could get them to elaborate." I take a breath. "That has to mean he's alive, right?"

Sydney rubs his chin, a habit he has when he's deep in thought. "That's what I suspected, although I couldn't be sure. Like I said, the bodies thing, it didn't add up. If they were dead, then something would have been left behind. This leads me to think you sent them to another dimension...a different realm. How Silas got sucked into it with them is the biggest mystery of all. Tremont fled. It was my parents who were taken, and Silas.

What connection do the three have, and how did I not get sucked up with them? I'm their own flesh and blood."

"This is crazy," Lillian says through the mouthful of food. She catches sight of the time. "Shit, I'm late. I was supposed to meet Ethan for dinner. He must think I'm becoming such a flake."

Sydney stands in a totally gentlemanly fashion. "You should go. You need to maintain your appearances, so we don't alert anyone to anything suspicious. If you need me, I'll be here or in the library. Otherwise, make sure you're eating and sleeping, and I'll see you after class tomorrow."

Lillian says her thanks to him and turns to me. "I might not be much help right now, but we're going to figure this out. Even if I have to be the cheerleader the whole time—which is something I despise, I might add—I'll do it. Whatever it takes." She wraps her arms around me for a quick hug and leaves me and Sydney alone.

A few minutes ago, I was ready to kick him out of my life for good, and now I want to grovel at his feet for doing such an incredibly selfless thing. He's sacrificed everything for me, the least I could do is put a little more faith in him.

"I owe you an apology," I confess. "It was uncalled for. Especially that bit with sealing your mouth shut."

"That was fucked up, Will." Sydney grins. "I don't blame you, though. It looked bad, it really did. I should have told you. I desperately wanted to. How do you tell someone you love that you have the tiniest hope of something completely outrageous even when you doubt it yourself? I thought I was grasping at straws."

I gently tuck my fingers around his palm, uniting our connection. *"I'm sorry. I don't expect you to forgive me."*

His mind wanders, and he brings it back. *"I'm terrified of losing you. I've never felt this before. Whatever we are, I cannot afford to let that go. I wasn't kidding when I said I'd do anything for you. I'll stop at nothing to find Silas; I promise you that."*

A lone tear rolls down my cheek, and he wipes it away.

I lean forward, pressing my lips softly to his. I whisper, "Thank you."

"Anything for you."

No one has ever done such noble and generous things for me as my men have. Each moment with them is a reminder that I have discovered something truly special and completely priceless. Not only have I been fortunate with one, but four exceptional true loves. I'll never be able to process how incredibly blessed I am to have found them.

And I will do everything in my power to hold on to that for as long as I can.

"How do we get him back?"

"If he's out there, we have to figure out where the hell he is. And in the meantime, we need to prepare."

CHAPTER 17

In order to venture in and out of demonic realms, we need to grow stronger—physically, mentally, and magically.

These types of journeys are not for the faint of heart or the weak. They're dangerous and deadly, often risking much more than one would imagine. At least that's what Sydney has told me.

Along with the secret of Lillian being a witch, we have to hide the fact that we're preparing to do things that the authorities at Harper Academy would never approve of.

And with that, we have our normal obligations, too.

School. Making sure I don't fail. Birthday parties and all that regular human stuff.

I even signed up to volunteer some of my power to help maintain the shadow realm. If I'm going to dabble in demon things, I'd like to be semi-certain the students here will be safe from a demonic attack. We don't need another repeat of a few months ago.

Not with so much on the line.

"I want you to start eating more. Protein and carbs specifically. We have to get some more meat on those bones." Sydney pokes at my arm. "Deghan is going to work with you on sparring and fitness. Cam is going to keep us fed."

At first, Sydney wanted to keep things between me and him. It took a little coaxing, but now he's on board with Deg and Cam being involved. I trust them, so he trusts them. Having them on the inside will help with our cover story if we're off doing angels know what. And it keeps Deghan occupied while Cameron works on his special day surprises.

"This is going to be fun." Deghan winks at me and takes a bite of a sandwich that seems to appear out of nowhere. That guy is always ingesting something.

Classes were nearly impossible to get through today with the constant nagging of wanting to be done to focus on more important things.

Silas.

The bringing him back from the dead, or wherever the hell I may have banished him to—given our theories that he and Sydney's parents are still out there somewhere.

I've tried to push away the pesky thought that keeps seeming to pop up.

How to save him without rescuing anyone else.

For now, I'll focus on one impossible thing at a time.

"I spoke with Walker and scored some extra shadow realm sessions. Told him the time difference between there and here will help you with catching up on schoolwork. It's not exactly a lie, but we're going to have to really micromanage our schedules to get the most out of this." Sydney flips through a notebook, scanning the pages with his pointer finger.

"What's on the agenda for today?" I sip from the cup of bitter herbal tea Sydney brewed for us. Supposedly, it's more potent than coffee and will aid in muscle recovery.

Sydney's attention settles on Deghan. "Tomorrow is the full moon?"

"Yup. Eleven fifty-three p.m. to be exact. Kind of annoying if you ask me. Couldn't it be at like nine in the morning to give me time to rage out and be back by dinner? Or at the very latest, bedtime." Deghan stuffs the rest of his meal in his mouth.

Leave it to him to be upset about missing out on food.

Sydney ignores his non-life-threatening complaints. "Okay, with that in mind, we should make an attempt to locate the fairies tonight. Tomorrow might be too dangerous if any of the wolves shift early." He glances at his watch. "We'll dedicate an hour to that, then meet in the realm for training. After that, we'll clean up, have dinner, and spend the rest of the day in the library studying. Sound good?"

Collectively we mumble some kind of agreement.

"Lights off by ten. Rest is equally important. None of this will go the way we plan if we don't recharge our own batteries." Sydney plucks two small brown satchels off his desk and tosses one at me and tucks the other into his pocket.

I peek inside to find sprigs of rosemary and fresh mugwort leaves.

"Fae attraction." Sydney gestures to Cameron. "You, food duty." He focuses on Deghan. "Go take a nap." Then finally, at me. "And you're coming with me."

"Roger that," Cam replies obediently. He winks at me and goes on his way with Deghan.

"What about Lillian?" I mutter to Sydney.

"She'll be joining us this evening. She's keeping Remi and Kyra occupied and then spending some time with Ethan." Sydney hesitates at the door. "What am I forgetting?"

I place my arm around his. "That you're incredible."

He rolls his eyes and blushes. "Hush."

We're the last to leave his room and head to our assigned tasks.

There is an added level of pep in my step as we make our way across the school. In the past, I've chosen to handle most of the challenges I come face to face with alone. I've never wanted to burden those around me out of fear that they might see me exactly that way—an excess weight they didn't need to carry. There's a level of gratification asking for help and receiving it without question or reservation.

When you love and care for someone, you do things without ever expecting anything in return. You fight for them and prove that they're worthy of being fought for. Relationships should be safe places where there is an excess of respect.

I've never known that. I've always been the one to lend a hand, to fix the problems, and be there for others. I haven't felt that in return, so it's a natural reaction to resist when it happens. That behavior is foreign. In the past, I've fought my own battles and those of others. Including the one person who should have been by my side from the start—my mother.

But instead, I blended in, I pushed away my own needs to put hers first and create minimal issues in her life. I became the parental figure. I took care of her. I got a part-time job. I sacrificed the biggest part of my adolescence to make sure she got the care she needed. I was forced to grow up and I became conditioned to relying only on myself.

I don't blame her for what happened. I'm sure she never meant for things to play out the way that they did, but it's hard not to have feelings of resentment toward her and wonder what I would be like if I had a more *normal* childhood.

Would I have more friends? Would I laugh more? Enjoy simpler things like music and fashion? Have fewer trust issues? Not be so afraid when someone wants to help me?

Maybe.

Living in the past isn't an option, though. This is the stack of cards I was dealt, and regardless of whether or not I think it's a fair hand, I'll play them out to the best of my ability. Sure, I'm going to screw up, like the numerous times I've let my friends down because of my own insecurities. I just have to overcome those experiences and do better.

You have to learn from your mistakes, not let them control and ruin your life.

"Where did you see them last?" Sydney interrupts my internal existential crisis.

"Over there." I point ahead through the thickly wooded area.

In a matter of a couple days, more reddish leaves have fallen and scattered across the ground. The evergreens seem to have swallowed up the new space, creating an endless depth of jade. The air is fresh with a nippy chill that makes my sinuses ache for the warmer days of summer.

Out in the open, I find the autumn temperature is tolerable with a light sweater. Here, in the coverage of the forest, it's drastically colder and much eerier.

"By that fork in the trees," I continue, except this time, I lower my voice.

I recall their fluttery, colorful wings appearing from the glowing moss-covered ground. A rainbow floated up and hovered near my face. It was equal parts alarming and magnificent. Not in a million years would I have believed they were real had I not seen them with my own eyes.

With each step closer, I spool my magic to the surface, willing them to answer my call for communication. I grip the herbs in my hand and surge the power into them. I fumble in my pocket for the small piece of clear quartz used for enhancing the strength of devices.

Sydney's anxious energy froths at the forefront of my awareness.

Placing my palm on his shoulder, I will him to be relaxed. The fairies seem to get spooked easily, so diffusing Sydney's nerves attend to multiple purposes.

He wraps his fingers around mine to initiate a private conversation. *"Thanks."*

Usually, if my magic was going to serve me, it would have

happened by now. With my increased abilities and connection to the earth, the fairies should have already shown themselves.

"Let's sit," I suggest, nodding toward a collapsed tree not too far from where we stand.

Sydney carefully obliges. He scans the vicinity and offers me his hand to steady myself.

The moments creep by with no sign of the fae.

First five...then ten. Thirty minutes of being so attentive that my eyes strain from paying attention to every single detail of the forest.

Dead leaves float by on the wind. A bird chirps to another. A small bunny hopping by without noticing we are here. The snap of a branch breaking from its old age.

The very normal sounds of the glorious thing that is called Mother Nature.

"Are you sure this is the spot?" Sydney asks.

"Yep. They were right here. Something scared them, and they took off in each direction." I urge my abilities to locate them to no avail.

"We can give it another twenty, but we have a tight schedule to follow." Sydney mentally pauses. *"This means nothing, don't get discouraged. We'll try again when we can. We'll exhaust every option."*

I should have chosen to go out here last night instead of staying inside. Maybe I lost my opportunity with them because I made the wrong decision. What if they're gone for good, like the angels?

A slinking loneliness settles its weight on my already too-heavy chest.

I close my eyes and let go of his grasp. I cup the herbs and crystal between my hands and beckon the fairies to me.

Please. I need your help.

A gust caresses my cheek from the pink magic sparkling around me.

Silence.

I'll do anything. Tell me how to find you.

Despite the growing confidence of my emerging powers, I'm massively defeated by not being able to reach out to the fairies.

A faint murmur brought in on an almost unrecognizably tender breeze tickles my ear. The single word, "Alone."

I swiftly look out into the looming dimness surrounding us. Not a blip of color in sight. They must not want Sydney to see them or recognize their proximity.

"It's time, Will. We have to go." Sydney rubs the small of my back.

Now I just have to figure out how to get around his rigid schedule and sneak out here on my own to have a little chat and get the answers I desperately need.

CHAPTER 18

"Catch." Deghan throws a rather heavy and grippy ball my way.

It nearly knocks me off balance with its weight. "Now what?" I shift my attention to the glowing purple seams holding our realm together.

"Throw it back."

I imagine tossing it at him, and a millisecond later, the orb is flying at him at a rapid speed.

"Not fair." Deghan manages to snag it at the last moment.

"Willow. That's cheating." Sydney looks up from his table in the corner where he's nose-deep in textbooks. "Don't use my temporary distraction as an excuse to cut corners. Being strong magically is important, but we need to up that physical strength, too. Package deal, remember?"

I sigh. It's much easier to will my mind to do the work for me, and since I'm fighting *supernatural* beings, shouldn't I fight with it, too?

"Again," Deghan instructs.

I heave when the thing makes contact with my chest.

"Come on, at least give me five minutes of an effort." Deghan tosses it through the air, making it appear to be a child's toy.

If this is what it takes to bring Silas back, I'll suck it up and play along. Plus, if I stay focused, maybe I can make enough progress to slip off and meet up with the fairies. It's been half an hour since Sydney and I left the forest, and yet the nagging curiosity of their behavior doesn't want to go away.

"You need to focus. Whatever you're thinking about, shut it down. In our training, I want your mind on what we're doing." Deghan's voice is strong and authoritative. Much more dominant than he ever has been with me in the past. "I'm serious."

He's right, he really is. While it's pretty damn obvious I have a lot of shit going on at once, I can't do my best at each one if I'm half-assing them at every corner. From now on, I need to focus on whatever it is I'm doing when it's that thing's turn.

So, during training, I need to train. During studying, I need to study. When I'm doing schoolwork... you get the picture.

Deghan's strong and muscular chest and shoulders bulge out of his snug grey T-shirt.

Concentrate, Willow.

Who could fault me, though? He told me to pay attention to training, and he *is* a very sexy part of that.

Deghan grins and chucks the ball back at me. "You're terrible."

"*You* are! You're going to have to wear something much less attractive next time." I anticipate the weight and grip the round sides better this time, absorbing the blow equally through my body.

"For someone so clearly distracted, that one was better."

"Do I need to remind you what's at stake here?" Sydney says overtop his book.

My entire soul, that's what. Or a significant part of it. And what's left of it is a worthless, blubbering mess.

"What are you studying?" I heave the mass at Deghan. "Shouldn't you be training with us?" I wipe at my brow and take in a steadying breath.

"I will. Prioritizing time. Trust me. I have a process." Sydney rakes his hand through his hair like he does quite often when he's frustrated.

To watch him be so intent on bringing Silas home from wherever he went is enough of a miracle to prove to me that literally, anything is possible. Those two are natural-born enemies, then conditioned throughout their lives to hate each other that much more. To see them come together, it's heaven to my aching heart.

If I didn't know any better, I'd say they're growing on each other. At the very least, the ice is thawing from their cores.

Believe it or not, they're more alike than they are different.

Sydney and Silas are both lost individuals, searching for meaning in their life. They're loners, and with their sort of rough exteriors, they're often misunderstood. Protective, incredibly passionate, intelligent. They're considerate and kind regardless of whatever front they put up. And they're both capable of so damn much. They're insecure despite having more than enough redeeming qualities. Not to mention, otherworldly good-looking.

No wonder they butt heads, it's like they're the same side of a magnet trying to connect.

Over time, I have hope that they'll realize how wonderful they are and maybe they'll respect and admire those qualities about the other.

It shouldn't matter whether someone is a witch, vampire, werewolf, human, whatever—it should matter what kind of person they are; how they treat others, how they show up in the world.

Maybe that's why I was attracted to both of them. They're

good people. Extraordinary, really. Deghan and Cameron, too. Better than I deserve, that's for sure.

I could spend until the day I die putting into words how noble and worthy these men are.

"You're doing it again," Deghan purrs.

"Shit, sorry." I lug the ball at him. "Hasn't it been long enough?"

He winks. "Sure. Give me twenty push-ups."

I exhale dramatically. "You're the worst."

"And that's why you love me."

Deghan has me running sprints through the room. He calls them *suicides*.

I totally understand the reference once I'm dripping in my own sweat.

At some point, Sydney joins us in the makeshift gym that both of them created by shoving the desks along the sides of the walls. It's not much, but it works, and given our pressing issue, we take what we can get.

We spend what seems like hours in the shadow realm, only for it to be a small blip in our days back in our normal dimension.

Once we're back, Cameron greets us with a gorgeous smile and three individual baggies. "For you, you, and you." He focuses on Sydney. "I included all the things you wanted. No clue how it'll taste. I did my best with tossing in some stuff I thought would make it more palatable."

I peek inside at the granola-looking thing and break off a chunk. I pop it into my mouth and immediately taste the sweet and acidic addition. My eyes go wide, and I snatch Sydney's before he gets it to his mouth.

"What?" Sydney calls out.

"They're blueberry." I hold on to the bar and keep it away

from him. Did it penetrate his skin? How is it that one of my favorite foods is his glitch?

"Will." Cameron places his hand on my back. "*Yours* is. Sydney's is apple, and Deghan's is chocolate. I went with things I knew you all liked. No cross-contamination, I promise. I'm always incredibly cautious about this. No alcohol, blueberries, or cayenne pepper."

I tilt my head at him. "Huh?"

He glances at Syd and then at me. "They didn't tell you? Lillian's glitch. It was the special ingredient in that honey mustard sauce I was messing around with. No biggie, though. I'm working on something else. That version wasn't my top pick anyway."

"We figured it out yesterday." Sydney avoids my stare.

What else have I missed out on because I've been so distracted?

How can I possibly make sure I'm covering all of my bases when things like this slip by?

"Oh, that's good." I try to mask my disappointment at being the last to know.

Deghan speaks up. "I think it's pretty damn good. I want another one. I'm starving."

Cameron grins and shoves him. "Go get cleaned up and it'll be time for dinner."

"Yep, let's keep on with the schedule. You have..." He checks his watch. "Twenty-eight minutes."

There is no way in hell I can shower and locate the fairies in that time frame. And if I choose to go into the forest without even changing, the guys will question me about what I had been doing. I'll have to figure out another moment to sneak off and ask the fae for information. I'm clinging to the small shred of hope that they'll have something useful to help us locate Silas, but I can't help but feel a bit skeptical. Call it intuition, nothing ever seems to come that easily.

Deghan leans over and whispers into my ear, "Want to save some water?"

I wink at him and shake my head, knowing damn well that's exactly what I want to do.

He throws his arm around me and drags me close to his side. The delectable aroma of his musky scent assaults me full force.

I may only have twenty-something minutes now, but I'm going to make the most of it. I pick up my pace, matching Deghan's normal stride through the north wing hallway and up the stairs.

Sydney funnels into his room, and Deghan pops into his to seize a change of clothing.

A moment later, we're on the other end of the building.

Deghan closes the door to my bedroom, his golden-brown eyes growing wild with want.

Not wasting another precious moment, I grip his face, pressing my lips firmly into his.

He lifts me off the floor and into his arms.

We stumble into the wall, turning and hitting another. We make it into the bathroom, and he frees one of his hands to crank the water on while maintaining his hold on my body. He sets me on the cold hard counter.

I rip his sweat-soaked shirt over his head and throw it to the floor. I trail my hands over his chiseled chest and along his broad back.

His mouth makes a frenzied path down my chin, across my neck, and onto my chest. He tugs my top to the side, revealing my sports bra. He grips the fabric and shoves it out of the way, pinching gently at me with his teeth.

The sensation sends sparks of pleasure throughout me.

I groan against his touch and reach to clasp onto him through his sweatpants.

Deghan emits a noise but pulls away. He traces his fingers along my sides and tugs at the elastic at my waist. He slides my leggings and panties over my hips, leaving me bare-bottomed on the vanity. He grasps at my belly and wrenches me to him, leaning my head into the steamy mirror. He takes my feet and brings them up to rest on the edge of the counter and spreads my legs. His face hovers over my most sensitive area, and he blows bits of alternating cool and warm air onto me.

I run my fingers into his chocolatey hair and mentally urge him to stop teasing me.

He plants soft kisses along my inner thigh and makes his way closer and closer to where I want him. Finally, his tongue playfully caresses me. He makes another deep moan, and like the animal in him is released, he applies more pressure and consumes himself within me. He licks up and down and from side to side, making sure to cover every single inch. He swirls around and flicks into my entrance.

"Deghan, please," I whimper, my head thrown back and hand wrapped forcibly into his mane. I drag him up and take his mouth against mine, tasting myself on his kiss. I maneuver my feet to his hips, drawing his bottoms down enough to free him.

His palms clasp onto me and yank me closer to his warm and waiting body. He manages to line me perfectly with him but slows upon contact to ease himself in.

I creep forward, desperate to experience him inside me once more.

Deghan fills every inch of me and still has more to spare.

I reach down and grip the base of him. I rock my body as best as I can from this angle.

He wraps his arm around my waist and lifts me from the spot and lowers me onto my back on the small bath rug on the floor. Gradually and with such restraint, he thrusts in and out.

The change in position brings a whole new level of gratification. I grip his back and dig my nails into his skin. A silent attempt to beg for more.

With our mouths and bodies intertwined, I ascend closer and closer to my peak.

Deghan picks up his pace while maintaining a gentle control.

I breathe in his salty sweetness mixed with the thick foggy air.

His teeth drag against the bottom of my lip, and the slightest new sense of pleasure sends me hurdling over the edge into a cosmic bliss.

CHAPTER 19

Remi narrows her eyes on us. "You two look rather...suspicious."

Leave it to Remi to publicly call us out on our pre-dinner-sexcapade.

"I don't know what you're talking about," I lie. My cheeks betray me and blush.

Sydney glances at his wrist. "You have less than a half hour to eat."

Deghan kisses my forehead and takes my hand in his, leading me toward the vast array of food. Tonight is one of his favorite dinners, not that he's very picky to begin with.

I grab a tray and a small piece of lasagna from the already plated and ready-to-go selection under the warmers. I scour until I locate the biggest one in the bunch and hand it to Deghan. I quickly find the runner up and give it to him, too.

"You understand me." He snatches up two side salads and accompanying dressing.

I secure our drinks. Sweet tea for him, sock water for me.

We approach our already eating group of friends and settle into empty seats.

"For the record," Kyra speaks loud enough for us all to hear, "I don't want a party. No surprises. I'd like to get through the weekend and pretend it's like any other. The only reason I'm saying anything is because I have a *feeling* that someone"—she elbows Remi—"is up to something."

Remi responds by kissing Kyra's cheek. "Whatever you say, babe."

I glance at Deghan out of the corner of my eye. He seems lost in his food, or desperately hoping no one saw him flinch at the mention of a birthday.

The rest of us stay quiet and pretend we have no idea what's going on.

"We could do another one of those movie nights," Ethan suggests from his place tucked in next to Lillian. "Something low-key."

"I approve of that." Kyra shrugs.

Cameron bites at his lip to hide any type of reaction. He's a bad liar and he's well aware of it. He's too damn pure and good-hearted to be dishonest.

"Any suggestions?" Lillian pushes her empty tray forward and leans her elbows on the table.

"We could go with a horror movie this time." Ethan scans the crowd for a response. "Or a thriller." When no one says anything, he adds, "Sci-fi?"

"Rom-com. Definitely." Remi grips her straw between her manicured nails and takes a drink of her water. "I'll come up with a list." She pulls her sparkly purple phone out of her back pocket and types a few things.

"I can't believe you carry that thing around with you." Ethan points at her with his fork. "Do you get service?"

"Nope, but a girl still needs to be able to take an impromptu selfie. Otherwise, I have nothing to post when I do get back to civilization." She tosses her perfectly curled blonde hair over her shoulder.

"Four minutes," Sydney adds quietly.

"What's the rush, Einstein?" Remi curls her fingers under and studies them.

Sydney doesn't skip a beat. "If we don't want Willow to fail this term, she has to maintain a strict studying regime to get caught up."

"That sucks," she says without shifting her focus. "If you have to run, I want to steal you first." Finally, she blinks across at me.

"Sure, yeah." I shove another bite of the warm and gooey creation into my mouth and stand, taking my tray with me.

When we're out of earshot, she flits her gaze back at Kyra. "I'm at a loss."

"What do you mean?" I wipe my face with my napkin and toss it into the trash.

We make our way across the dining hall and into the main area of the school. The massive ever-changing garden threatens to steal my attention with its questioning glory.

"I can't come up with anything *special* to get her." Remi clutches my forearm. "Please, you have to help me. Do you have *any* ideas?"

I rack my brain and sigh. "I'm quite literally the *worst* person you should be asking this kind of advice from." I note her frown and force myself to think of something. "What is she into? Stuff that's specific to her. I'm talking coffee, preferred scents, foods, music..."

"She likes *me*." Remi anxiously lets out a laugh. "I'm doomed."

"No, you're not. I'll tell you what, talk to Cameron. He's the king of romance. If you want something mind-blowingly awesome, he's your guy." I scan the distant group of people and settle my sights on his dazzling smile.

His blue eyes glisten even at such a distance.

"He's already doing so much. He probably has his hands full with Deghan." Remi paces in front of me.

"Bounce some ideas off him. That won't be too much." I reach out and touch her shoulder, begging her to calm down and not overly stress. "What about a date? Plan a day and do all of her favorite things?"

She places her hand on top of mine, her eyes growing wider as her head bobs up and down. "That's actually pretty good. I can work with that."

I smile at her obliviousness to my magic and lower my voice. "Keep in mind what she wants, though. What's up with her shutting down a party? I pegged her for one of those girls who loved their birthdays. The *it's my month* kind of gal."

Remi exhales, and her energy turns to something dark. She flits her gaze in Kyra's direction and speaks low. "A few years ago, I guess her dad left her mom. Said he had enough of pretending to be a happy family. Completely ruined her special day. That's why I want to go above and beyond and try to replace any negative thoughts she had and prove to her that she doesn't need that lowlife loser in her world. He doesn't get to control her like that. How is that fair to her? I won't let him continue to sabotage what he chose to leave behind."

"You're a good girlfriend, Rem. She's going to love whatever you do." Kyra may still be pissed about Remi going against her wishes, but I think Remi is onto something if she can pull it off successfully.

"Time's up." Sydney approaches. His forest-green tee brings out the emerald in his eyes and shows off his subtle build. He tucks his fingers into the pocket of his dark jeans. "Everything okay?"

Remi lightly slaps his arm. "Top secret stuff, you know." She winks at me. "I'll see you later, Will."

"What are we working on?" I ask him on our way to the library.

"We're splitting our time between normal stuff and other things. You need to get caught up on school as soon as possible. I don't doubt that you'll rebound on your classwork soon—I'm sort of counting on it actually. Then we can focus all of our attention on, well...you know."

I spend an annoying amount of time straining my brainpower on learning what I was behind in statistics. It's hands down my most difficult and time-consuming course—hence why it gets priority. If I can manage to pass this one, I should be good with the rest of them. Marketing and intro to management both have projects that count toward the majority of the final grade, and given most of the students haven't even started on them yet, it's safe to say I'm still on track. Sure, I missed some participation points, nothing I can't make up, though.

I do my best to avoid thinking about speech since it throws my mind spiraling into sad-and-helpless-Willow mode.

"Do you think you understand the p-value?" Sydney studies my face to determine whether or not I'm about to lie or tell the truth.

"Yes, it's a fairly simple concept." With all things considered, the work isn't too difficult. It's mostly about absorbing the required information and then applying it. I can absolutely see where it can become challenging if you aren't acquiring each step.

"Good." Sydney shuts the text and slides another book from the stack at the end of the table. "I want you to scour this, see what you can find on the other dimensions. Because of your connection with Silas, I'm hoping that something sparks and gives us a lead to chase."

I flip the old dusty thing open and peer inside, taking a breath to calm and steady myself for the task at hand. "Okay."

Sydney fumbles through the heap until he finds one for himself. "I'll be doing the same...minus the being fated to him and all."

I suppress a sigh that comes from the empty nothing inside my soul. I haven't sensed Silas in such a long time that I'm convinced we're no longer linked.

I let my gaze wander along the first page, then the next. I skim the words, not totally caring how the other dimensions operate or are formed. My foremost goal is to figure out where Silas is. The other details are seemingly unimportant for the time being.

Traepadeo realm. Thirteen folds over. I blink in confusion.

"What's a *fold*?" I ask Sydney.

"If you read the beginning you'd know." He settles back into his chair. "Although, it does explain it pretty poorly. It's basically the distance from us. Maybe think of it like a light-year. The farther away, the more difficult it is to reach, and that typically means the more dangerous the lifeforms are. But don't let that fool you, there are deadly demons right on the outside of ours. You have direct experience with that."

"Interesting." I glance at the page again, but a question nags at me. "How many are there?"

Sydney exhales. "Perhaps infinite. It's hard to tell for sure. Research and discovery are difficult, considering how unsafe it is to travel to those places. No one really wants to volunteer and risk their life. Some witches had developed a plan B in case something had gone wrong on an exploration of a new one. Basically, if they didn't make it, their encounter would be sent to this magical computer, so their sacrifice wasn't for nothing. Well, they ended up biting the bullet, and what the remaining people found was unlike anything they ever imagined. Gruesome. The worst of the worst. No one has traveled any farther outside of the known folds since then."

"Wow." It's a bit alarming at how incredibly endless and terrifying the universe is.

I shift my focus to the opposite page. *Fuwno realm.* Six folds.

There is a black-and-white photo of man-like creatures with animal paws on their hands and feet, and long spirally tails. Nothing is intimidating or scary about this one.

"Are they all bad?" I study the picture and find nothing menacing.

"Not all of them. Some have beings that mean us no harm. With that, though, other demonic realms prey on our naivety and pretend to trick us. Which makes it that much more difficult to comprehend which are safe or not." Sydney traces his finger along the line of text on his book.

Kuhqn realm. Twenty-nine folds. The image depicts a vast mountain range with snow-covered terrain, the words *unhabitable by man* scribbled in the margin.

A light shuffling of feet steals my attention.

I look up and wait for the person attached to the sound. Nothing.

A pen clicks, and I assume it's Sydney. I realize all too late that it's Lillian. She fooled me at my own game. Granted, I only had the device for a few months, but I put that thing to use. Now, my mind can't seem to keep up with it not being in my hands for a change.

"I kind of love being invisible." Lillian grins.

I understand that declaration all too well. It's freeing and exciting being able to walk through a crowd without a single person having a clue you're there.

Except Silas. He always seemed to notice me, even when I was hidden from everyone else. Our connection and his innate perception made it nearly impossible to sneak by him unnoticed.

If he could sense me so easily, surely, I can find the needle-in-a-haystack version of him that's lost out there somewhere.

CHAPTER 20

Another day full of the same tasks, except today, I have to find a window where I can sneak off and try to locate the fairies. Only this time, it'll be a bit more dangerous considering the full moon is only a few hours away.

Despite getting the full amount of sleep that Sydney recommended yesterday, I'm incredibly tired. It's either the additional training on top of the endless stress or the nonstop nightmares that hover through my mind.

I had opened my eyes to a steaming cup of coffee and a fresh muffin on my nightstand. Whoever dropped it off did a damn good job at not waking me.

Sydney and I studied the same crystals and herbs today, going into more detail on what each of them offered. That led to my mundane classes where I have a decent understanding of all of my course material enough that I'm not completely lost during each of my lectures. I add the current homework to my school to-do list and go about my day.

Now, I'm doing my best to pay attention to my teacher while I block out the chatter of the girls at my sides.

"I heard she's going to drop out," Remi whispers.

"No way," Kyra responds.

I'm not sure who they're talking about, but it seems highly significant to them.

"Paige told Sarah who told Billy who told Ethan that she's losing her mind," Lillian chimes in.

That first name of the gossip train catches my attention. I pivot at the waist to face Remi. "Who are you talking about?"

The corners of her lips turn upward. "Allie."

Someone claps. "Girls, if I could have your attention at the front of the room, that would be great. And while we're at it, how about one of you give me the definition to tactical planning?"

My gaze falls on the panicking friends around me. I clear my throat. "It's a middle-level process that converts a business's plans into more precise goals."

"Very good, Miss Oliver."

I swallow the nerves of being called out in front of the class and let the sense of pride wash over me at having known the correct answer. I got lucky, but I'll take it.

I allow my mind to wander away from the material. Is what they're saying about Allie true? And if it is, did I cause this to happen? Part of me can't help but feel like I may have been a bit too harsh on her in the bathroom. The other part is totally justified based on her completely horrible behavior toward me since I've known her. I haven't done a damn thing to her other than exist, and she's been such a stuck-up snob.

Maybe she deserved what she had coming to her. From the little bit I have learned about her, I'm not the only one she treats poorly. Allie is very much a bad person.

But those kinds of people are either born that way or are

conditioned by their environment and upbringing. And usually, it's the latter. Treating Allie poorly is only continually engraining in her mind that this type of behavior is acceptable and merited. Allie might be facing demons that I could never imagine, and without breaking the cycle, these types of situations will only continue.

"Earth to Willow." Remi snaps her fingers in front of my face. "Are you coming?"

I glance around to see the class emptying. "Yeah." I shove my notebook into my backpack and sling it over my shoulder.

Because of the upcoming full moon, Deghan was excused from today's shadow realm session. I was instructed to meet Sydney at the library when class let out, given he would already be there. We're supposed to study for a little while there and then travel to the other side to do one-on-one training.

With my hand firmly gripped around the rosemary in my pocket, I make a beeline straight for the exit. I pop out of the front of the school, making my way around the side of the building along the stone paver path. I could have asked to borrow my invisibility pen back from Lillian, but it may have come across as suspicious, not to mention, she seems to be using it quite often to hide her witchiness.

I grip the cold corner of the building and peer to the back. A few students stand on the patio, chattering to one another about this and that. Here's to hoping their conversation is enough of a distraction, so they don't spot me randomly walking into the woods.

I pick up my pace, almost running across the sort of wet ground. Taking in a deep breath, I reach the coverage of the forest. Now, the only eyes I'm concerned about are those of the wolf-nature. I'm basically in the belly of the beast and while I'm not totally scared of them, I still need to be careful. My magic could fail me, or I could be distracted when one of them decides to attack.

They're dangerous and volatile creatures that cannot be reasoned with in their animal form.

I look over my shoulder and watch the school grow smaller and the babble get quieter. I focus on the crackling that each of my footsteps makes on the earth. A snapping of a twig, a crumbling of some leaves. I have to work on being able to get through these types of areas more discreetly. Perhaps that's something I can ask Deghan for help on.

I cautiously walk toward the area Sydney and I visited yesterday. Despite being only mildly confident the fairies will appear, I take the risk anyway. Anything that could potentially bring me closer to Silas is worth any price.

A faint rustling in the distance confirms that I'm not alone out here in this space of many possibilities.

I swallow my nerves and keep on my path until the small clearing comes into my sights. I activate my powers and call forth the fae. I take the rosemary out and sprinkle it here and there.

"Please," I whisper. "If you're out there. Come forward." I gaze around. "It's only me."

Minutes pass with nothing but the occasional gust of wind taking a string of leaves with it.

I sit on the same fallen log Sydney and I had taken up post on. I'm not sure how long I have until he realizes I stood him up. I could have told him about the fairies wanting to speak to just me, but he would have wanted me to wait until the full moon had passed. Until the wolves were at a lower chance of prowling around looking for something to satiate their animalistic hunger.

That's time I'm no longer willing to sacrifice. If Silas is out there, I need answers on how to find him.

Something flickers in my peripheral. I find nothing when I turn. Then again, out of the other corner. I move slowly this time, hoping like hell it's not some wolf trap. The more I'm out here, the more I realize how dumb of an idea this might have been. I could have chosen any other night and put so much less on the line.

"It's not safe," a tiny purple flying creature says. Daphne, if I'm remembering correctly.

Her words send a weird chill over my body. It's the same thing Silas spoke to me of not too long ago out here when we first met. The memory unsettles me and throws me off.

"I was hoping to talk to you. If you don't mind. I have some questions." I speak quietly in an attempt to not scare her.

"You wish to talk to me?" She flutters about a foot in front of my face.

"Yes. Your red friend—"

"Astrid," she interjects.

"You two said that I didn't kill the bad woman, that I only sent her away."

The sound of howling forces our attention into the woods.

"You mustn't be out here," she continues.

"I have to know what you meant. Can you please tell me?" The truth is so close I can taste it, and no matter what kind of trouble is lurking through those woods, I refuse to give up now.

Her small face is strained with worry.

Is it possible for me to use my calming powers on fairies? It seems to work on other supernatural folk.

She opens her tiny mouth. "You are correct. You did not kill her. She's only gone."

"What exactly does that mean?"

"Gone means she can come back. She's not dead, you sent her away."

And if what they're saying is true, that could only mean one thing.

If it's possible to bring her back—then there is hope for Silas, too.

"Where is she? How can I find her?"

"You wouldn't." The beautiful creature's face strains. "Please tell me I'm wrong. You are our savior, Willow. You would be betraying us." She floats a little farther away.

I shake my head and hold out my hand. "I'm not, no. Please

believe me. Someone I love was taken with her. I'm trying to rescue him. I'm begging you." My voice cracks, and tears threaten to escape. "Help me find him."

Her expression softens into something else. It's the look you give someone at a funeral, when you're not quite sure how to comfort a person who has suffered such a loss.

"He's gone." Her voice is delicate and somehow still slices through my heart. "The place you sent him. There is no coming back from that Hell."

I haven't registered her words long enough to make sense of the devastating truth before a thudding of footprints fills the area.

She buzzes merely a breath from my face and urges, "Run!"

And despite my body and mind and soul and heart not having the strength or will to do so, I stand and do precisely what she says.

I sprint all of the way to the school, mindlessly following the glittering path that Daphne supplies graciously to me.

I make it to safety, collapsing into the side of the building where no wandering eyes can watch me suffer the loss of Silas yet again.

CHAPTER 21

"You did what?" With his eyes wide, Sydney clutches his chest and drops to the ground beside me. He rubs my shoulders. "Why would you do such a thing? Are you okay? Are you hurt?" He looks to the woods and follows the path with his gaze.

I shake my head. "Not physically."

"Willow. Tell me. What happened?" Sydney unzips his sweatshirt and lays it over my shoulders. "You're freezing."

I finally meet his stare. "He's...he's gone." Tears roll down my cheeks uncontrollably. The pain in my chest rips me wide open. Silas is lost forever, and it's all my fault. I did this, and I have to live with it for the rest of my pathetic life.

Why should I get the chance to live and he doesn't? What

could he have ever done to deserve this? Why did it have to be me who did it to him?

He had only just found me, and I sentenced him to an eternity of what? Hell?

I had to play the hero. I thought I could save the day, rescue the Olivers from the ancient curse plaguing them for centuries. I did exactly that and ended up destroying Silas in the process.

How is that justice or vindication?

Is this supposed to be some fucking *greater good* situation? One for the many?

Why couldn't it have been me instead? I'd give anything to trade places with him.

Sydney wraps me into his arms and rocks me lightly. "What makes you so sure?"

I pull away and look into his achingly beautiful green eyes. "That's what she told me. Daphne. The fairy." I wipe at my runny nose and choke down a sob. "He's not dead."

"Will, that's great news. We just have to find him. That should give you hope." Sydney tries to understand what I'm not saying.

"You don't get it, Sydney. I sent him somewhere he can't return from. It's impossible. He really is gone forever." And somehow, the realization that he could be potentially suffering makes this all that much worse. It's one thing for him to have been dead —this is entirely different.

How can I live with myself knowing what I've done?

I should walk back out into those woods and let the wolves rip me apart. I glance in that direction, the irrational thought incredibly tempting. If I made a move to go out there, Sydney would stop me. It's not like he's going to leave me now that I'm a blubbering mess hunched into a ball beside the school.

"How did you even find me?" The idea suddenly strikes me. Why would Sydney have ever ventured along this random path? I've only ever noticed him going out of the rear exit of the building, never the front and around the side.

He clears his throat. "I, um, I've been working on my locating abilities."

"Why do you sound so suspicious?" I narrow my gaze.

"It's embarrassing is all...you've found your powers a few months ago and you're stronger and more capable than me. I was just trying to catch up. I've never really been that great at tracing. I've been working on it, especially considering the whole Silas thing. When you didn't show, I got curious."

"Oh. I didn't mean to make you feel inadequate. If it's any consolation, I have no idea what I'm doing most of the time."

"That's probably worse." Sydney smiles and cups my cheek in his hand. "Anyway, business time. I want you to focus. What exactly did this fairy say to you?"

I let out a breath and will myself not to grow hysterical. "Other than the obvious? Your mom is someplace terrible. Silas is with her. They cannot return. And I think I pissed them off for a minute."

Sydney frowns. "The fae? Why?"

"She thought I was trying to locate your evil mother to rescue her. She said I would be betraying them, whatever that means."

He nods in some kind of understanding. "One of the reasons the fae are so elusive is because of dark witches. They're cruel and vicious and prey upon the fae for their powers. If I'm not mistaken, you took out the queen of the bad guys and rescued them along with the Olivers. That didn't register to me until now, but you freed more than just your own bloodline. Many creatures were under their abusive reign."

At least some kind of good came out of this shit situation. An added silver lining to this terribly tragic outcome.

"Was that it?" Sydney scans my face.

I recall the very short conversation. "Yeah. I think so. I mean, she told me it wasn't safe out there. That much was obvious. It's a full fucking moon. I was an idiot for going into that hell of a woods alone. Wait." The memory strikes me. "She said 'there is no escaping that Hell' or something like that."

Sydney blinks at me as the comprehension hits him. "Didn't you say you've been having nightmares where you're in a fiery inferno?"

I nod, the awareness coursing through me, too. Have I really been dreaming of the actual place that Silas was sent to? He's been there every time, calling out to me, begging me to save him. I make attempt after attempt to get to him, failing over and over. The flesh melted off my body, and somehow the pain of losing him is worse than the flames that consumed me.

"I know you're defeated right now." Sydney stands, extending his hand my way. "There is no giving up, okay? We exhaust all options."

I let him help me to my feet.

Sydney brushes the dirt off my side. He grabs my shoulders. "How many times have you overcome the impossible?"

He's not wrong. I really have. Time and time again, actually. Every single Oliver curse was infallible, yet I eliminated each one. Silas couldn't touch me without causing fierce pain rippling through his body, and somehow, I figured that out, too. Accidentally maybe, but still. There hasn't been a single obstacle in my way that I haven't eradicated. Why would I back down to a challenge now? Giving up isn't an option, and no matter what a fairy or anyone else has to say, I will see this through.

"You're right." I weave my hand through his and lead us toward the front of the school.

Sydney glides into our reserved library space and ignores Lillian on his way to the far corner. He floats his finger along the spines and pulls book by book out, stacking them until he can no longer hold his selections.

"I take it he found you." Lillian peeks her head over the text in her grasp.

I ignore the elephant in the room. The one that left my face tear-stained and puffy.

I watch the recognition settle on her face and, without giving her the chance to ask me if I'm okay, I speak first. "What are you studying?" I do my best to keep my voice and composure natural.

Her eyes light up. "Did you know there are a crapload of *types* of witches? Like, endless, really. Cosmic and green and hedge and sea witches. The list goes on and on. And get this, they're all either descended from angels or devils. Isn't that nuts?" Her voice lowers when her train of thought shifts. "I wonder what I am?"

Sydney places another few books on the table next to his initial pile. He glances over. "It's not that simple, though. Only a few have direct bloodlines." He meets my gaze for a slight second. "The rest are sort of...mutts. A mix of both. It's rare to figure out with certainty which lineage one has."

She looks between us. "Do you?"

Sydney swallows his uncertainty. Until recently, he was under the impression he might have been a dark witch. And then his mom threw us the curveball that he wasn't, and she basically disowned him for it.

"I...um..." I should probably tell my best friend that I'm a direct relation to the angels, right?

Sydney interrupts. "We aren't completely sure." He lays a hardcover in front of the seat next to his. "Here, I have a hunch."

I plop down and slide it toward me. I wipe the dust off the old, battered thing.

Hell, the infinite unknown.

I suck in a breath and flip it open.

Creatures with horns protruding from their skulls. Long, fang-like teeth and sharp curved nails. One beast has translucent wings, similar to a fairy, just much larger. Glowing orbs where eyes should be. Jagged blades with skulls on the end, clearly made for inflicting the most pain possible. And to top it all off, tridents...more commonly known as pitchforks.

It's incredibly unnerving to think that Silas might be mixed up in this domain. That I put him there.

I turn the frightening page and skim the text.

Hell, the farthest fold away. Although, there are numerous realms of Hell, governed by different princes that are said to be closer than others.

Maybe the reason I can no longer sense Silas's connection is because he's so fucking far away. The farthest place in the universe to be exact. And the most torturous.

There are three main jurisdictions of Hell with various subsectors.

Leviathan. Known as the seaman, with hands like tentacles that will latch onto you and suck the life from your body. Third of the princes to come into existence.

My mind wanders back to when I had studied symbols and found the one named after this guy. I hop up from my seat and stroll across the room to pull out that book. I float through the pages until I land on that one. An infinity sign at the bottom, and coming straight out of the center are two crosses stacked on top of each other. I knew the name seemed familiar.

"What did you find?" Sydney asks.

Lillian eyes us curiously.

"This Leviathan dude. I had read his name when I had done research in the past. Sure enough, I was right. Apparently, he's one of the lords of Hell." I take the text back to my seat with me to keep it handy.

"Do you think that's where he is?" Sydney runs his hand through his hair and drags it from his face.

"I'm not sure."

Lillian sets her pen down. "Wait, you guys think Silas is in *Hell*? That place legitimately exists?"

"According to our ancestors, there are many versions of it. Nobody has made it there and back to tell the story, though. I'm not sure where the legends come from. To sum it up, though, it's highly probable. That it's real, and that Silas is there." Syd gives his attention to the barely bound manuscript on his desk.

I scan the page of mine and find Leviathan's name and settle on down further.

Mammon, often associated with the sin of greed. If Ophelia LeBlanc is anywhere, this seems like the place she'd be sent. That bitch is one of the most self-centered, egotistical, completely gluttonous people in existence. It would only be fitting for her to spend an eternity in the company of the guy in charge of punishing that exact kind of person. A sense of certainty hits me.

I let my gaze wander down.

Balial, chief of all devils. I shake from a random chill and glance around, glad that no one saw my weird reaction to simply reading this person's name.

The ruler of everything that is Hell. The most sadistic and heartless being known to all. He stepped foot in our realm on one occasion, along with his brothers and others like him. Each of them procreated with human women, creating the very first of the witches. Those witches went on to reproduce with other humans or those who had been born with angel blood. Some light and dark bloodlines were preserved, with most dissolving over time, making it impossible to determine the origins.

Could it be that Silas is in one of these Hells? And if that's the case, how will we ever travel there and be able to return? Speaking of impossible things, this seems to be at the top of the list. Not a single person known to man has ever been able to pull such a feat off.

But no one has ever had this much to lose. I'd go to the ends of the universe to get him back, and if traveling to the farthest reaches of Hell is what I have to do, sign me up.

Now I just have to figure out which one of these he's been sent to. Clearly, taking turns exploring the depths of the underworld isn't an option, so we'll have to narrow it down and do our best to nail it on the first go.

How can we be so sure when there are nearly no more leads to chase?

"What I don't understand is why he got sent with them? Obviously, my parents got sucked into oblivion. Tremont didn't, though, he fled, and he was part of the cause. What linked Silas to them in a way that tied him up in all of this?" Sydney scratches his chin.

I rack my brain. "Silas had no connections to them, did he? I mean, he's a vampire. He was just as much a part of things as we were, and none of us got sucked up."

"I can't place it. The piece we're missing."

"Me neither." I hate not being able to figure things out, especially when they're this incredibly important.

"Think back to the ceremony, what do you remember? There was a pentagram. You needed her blood. What about the spell? Do you recall any of the words you chanted?"

I had been hit and knocked temporarily unconscious. The angels appeared, and I begged them to help, to assist me in defeating Ophelia. They showed me a vision, they filled my head with a strange realization of what I had to do. It was like they planted these seeds into my mind that bloomed and did whatever commands that needed to be done. How Silas got roped into that makes no sense at all.

And then it dawns on me.

"There was something you had said to me before...that they were your own flesh and *blood*. What if that's the key? Silas sliced your mom with his fangs to draw what I needed for the ceremony. What if he ingested some of it and that tied him to the ritual?"

"How does that explain me? I'm their son."

I shake my head. "But you're an anomaly, remember. You have angel blood." Immediately, I clasp my hand over my mouth, only now realizing what I said out loud in a room where we aren't alone.

I guess the witch is out of the bag now.

CHAPTER 22

"You can't say anything," I blurt out.

Lillian narrows her gaze. "Seriously, Willow? Who exactly would I tell? You've already sworn me to secrecy about myself. I haven't told anyone. I've been careful. Ethan doesn't even know. My own *boyfriend*. I can't believe you don't trust me. Everything we've been through and you continue to keep secrets from me?"

I frantically look to Sydney for some backup.

"It's not that simple, Lillian," he admits. "This *information*… it's dangerous. Not just to me and Willow, but to anyone who knows it. People have killed to find purebloods or even reasonably distinguishable lineages. That's why Willow's powers were suppressed her entire life. Her magic was hiding itself to protect her."

Lillian sits up in her chair. "Wait, you have it, too?"

I nod hesitantly. "Yep."

Sydney continues. "Willow was born from the lightest of the light, and I was born from the darkest of the dark. My parents were bad people, and something, or someone, spited them, causing me to be born a complete opposite of them. Despite them being descended from the Devil, I have angel blood running through my veins. I think that's why they hated me so much."

I pick up where he stops. "Demonic witches have gained their power by stealing it from others. My ancestors were some of the most powerful of all, and a long, long time ago, they were cursed —all of their magic stolen and funneled into the darkness." I glance at Sydney and back to her. "I didn't even tell Syd when I found out. Silas was the only one to know for a while. And it's not something we openly talk to Deghan and Cam about. It's more of an unspoken agreement to keep it between us. It's safer for us all that way. It's incredibly rare to randomly find out you're a witch, and then that you're related to the angels. And I happened to do both. The moment the dark forces found out where I was, they started planning their attack against me to steal my magic. I was fortunate to have come here, under the protection of the school. Sometimes that isn't enough, though. That's why you can't tell anyone, not about this, not about your powers. Not until we can be sure that we trust whoever it is."

Lillian's expression softens. "What happened? Like, to the curse?"

The events from the last few months that led to today quickly assault my memory. Killing my first love. Shattering the shadow realm in the process and defeating that disgusting demon. The insistent bad luck, and my mom going missing. Battling the endless Silas's that wouldn't stop coming. Somehow going into my own mind and conquering another intense beast. The evil teacher who was gaslighting me and suppressing my powers from the inside. Directly speaking to the angels and the fae and fighting off werewolves and that incessant vampire who nearly killed me. Slowly watching Silas succumb to the darkness of the Reperio stone and nearly losing him, time and time again, only to have lost him in a more final way.

"I broke them, one by one." I expect to feel some sense of relief; instead, it's only remorse that comes. If Silas were here, there wouldn't be much more in life that I could ask for. I'd have my magic, my guys, my friends, and a chance at a future. I'd finish my schooling and magical training and figure out what I would pursue as a career. I'd have endless possibilities. Now, there's just the aching pit of despair that will never go away. If I had lost Silas in any other way, maybe I'd be able to cope with the loss. Knowing it's at my hands, though, that's something I'll never move past. Not in a million years.

"Did they get their powers back? The Oliver witches?" Lillian asks.

I recall my mother dancing in the living room, floating through the kitchen, and her beautiful rippling of power skipping across her skin. "My mother did, yes."

Lillian's energy shifts to something else I can't quite distinguish. "There aren't any others?"

I shrug. "I'm not sure. I don't think so. My mom never really talked to me about our family. She had told me that my grandma died from a broken heart. She never met my grandpa. My uncle, well, he's adopted. My grams thought that maybe having another child would remedy the ache in her chest. It didn't."

Sydney takes in a breath, and Lillian and I turn our attention to him.

"What's wrong?" I study his face, desperate to figure out his unspoken quandary.

"I can't believe I hadn't thought of this already." His eyes glisten with excitement. "Okay, this might be a long shot. Hear me out. What if"—he pauses for dramatic effect—"the reason why Lillian suddenly came into her magical powers is because she's tied to the Oliver bloodline?"

My eyes widen, and my heart picks up its pace. "You think...?" I turn to Lillian.

A smile spreads across her face. "That we're related?"

She and I hop to our feet at the same time, meeting each other in the middle for a giant hug. We bounce up and down and must look like complete fools.

"Now, don't get ahead of yourself, it's a theory. A highly probable one." Sydney can't hide his enthusiasm either. "I wonder if there are others?"

Lillian and I are all smiles—arms interlocked—on our way to the dining hall.

"You two seem awful chipper." Remi examines us like we're foreign objects to her. "Spill the details."

"Oh, I—um." I fail at coming up with an excuse.

Lillian doesn't skip a beat. "Wills passed her practice stats test with flying colors, meaning all the extra studying is paying off."

"Yeah, that." I nod enthusiastically.

"Uh-huh, okay. Whatever. Weirdos. Anyway." Remi glances across the room at Kyra and lowers her voice. "Everything is nearly set for Saturday. Cam is working on the cakes. I found a DJ and scored some booze. We've managed to invite the people we want and sworn them to secrecy. This will probably be our last outdoor party of the season, considering the crappy cold weather that is upon us." She lets out a sigh. "Couldn't our parents have birthed us somewhere warm, like California? Or Tahiti. I mean, come on now, is that too much to ask for?"

"I hear Costa Rica is nice," I add. Anything to keep her mind off of our lying trail.

Cameron slides his arms around my waist from behind and kisses my cheek. "There are a lot of mosquitoes there."

Lillian lets go of my arm in time for Ethan to grab her into a hug. The two of them are adorable together, despite all of the secrets she's hiding from him. Maybe one day, when we are no longer here at Harper Academy, she can fill him into this crazy *other* part of her life.

The oath doesn't exactly apply to her because she never signed it, but to protect the rest of us who have, she has to keep things to herself for now.

"Hey, you," Cam whispers into my ear. "I missed you."

I close my eyes and lean into his embrace, suddenly realizing how much I missed him, too. I rotate my body and bury my face into his inviting chest. "Mmm, this is nice," I mumble into his shirt. I wrap my arms around him tightly and wiggle one of them down and under his shirt, touching the base of his bare back.

Something electric comes to life for a brief moment. It's not what I notice when touching a vampire, witch, or werewolf, it's different. When I interact with humans, there is nothing there. With Cameron, there is definitely an obvious variance. Does Deghan have this same experience with him? Or is it only me? This isn't the first time I've felt whatever *this* is, so it can't be merely a strange coincidence. I could ask someone—Sydney may help figure it out. How can I explain something I'm not so sure about myself, though?

"You hungry?" Cameron asks into my hair.

We make our way into the crowd, loading our plates full of grub and finding seats around our friends.

Cam settles in next to me, and I'm relieved to have a moment to catch up with him. With everything that's going on, I feel out of the loop with the more human side of my life.

I take the top off my burger and squeeze some ketchup on it. "What have you been up to?"

Cam sips his drink. "Other than the obvious? Not much. The usual. Hanging out with Deghan. Studying. Cooking and baking when I can."

I can't shake the impression that there is more to what he's letting on. "What about with your brother?"

Cameron tenses at the inquiry. He flits his gaze to those around us. "He got out. He's home now."

"That's good, right? Why does it seem like that's bad?"

"He's mooching off the money we raised to pay the bills. I keep trying to get him to get a job to pick up the slack. I've told him I can't do it all myself. He claims he's tried. That no one is hiring. I call bullshit."

This explains why I've noticed the difference in Cam's energy lately. It doesn't rationalize the sensation of touching him, though.

"What kind of work is he looking for?" I stuff a few French fries in my mouth.

"Construction, I suppose. Something that doesn't require a drug test would be my best guess. He hops around from position to position because no one will keep him on very long. He's unreliable. It makes no sense. The guy used to be such a hard worker. Now, he's lazy and entitled. Completely selfish. I really don't think he cares if we lose the house." Cameron keeps his voice low to not draw any attention to the private conversation we're having out in the open.

"I'm sorry, Cam. You don't deserve that." I place my hand on his shoulder in a weak attempt to comfort him. I wish there was something I could do to help him. It's typical Willow to want to fix someone else's problems. And Cameron's brother, he is definitely a problem.

"It is what it is." He wipes his face with his napkin. "I'll figure it out."

"Is there anything I can do?" I offer.

"Unless you can magically kick his ass into gear, I don't think so. Thank you, though."

What if that's something I could do? If I could figure out what made Cameron's brother change from being a productive part of society to the lowlife he is now, maybe I could get him back on his feet.

What's one more thing added to my endless pile of seemingly impossible tasks?

"Five-minute warning," Sydney calls from across the table. "We have work to do."

I spend the time shoveling the rest of my food into my mouth, desperate for any ounce of strength it will give me in preparation for the training Sydney has prepared for me today. He warned me that it might be brutal, and for once, I actually believe him.

"Infito grantum modem," we say together.

Crossing over into the shadow realm never gets any less weird. Every time, I expect to have some out-of-body experience, and every time it's like I'm walking through any normal doorway. Except this one leads to another dimension, right outside of ours, that happens to have a completely different sense of time, and if the seams are severed, gives way to a demonic world.

I examine the integrity of the joints in the manner I always do. One should never be too certain of such things. Especially given my past with this place.

"I did some digging and found this spell," Sydney begins. "It's basically a magical hardcore workout. I want to try it out today since Deghan isn't here."

"Is it safe?" I ask, hesitant of some strange unknown thing.

"Yes. Although, it will be intense from what I've read. It's a more advanced incantation, so I'll need your assistance. To ensure it's not done alone, it requires two magic sources."

"This seems sketchy," I confess.

"Desperate times call for desperate measures. We need to get whipped into tip-top shape if we're going to rescue Silas."

Sydney is a fairly cautious and reserved guy. He's all about limiting risks and thinking things through thoroughly. I can't imagine he wouldn't have done the same with this. He's never once not proven to be a man of his word.

"Okay. Let's do it." I extend my hand. "What do you need me to do?"

He wraps his palm around mine and hands me a slip of paper with the other. "Recite this with me."

I do exactly what he says.

Our magic spins together in a beautiful mix of pink and green. It swirls up, and then cascades down like a glittering of colorful rain around us.

A small gust of wind knocks a stack of papers off the desk, and a moment later, an apparition appears.

CHAPTER 23

"**I**s that normal?" I blurt out.

Sydney nods. "Yes."

"Good day, sir, ma'am." The floating and translucent figure glides over to us.

I take a hesitant step back and study the suddenly appearing being. He hovers atop the floor of the room, his body completely transparent and masked in shades of the dullest grey. He appears to be a man in his fifties with wrinkles lining his aged face.

"My name is Charles—I'll be your instructor this evening."

"I'm Sydney, and this is Willow." Syd points to me.

"I'd shake your hand but, well, you know." He lets out a small chuckle, apparently pleased with his joke. Charles clears his throat. "Now, to business. May I ask the purpose of requesting me? Ergo, what goals are you hoping to achieve with my service?"

"Strength, mostly," Sydney speaks up. "We'd like to build our overall combat skills."

"Mmhm, I see. Stamina is of importance, too. Is there a specific type of demon you're battling? That will help me narrow down our training program." Charles runs his fingers through the air at nothing, as though he's scanning an invisible database for the proper plan.

"This is all hypothetical, obviously. We want to prepare for the worst of the worst." Sydney attempts to lie to the ghostly man.

"Right. A theoretical situation. Clearly." Charles winks at me. "And do you have prior experience fighting enemies? What do you have in this realm, vampires and wolves?"

"We've fought greater demons." I remain stone-faced despite Charles eyeing me like I'm lying.

"Have you now?" He inspects my serious expression.

"She's telling you the truth." Sydney moves forward defensively.

"Okay. Okay." Charles blinks dramatically. "I've found our regimen." He moves to the far corner of the room. "It's not too late to change your mind."

"Never." I stay standing where I am, unsure if I'm supposed to follow him. "What do you want us to do?"

"If I've done my job correctly, I've come up with a design that offers you a very hands-on approach. I'd like to start by saying, these are simulations, they are not real. You are only in danger of yourself, not the creatures that will spawn. I'd like you to forget that, though, and treat each scenario with a life-or-death mentality. If you assume you are in no danger, you may react differently than you would if faced with these in the real world. Injuries that you sustain within the construct are merely fictional and will revert once the time limit is complete. For our first lesson, you'll face a...let's call him an entry-level demon, to warm you up. Depending on your response, things will progress accordingly. Your magic is at full power, so use it how you prefer. Work together to defeat the demon. Each time you've completed your task, you will return to this room. Do you have any questions?"

"When do we start?" I glance around the class, wondering where the beast will come from.

"No, none from me." Sydney presses his back to mine, and a second later, our entire surroundings change to an industrial building.

The space is dim, barely lit by some low-hanging single bulb light fixtures. The air is stale and reeks of chemicals. How is it possible that I can *smell* the difference if this is just pretend?

My investigation is halted when a furry, six-legged thing walks out from around the corner of some stacked shipping crates.

I focus on the black-and-orange animal, willing it with my mind to be gone.

Somehow, the thing explodes.

I blink, and we're back in the classroom, standing in the same spot, backs pressed together.

Charles has a sly grin on his face. "I must have underestimated you, Willow."

"How?" Sydney stutters. "How did you do that?"

Charles points to his head. "She thought it. Isn't that incredible?" He chuckles. "How about I crank it up a few notches this time?"

I nod, waiting for my next task.

We blip to the building, that growing familiar scent assaulting me again.

This time, four beasts appear. Two on my end, two on Sydney's.

I force my train of thought on them and grit my teeth in effort.

A few whimpers and a splattering later, we're standing in front of Charles.

"I think I want a refund," I tease.

Charles pokes a few imaginary buttons, and we're sent to the same building.

The aroma is more like rotting flesh this time, with a tinge of dead fish. If he was trying to throw me off with a disgusting smell, it may be working.

I clamp my hand over my mouth and nose from breathing in the putrid odor.

Sydney follows suit and does the same. "Where are they?"

We spin slowly around in what is referred to as a death circle.

The floor shakes with approaching footsteps. A giant creature rounds the corner on all fours. Large horns layer the top of its body, with the biggest one coming from its forehead. It's reptilian with thick scales coating its sides. The arms and legs are made out of pure muscle and have no skin covering the meaty fibers. There is nothing except deep endless dark pits where the eye sockets should be. Its mouth opens, revealing infinite fangs and a long lizard-like tongue.

It roars, and the floor where its saliva hit melts away.

I summon my mental power in the same manner I had the last two times.

Nothing happens. No exploding creature, not even the slightest flinch.

Charles must have realized my strength and found a creature that couldn't be defeated that easily. It's clever really. How many times would I face such a being? I have to learn how to be resourceful and not always rely on the same methods.

"My mind power doesn't work on this guy," I inform Sydney.

He comes around and stands firmly beside me once he's decently confident there isn't another one coming in his direction. "What's the plan?"

I shrug. "Improvise?" I wrap my hand around his, channeling my power through him and his through me. The green and pink magic shimmers on my skin. "Follow my lead." I ball it up at my fingertips and wait for Sydney to do the same.

At the exact time, we launch our balls at the demon.

The creature winces and rebounds quickly. It stalks toward us, each footstep rattling the building and chattering my jaw.

"You take its back; I'll get the front. Try to find its weak spot." I shove Sydney out of the path of its airborne spit. I creep forward, examining its features from a closer proximity.

Despite not having visible eyeballs, the beast is attentive to Sydney running around to its rear. It snaps its mouth and throws acidic juices toward him.

I fire two rapid orbs of power to grab its attention.

Charles told us that this was a simulation, and although I want to believe him, this seems hella real to me. I can't lose Sydney to some disgustingly deadly demon fluid. It's hard to think this is anything other than reality when I can literally feel the foul breath of this monster.

I step closer, careful to watch for any flying debris. I survey it in an attempt to find anything I can deem useful. "Syd, I need a distraction."

"On it," he yells from behind the massive thing.

The demon must be thirty-foot long and twenty-foot tall.

Sydney nips it with a green blast, causing it to raise its chest, revealing a small glowing red ball in the middle.

I summon my power, creating exactly the weapon I need. A sword appears in my hand, embellished with every color of the rainbow. I take off in a sprint and hold the blade at my side. The beast roars, throwing a stream of killer spit in my direction.

Sydney screams, blasting it with everything he has.

Like I'm playing a game of ball and I'm trying to get to home before I'm called out, I drop and slide my body along the slick concrete floor and under the demon. A bit of its saliva touches my bare arm, sending spikes of pain through me. I heave my magical knife into the ruby sphere, disintegrating the thing in the process.

Goo covers me from head to toe, and a smile spreads across my gross face.

I blink again, and Charles is slowly clapping his transparent hands in front of me, clearly pleased and proud of the performance.

CHAPTER 24

"You're really something else, aren't you?" Charles crosses his arms and floats toward me. "How did you learn how to do those things?"

"I didn't." I bite at my lip, suddenly embarrassed about my success.

"That was...incredible, Will." Sydney nudges my shoulder with his fist. "Trust me, I knew you had it in you. Watching it happen, though, was intense."

I abruptly turn up my arm, trying to find the spot that had been singed by the demon's spit. Nothing is there. I'm perfectly unscathed.

"I told you. No harm will come to you regardless of how very real it seems. I'll have to work on finding you proper competition next time. Give you a real challenge for a change." Charles's original monotony is replaced by excitement at having his work cut out for him.

Sydney glances at the clock on the wall. "We're out of time for today."

Charles nods and floats a few feet away.

"Wait. Will it be you who comes when we do the spell?" It's only been a short while, but I've already grown fond of Charles and his understanding of our needs. I don't want to start over with someone new each time.

"Oh, I assure you. I call dibs on your case. Anytime you ring, I'll be here."

"Tomorrow, then," I confirm.

"Tomorrow." Charles's already dull body fades completely away, leaving me and Sydney alone in the classroom of the shadow realm.

A few words and a flicker later, we're standing in our home dimension.

Exhaustion and hunger hit me full force. "Damn, that wore me out." And made me somehow feel more alive than ever. Where has this magical training been all my life? This is the kind of stuff that Abigail and Walker should be teaching their supernatural students. Enough with this crystal and herb stuff. Demons and enemies lurk around hidden corners, and these students need to be capable of fighting them off.

"Let's stop by the kitchen, see if there is something to eat, and then it's off to showers and bed." Sydney takes my hand in his. He's growing more comfortable with his public displays of affection, and I am definitely here for it.

"I hope Deghan is okay." I'm fully aware he's a werewolf and qualified to defend himself, but the thought of him being out there with a bunch of unrestrained idiots is heavily unappealing. What if he turns into his human form and one of them attack him?

Sydney enters my mind space. *"He's a big boy, I'm sure he's fine."* He pauses and then continues. *"I wanted to tell you that tonight, you're stuck with me. I can't be up at all hours worried that you've ventured into the woods again."*

I roll my eyes. It's hard to be mad at him when he's completely justified in his thought process. Not to mention, his protectiveness is a heavy turn-on. *"Your place or mine?"*

"Yours. I wouldn't want any of the guys to worry the same thing if they stop by and you aren't in bed. We'll go to my room to grab a few things. Do you mind if I shower in your dorm?" He does a better job than me at maintaining pure thoughts.

I have to let go of his hand to avoid any embarrassing things to be heard.

He snickers and shakes his head. "I'll take that as a..."

"Yes." How is it possible that I am so endlessly insatiable?

It's not like any of my guys are lacking in that department. And considering my very limited past experience with men, I definitely got lucky in their ability to perform. Each one of them brings something different to the bedroom and never fails to satisfy my needs.

Sydney breaks my train of thought when he knocks on the side door to the kitchen.

Cam peeks his head out and verifies there is no Deghan in sight. "What's up?"

"Food. Is there anything quick we can grab?" Sydney steps inside and closes the door behind me.

"Yeah, totally. If you're wanting to eat on the go, I think there are some ready-made sandwiches in there. I threw together that pasta stuff you guys like, too. I figured Deghan would be starving when he was done with the whole wolf thing."

That was the dish that Silas complimented Cameron for, and Cam nearly fainted from the infamous Silas Harlow not being a grump for once. Oh, what I would give to have his broody ass prowling around the halls. Even if he had no idea who I was, just to feel his presence again would be everything.

"Which would you prefer?" Sydney places his hand on the refrigerator door in anticipation of my response.

"Surprise me." My indecision makes a grand appearance. I'm too tired to make a choice about something so insignificant.

Once we're closed inside my bedroom, Sydney sets the bag full of grub on the small table. I assume he's going to divvy up the food for us to eat; instead, though, he turns and walks across the space until he's right in front of me.

He pauses and raises his hand to my face. Sydney tucks the wild strand of silver hair behind my ear. "You were incredible today." His voice is barely a whisper.

I dig my finger into his pocket and pull him to me. "You weren't so bad yourself."

The moment the words leave my lips, his mouth is on mine. Slow and steady, building up to a sizzling hunger that no type of food could appease. Our bodies stumble back, bumping into the wall.

I open my eyes to locate where we are and find the closest bed. I drag him over to it and tug him down on top of me as we fall onto the mattress.

He smiles and continues to kiss me deeply. He runs his hand all through my hair, along my cheek, my neck, down my frame.

I match his movement, exploring his physique, too. I lace my fingers under his shirt and lift it over his head. I toss it to the side and then rip mine off and throw it in that direction.

Our bare chests touch, and it's everything I can do to not tear apart the rest of his clothing to give our bodies the chance to be that much closer.

I wrap my legs around his waist and grind into him.

He takes the opportunity to hook his arm under my waist and spin me on top of him. He grows hard against my movements.

I decide I can't take it any longer. I break away and unbutton his jeans.

He kicks off his shoes and wiggles out from under me to stand at the foot of the bed. Sydney drops his pants and releases himself.

I inch to the edge of the mattress, and he reels me in for another kiss.

His hands trail my body, finding their way to my leggings. He wrenches them down and over my ass and onto the floor. He leans me back and traces his tongue gently over my skin.

The impatient version of me grips his face between my palms and tugs him up to me.

He lifts me by the waist again and tosses me a little farther on the bed to give him room to climb on top. Sydney presses his mouth to mine at the same time he slides his length over my very ready entrance.

I suppress a moan upon his admission, a moment I find myself to thoroughly enjoy. There's something to be said about that first second when your man enters your body. It's like all of the build-up finally leads to this incredibly rewarding instance. I definitely rate it up there with the actual climax itself, just for different reasons. Obviously, it's not a freaking orgasm but it's pleasurable all the same. I'm fairly certain if that occasion was played on repeat, slow and steady and over and over, I'd absolutely come undone.

Sydney picks up his pace without becoming too aggressive. He's a tender and passionate lover, something I absolutely love about him.

We stay like this for a while, our bodies finding their perfect groove together, our lips dancing to the beat of this seductive lullaby.

Completely lost in each other, we climb the mountain of bliss.

CHAPTER 25

It's everything I can do to stay focused on my classes again, knowing damn well there are clearly more important things I could be doing.

Luckily, today is Friday, and aside from the joint birthday party that Cam and Remi are planning for Deghan and Kyra tomorrow, I have the whole weekend to train with Sydney and hopefully make some progress on locating the long-lost Silas.

I'm fairly caught up on my outstanding coursework. Sydney has been a great teacher and never fails to surprise me at how scholarly he is. He says I'm a fast learner, but I owe my success to him and his patient tutoring. There are only a few more small assignments to complete and then the bigger projects for finals. The load is reasonable if I continue on the path I'm on, which should be possible, given all that I've managed to juggle thus far.

Deghan grabs me from behind and spins me in a circle. "Princess."

"Put me down, you big buffoon." I laugh, and my cheeks redden at the sudden surprise.

He refuses, twirling me into his arms and carrying me. "Nope."

I bury my face in his chest and absorb his woodsy scent. "You're absurd."

"Yeah, yeah. You love me for it." Deghan kisses the top of my head.

Remi calls across the foyer, "Why don't you two get a room?"

Deghan smirks. "Don't tempt me."

"We might have time," I suggest sarcastically.

He glances down and shakes his head once he registers the not-so-serious smile on my face. Deg plops me onto the floor and places his hand on my lower back to guide me into the classroom where Sydney stands.

"Snacks." Syd points to the table where there is a selection of those special granola bars he had Cameron create.

I munch on one of the blueberry kind while I wait for our instruction. I mentally cross my fingers that we'll be doing the same type of training we did yesterday. It was pretty hardcore but highly effective.

Deghan quickly polishes off his food, so I offer him some of mine.

His eyes glisten with delight at getting more to eat. His metabolism must be incredible considering how much that guy can put away and still maintain rock-hard abs.

"Today we're going to be doing something different," Sydney begins.

I try not to feign disappointment.

He continues, "Yesterday, Willow and I summoned a magical coach who put together a personalized training program to help with what we're working toward."

Oh, he meant new to Deghan, not us.

Deghan nods. "Sounds fun. How was it?"

"Interesting to say the least. Willow kicked major ass, as per usual." Sydney winks at me.

Deghan nudges my shoulder with his elbow. "Atta girl, princess."

I grin and point to Sydney. "Syd did, too." My attempt at getting the focus off me fails.

Sydney shakes his head. "You literally disintegrated four demons with your mind."

Deghan's eyes go wide. "No shit? Really? That's awesome. Man, I miss out on all the fun."

"If you're on board, we can cross over and summon him. We have time to go through a few simulations." Sydney studies Deghan's reaction.

Deg hops up from his spot where he was leaning against the table. "Absolutely. Sign me up." He walks to the door and says the three magic words.

Sydney and I follow him through a millisecond later.

I quickly verify that the seams are intact and walk to the center of the shadow realm class where the guys are.

Sydney hands us individual slips of paper and tells us to join hands.

Wind swirls in the room, and a rainfall of pink, green, and gold glitters around us.

"Good day," Charles speaks. "I see you've brought a new recruit."

Deghan doesn't skip a beat, he walks right over and extends his hand. "What's up, man? I'm Deghan."

Charles chuckles and looks to Sydney and then me. He points to Deghan's outstretched palm. "I like this one."

"What?" The realization registers within Deg. "Oh, you're a ghost or something. Got it."

"Why, yes. *Something* like that. Anyway, I'm Charles. Have your friends filled you in on how this works, or shall I give you the spiel?"

"Um, simulations and Willow exploding some demon dudes." Deghan shrugs. "Did I miss anything else?"

Charles hovers in place. "That's about it. I'll add that these are in no way real. You will benefit from them, but you will not become injured. I clarify that because they can become incredibly intense. You will register pain and fear the same, it is only for learning purposes, though. It creates an appropriate environment to utilize your skills genuinely. Without the whole dying thing. Please use that information accordingly, though. You should react to how you would in any other setting."

"Got it. Be brave, not reckless."

Charles examines Deghan for a second then focuses his attention on me. "We'll start slow for your friend here to catch up. I have some things in store for you, though, to test your capabilities. Be prepared for the unexpected." His words are calm and considerate, a gentle caution of what's to come. He's respectful with his forewarning.

I nod, ready and willing for whatever challenge he has in mind.

"Are we set?" He meets each of our gazes. "And, go."

We appear in the same industrial building from yesterday. We back ourselves into a three-sided death circle. The gross aroma from our first encounter fills my lungs. It's those stupid creatures again.

"Um, this is weird," Deghan says with a slight humor in his tone.

I take pause, knowing how easy they are to defeat. I let Sydney and Deghan figure this one out on their own for a change.

"Ew, what are those things?" Deghan asks.

"Demons," I respond, matter-of-fact. "Kill them."

"I see how it is," Sydney adds. "Making me put in a little effort this time." He takes a cautious step from our tight group, inching closer to the two mutts approaching his side.

Deghan looks over his shoulder and follows suit.

I take turns eyeing them both cautiously, not wanting either one of them to get hurt in my attempt to allow them this battle.

A different sound rattles my ears. I scan the building to locate the source. I dislike how it shifts my attention from the guys. I could easily end this right now with a mere thought of destroying the monsters—instead, I stay firm on giving them their chance.

A giant, dragon-like thing skulks out of the shadow across the way. I take in its size, craning my neck to locate its head. A mane, similar to that of a lion, flows around its face in a very confusing manner. Demons really are creatively strange with their appearances.

It exhales, opening its mouth to reveal no visible teeth. A foggy mist floats out slowly.

Okay, Willow, time to get to business.

I focus my power on it, desperate to end it with one mental blow.

Instead, it growls in a pissed-off kind of way.

I guess my mind control doesn't work here either. I'll have to get resourceful instead.

I waste no time, charging it and throwing rapid-fire shots of pink magic at its massive frame. I do my best at scanning the beast's underbelly for any indication of weakness. I find nothing.

The demon turns abruptly and whips its gargantuan boney wing at me.

I go flying across the space and slam into a cargo container. This might not be real, but fuck did that hurt. I grab my shoulder and yank it back into its natural position. I attempt to look around it to check on the guys.

It blocks my view and ambles toward me. The ground shakes, and the vibration settles in my chest. Another current of vapor drifts from its mouth. This time, I don't get out of the way quick enough before it makes an impact with my left leg.

The pain ripples up my body.

I have to end this now.

Rage builds inside me, a fit of bubblegum-colored anger that swells and leaks out on my skin like sweat on a hot summer day. I channel it into both of my hands, forming a massive sphere of pure power.

In anticipation of my attack, it leaks more of its gas in my direction. It flaps its wings, hovering barely off the concrete floor and almost touching the incredibly tall ceiling. The wind from the wake sends the poison in bursts all around me.

More stinging drips its way down my arms and legs. My clothes melt in the spots it hits, and I fight to hold on just a little longer.

There is no more time to waste, the ball of magic must be enough. It has to be.

My diaphragm rumbles, this time from a low growl that forms in my chest. It converts into an ear-curdling scream as I release the wrath on this unbelievably large thing.

A solid line of pink flows from my hands leading to the seemingly slow-motion ball that crashes into the neck of the demon.

It cries out in agony and attempts to retreat from my attack. There is no use, it's a direct impact, rendering the creature helpless to the deadly blow.

I drop my hands to my sides and slump from the exhaustion and cascading pain. A second later, it's like nothing at all had happened. I flinch at the memory of moments prior.

Back in the classroom, Deghan grabs my shoulders. "Holy shit. That was *insane.*"

I flit my gaze to Sydney's smirk of approval and turn to the man in charge. "Thanks for that."

"Now, now. Don't be mad. You had it under control." He huffs. "Although, you managed to surprise me again with your determination and perseverance."

I realize I'm missing a few details. "What happened with you two? I didn't get to see."

"Nothing compared to you, warrior woman." Deghan leans his weight to one side. "Took some effort, but we managed."

"Good. I was worried." I regret saying the last part once it's out. I have full confidence in their ability to protect themselves, it's just hard to not want to fight their battles for them. I love them too much to let anything happen to them, especially when I could have prevented it myself.

"I'm hiding behind you next time. You're a freaking badass, Wills." Deghan is truly so happy for me that it warms my aching heart. He's the kind of guy who supports his friends no matter what, even if it means taking a backseat to them. There's something honorable about being able to celebrate someone else's successes and achievements.

Sydney places his hand on my forearm. "You good? You seem a little shaken."

I force away my crummy vibes. "Yeah. That one felt awful real."

"It was a difficult one to watch." Sydney's face tenses. "When Deghan and I defeated our demons, we transferred back here and saw yours play out like a movie. I hated not being able to help you."

"Freaking crazy," Deghan adds. "You're unstoppable."

Sydney is focused on making sure I'm all right, and Deghan is in awe of my performance. And somehow, I adore them both for their reactions.

"I'm okay." I turn to Charles. "Got another one for us?"

A smile spreads across his dull and see-through face. "As you wish."

When we get done in the shadow realm, to say I'm ready to sleep for a thousand years would be an understatement. I'm tired, hungry, physically and mentally exhausted.

"Time for dinner and then to the library." Sydney leads the way to the dining hall.

Each step feels like I'm weighed down with sandbags, and the gravity is turned way down, making everything so much more difficult and thicker to get through.

"I am starving," Deghan whines. "For real. Not my usual non-stop eating. Full-on, *I'm going to die if I don't get a cheeseburger soon* kind of thing."

Sydney looks back and rolls his eyes. "We're almost there."

I study the pep in his step, unlike that of me and Deghan. "How are you not equally dying right now?"

"Trust me. I'm fatigued, too." His posture and liveliness tell a different story. "That was invigorating, though. It's like we might actually have a chance, you know?"

Sydney is excited because we can potentially save Silas.

He's thrilled to rescue someone he absolutely despises.

If that doesn't jump-start my heart, I don't know what will.

I can't help but smile at him and absorb his happiness at such a bizarre-for-him kind of thing.

Here's to hoping the nagging thought that keeps popping up in my mind is wrong.

There's still the chance Sydney is doing all of this to liberate his parents, not Silas, and he could be using me to do that very thing.

For now, I'll push it away and revel in the possibility that he's being truthful, because I couldn't stomach any other reality.

CHAPTER 26

I'm stuck in another terrible, fiery inferno. Reaching for Silas. I'm well aware I'm having a nightmare, but that doesn't mean I don't fight for him every single time. I'd do everything for any version of Silas, and this is no exception.

My skin is licked by the flames, and my lungs are filled with a thick smoke. I clench my eyes barely shut to see through to the other side where Silas is cowered on the ground.

His leather jacket is torn and damaged from the fires. His perfectly sculpted face that was once flawless and impeccable, is now covered in soot. He trembles from either the fear of being in such a place or the pain he's experiencing.

He slowly tilts his face upward, meeting my gaze. His familiar purplish and silver eyes rip my heart apart with the sadness that consumes them. He looks hopeful for a slight second.

I take a step toward him and into the intensive blaze.

"Stop," he calls out. "Don't come closer."

I keep on pushing through. My body is continuously ravaged. I block it out. No amount of pain could ever supersede a life without Silas. If he dies, I go with him.

That was his plan, and now it's mine.

He told me that he would never live a life without me.

I didn't fully understand that sentiment until I lost him.

I had believed that I had forever with him, given he's immortal. Never did I consider that he would be taken from me in such a tormented way.

Silas is a strong and determined man, and he's lived countless years on this planet without meeting his end.

I was confident in his ability to at least live long enough to accompany me through my mortal life. In reality, had he never met me, he'd be perfectly unharmed, living and doing his vampire thing. It's my fault he's gone, and that has to be one of the most difficult parts of this new reality.

I ruin good things.

"Please, Willow, I'm begging you. Go back." Silas attempts to bring himself to his feet, except he can't find the strength. "You'll be stuck here. There is no getting out once you cross over." He crawls forward a few inches. "For me."

My heart breaks when I register his fear. It's not for himself, it's for my life.

In that moment and all the rest, there's nothing that could stop me from going to his side. I continue toward him. My flesh is torn apart, and I fight back the urge to scream.

I will save him. I have to save him.

"Willow," a different voice rings out.

I pause and grit my teeth against the agony.

"Will." It's Sydney.

He's not here, he's back in the waking world.

I focus on Silas, knowing my time with him is limited. "I have to go."

He slowly nods, and a tear rolls down his cheek.

I barely get my last sentence out. "Don't worry. I'm coming back for you."

My eyes open and register Sydney's frantic face over my body.

"What's wrong?" I spit out in a hurry.

"Nothing, really. I have an idea." His lips turn up and into a mischievous grin. "Want to do something crazy?"

I sit up and scoot against the wall. The time on the clock is a quarter past two in the morning. "I live for crazy." I yawn widely and hop out of bed.

***

I follow Sydney downstairs to what I assume will be the library, still unsure of what the heck we're doing up in the middle of the night, especially following such an intense training session with Charles.

I put my faith in him and tag along anyway.

"Let's make a pit stop first." He weaves his fingers around mine and tugs me toward the north wing.

The building is quiet and a little bit creepy at night. The lights are dim, and it's damn near silent, minus the generator-like humming that comes from the energy created by the supernatural side of the school. I've grown used to that sound, although it's much more obvious when everything else has been silenced.

Sydney carefully opens the door to the teachers' lounge and motions for me to enter. He strides directly to the espresso machine and pushes a few buttons. He grabs two to-go cups and makes quick work of creating a delicious pick-me-up for each of us.

"For you." He hands me one. His energy is buzzing with excitement.

I grow anxious about whatever the heck is going through his mind. I have the inclination to press our hands together and pop into his head and figure it out myself but choose not to.

I take a different approach. "What are we doing, Syd? You're kind of freaking me out."

"Oh, duh, right. You're probably wondering why the hell I woke you up for coffee." He puts the lid on his cup and faces me. He glances to the door and lowers his voice. "So, get this. I've been researching interdimensional travel. Like, to the folds."

I bite at my lip to hide the shot of adrenaline that instantly flows through my body.

He continues, "Obviously, short distances are no big deal. A newbie witch could figure it out. Longer, though? That's much more challenging. That's why we don't read about it often in the history books. It's possible, though, despite what everything we read tells us. The stories are so terrible that they try to make us believe it isn't feasible. Then we won't try anyway and cause any issues. Clearly, this kind of travel has consequences. It creates energy voids and can give demons vulnerable access points to enter our realm. But, and I mean a big one, on top of actually being able to *for real* make the trek, there's a different way."

Sydney pauses for dramatic effect.

I lightly smack him. "Well, what is it?"

He extends his hands to enunciate the words with them. "*Astral projection.*"

I process what little I have stored in my mind about the term. If I'm not mistaken, it's an out-of-body type thing where you can keep your physical body in one place, and travel with your mind and soul to another.

Is that what Charles does to join us for training? He had never really clarified what he was and how he appeared to us. I guess I just assumed he really was a ghost.

I finally speak up, "And you got me out of bed to tell me about one of your theories?"

Sydney grins and shakes his head. "Nope. Not *tell* you. I want to test it."

My eyes go wide in shock. My heart pounds. My palms sweat.

Could this possibly be happening?

If we pull this off, I could potentially be seeing Silas in only a short matter of time.

I cautiously set my mug on the nearby desk. Once it's secure, I throw my arms around Sydney and squeeze him tighter than I ever have. "You're a freaking genius, you know?"

He hugs me back. "Don't praise me yet. Let's make sure it works first."

I break away from him. "Where do we go? What do I need to do?"

"Remember that place we used the Reperio stone? There. I had to wait until the last of the wolves were accounted for until I felt safe enough to go out there. Well, they're officially all in, tucked away in their beds, sleeping soundly post carnivorous rampage."

I grab hold of my warm cup of coffee and make a beeline for the door. "What are we waiting for now?"

<hr>

The walk through the woods behind the school is brisk and dark, despite the sky being brightened by the full moon. Under the coverage, barely any of the light shines through. I don't bother paying much attention to my surroundings, considering all I can concentrate on is seeing Silas's face.

Sydney and I approach that familiar building where I was able to sort of locate the whereabouts of my mom and dad. Little did we know, in that same moment, Silas linked himself to that stupid rock and would suffer the torment of its power in the following days.

I was rapidly losing him by keeping the stone intact in hopes that it would recharge so I could do another location spell. What an incredible lose/lose, given he underwent that torturous trauma for nothing, being that I destroyed the ruby-red nugget before I could use it again.

"Are you sure about this?" Sydney closes and locks the door behind me.

I breathe in the musty air and blink to adjust my eyes to the darkness. "Is that even a question?"

Sydney strikes a match and lights a few candles, bringing a calm glow to the sacred place. "First, we're going to throw a protective barrier on the building in case someone attempts to enter prior to our return. Our bodies will remain in this dimension while our minds will ascend. I'd like to make sure we're sheltered in case that happens."

"Okay." I stand by a long table with various crystals strewn about, waiting for his instructions. I dislike feeling helpless, but it's best if I let Sydney lead us through these tasks rather than risk doing the wrong thing and prolong my chance of getting to Silas.

Sydney glides around the room and ignites more of the wicks. He secures a bundle of sage off the stand and burns it, too.

It's not long until a wafting of earthy smoke fills the space.

"To clear out any impurities." He opens the small window and lets the breeze carry away the bad energy.

"Can I do anything?" I offer.

Sydney motions for me to meet him in the center of the area. He takes my hands within his. "This is for protection. All I need is you to repeat what I say."

I allow my magic to flow through my fingertips and into his body, creating a beautiful current of power coursing within us.

"Uhyn bram motif ret weh breh," he speaks slowly.

We repeat the chant together. Our energies swirl around and create a tiny tornado of pink and green. Again and again, we pick up the pace and recite the incantation louder and louder.

Suddenly, a bright burst of magic explodes and cascades down around us, enveloping us in its grace.

Sydney's gaze meets mine, his emerald eyes seeming to melt through me like they always do. "We did it."

"That was incredible."

"This next part might come across a little weird." Sydney

hands me a small chunk of white chalk. "We're going to trace an outline around each other on the floor. Go ahead and lie down and I'll show you what I mean."

I do what he requests and position myself flat on my back on the hard wood surface. The boards creak when I settle all the way against them.

Sydney sketches a loose shape along my frame, completely circling and encasing my body. He motions for me to sit up. "See."

I study the blob and firmly grip the piece in my hand, ready to repeat the motion for him.

"Right here, though." He points to where my left hand was and wipes a part of it away. He draws a bigger tunnel-like area to where he is. "We'll be holding hands to maintain a tether to each other."

I nod and complete his shape.

He takes the writing utensil from me and tosses them both out of the way. "Ready?"

"Yep." I tuck my hair under me to make sure it's inside the confines. I tilt my head to get a better look at Sydney while he lowers down, too. I fight nervous energy that threatens to devour me.

Is it worry that I'll be seeing Silas for the first time in a while or of this not actually working? What if something goes terribly wrong? What if this is a trap? What if Sydney really is using me to get to his parents? I don't even understand the logistics of what we're about to do and yet here I am, going into it with a blind faith that everything will go the way I hope.

I push away the rampant worries as Sydney's cool fingers caress mine.

"I know it will be difficult, but try to clear your mind. Open yourself up to the universe, to your powers. Allow your true potential to come to the surface. It helps if you close your eyes."

I let the sound of Sydney's calm voice lull me from my irrational fears.

Silas pops up into my line of vision, and I shoo him away in an attempt to follow through with what Sydney is asking of me.

"Bronta bur tey magna plak fie…" The words roll off Sydney's tongue and find their way onto my lips.

I repeat them and completely open up to grant the magic free rein over my body and soul. It's a strange sensation, giving up and not resisting the intense flow that courses through my veins. The sheer volume that rattles my interior is incredibly liberating and astonishing.

He rattles off more, and I shadow him without second-guessing a thing.

A light breeze kisses my cheeks. I keep my eyes glued shut. I mutter the spell, hoping like hell it'll take me to Silas.

What an ironic statement.

Hell.

I take in a full breath through my nose then exhale deeply out of my mouth to calm my wandering mind. The air is surprisingly different. Hotter. Rancid. I clench my jaw, afraid to open my closed lids. It dawns on me that I'm no longer horizontal. I'm very fucking vertical.

I do the thing I'm most afraid of. I look.

Sydney is still holding on to my hand, an expression that registers as both shock and terror on his pretty face. His body appears a little translucent. Not like Charles's, though, much less.

I lower my gaze and find my body is also a bit see-through. I raise my hand and wave it in front of my body. The wind registers against my skin. Apparently, during astral projection, you still have access to all of your senses.

The heat whips at my flesh, nothing similar to that of my dreams. For a moment I'm concerned about the very real whipping of flames and infinite Silases I've never been capable of rescuing. That second is fleeting, given the incredible certainty that washes over me that this is *not* the same place. I've relived that nightmare enough over the last few weeks to know that with certainty.

"Where are we?" I finally ask. I scan the distance, only catching sight of an endless cave structure with glowing walls. They resemble hot lava rock...or burning charcoal.

Someone lets out a low laugh, and the sound is carried through the hollow and dances around my body in a taunting manner.

"How rude of me. It's not often that I get visitors. Usually, I take in more *permanent* guests. Shall I introduce myself?" The person's tone is guttural, profound, frightening.

I tighten my grip on Sydney's hand.

"We'll be all right," he whispers a weak reassurance to me.

I forgot to ask him what to do if we need to get out of here. And here I am, ready to pull the fucking get-home-quick lever.

A man, tall and well-built with a strong jawline and eyes made of onyx strolls out from the shadows. His immense beauty sends a creepy chill down my spine. Isn't there a saying that the Devil often disguises himself as an angel? This guy is most definitely doing that.

He's threatening and commanding and somehow, absolutely alluring. His skin has a faint glow of blue, and although it's strange, it works for him.

"I'm Mammon." He bows at the waist.

Screams ring out in the expanse, and I try to place them, failing miserably. Other than this gorgeous guy, there appears to be no one else in the close vicinity.

Mammon walks within about ten feet of us and sniffs the air. "Angel blood, interesting." He crosses his arms over his chest. "Sydney LeBlanc. Willow Oliver. What can I do for you? You haven't come here on a pathetic rescue mission, have you?"

My heart picks up its pace. My doubts from earlier about this not being the right place are immediately erased. Maybe my dreams weren't leading me in the correct direction. How foolish of me for wanting to pull the plug on our visit to Hell without following through with the reason we came.

"I sense your pain, child." Mammon narrows his gaze at me

and comes closer. "It's quite delectable." A devious grin spreads across his face, revealing his perfectly straight and white teeth.

Sydney pushes me behind him and stands in front of my transparent body.

Mammon chuckles. "Oh, I see." He whips his finger forward, and another scream rattles my ears.

I blast an orb of protective power around Sydney's form, quickly realizing it wasn't him who made the sound.

A frail form is dragged from the darkness and plopped in the space between us and Mammon.

"Is this what you came for?" Mammon teases.

The crumbled person slowly looks up. Tattered and dirty clothes. Hair matted to their head. Pain and anguish exuding from it in heaps.

I gasp, not believing my eyes.

Sydney tenses, and I'm not sure whether it's in surprise or anticipation.

A single word leaves his mouth, "Mom."

CHAPTER 27

Sydney did what I was afraid he would do, and now here I am, stuck at his mercy. What am I to him? Some kind of pawn in a sick game his twisted parents put on? He manipulated my desire to do anything for Silas and stole my magic to save his malicious mother.

Sydney betrayed me in the worst of ways. And for this, I will never forgive him.

I rip my hand away from his and hold it close to my body. "Sydney what the fuck is going on?" I blurt the question out and examine the way his body shifts.

"Willow, I..." He's at a loss? How convenient.

I glance at Ophelia and take in her aged features.

She's only been gone for a few weeks, and somehow, she appears twenty years older. Her once shiny black hair and perfectly maintained exterior is crumbling. Wrinkles line her face, and she's lost quite a bit of weight. Her lips are dry and flaky. Her skin is ashy and covered in dirt. Her eyes are red and dark, and if she weren't dehydrated, she'd probably be crying.

"What happened to you?" I ask her with more pity than I mean to let on.

She's a vile human, she deserves whatever torment Mammon sees fit.

"Oh, don't you worry." Mammon purrs. "I've taken *great* care of this one."

Ophelia opens her mouth to speak. Nothing comes out.

Did he take her voice, too?

I scan the vicinity again. "Where is Silas?"

Mammon puts his finger to his chin. "Hmm, could you be more specific?"

I narrow my eyes at him. "Silas Harlow. Vampire. Grumpy loner type. Incredibly attractive and covered in tattoos."

Mammon shrugs. "Doesn't ring a bell."

Anger rises inside me. Partially at being betrayed by Sydney, the other half by this arrogant devil. "So help me, angels, if you don't—"

Mammon cuts me off. "They won't help you here. Don't waste your breath. That sad attempt at..." He waves his hand at me. "Whatever this is, won't work here. I'm the Prince of fucking Darkness. You're a fool for stepping foot in here."

He snaps his fingers, and a familiar set of dark and orangish demons appear from all around us.

I have the audacity to actually let out a laugh.

Thank you, Charles, for your heads-up at what was to come.

"Something funny?" Mammon barely lowers his head up and down to give them the approval to attack.

I glance from side to side and behind us. Although I'm here without my physical body, my magic flows through me regardless. I take in a breath to steady the channeling of energy and focus my thoughts on the creatures.

I release the mental command, and not even a second later, each one of the mutts explode and splatter us with their remains.

Mammon flinches in the slightest, hardly giving away any sense of surprise. "I quite liked this suit." He pulls a handkerchief from his jacket pocket and wipes some of the ooze off him. "You're not much fun, are you?"

"I'll ask you again. Where is Silas Harlow?"

Sydney finally snaps out of his stupor. "Answer her. Where is he?" His question seems to surprise us all.

Ophelia lets out a whimper.

Sydney doesn't break his concentration from the master of Hell.

Mammon straightens his shirt collar. "While this is rightfully entertaining my incredibly dull and monotonous life, I am speaking the truth. This Silas Harlow you request is not here."

A newfound wound rips open in my chest. Sydney and I traveled to an unspeakable place and risked creating weaknesses in the balance of power, and all we have to show for it is Ophelia LeBlanc? If Silas was sucked into this mess with her, why isn't he here?

"What about his father?" It could be possible they were all sent to different places. I'm grasping at straws and hoping I grip one.

Mammon claps lightly once, and another crumbled form is hauled from the unknown by an invisible force. "He's here, too. I'm taking great care of both of them. You should really thank me."

I make eye contact with the twisted man lying in a heap on the dirt-covered ground.

It's definitely Sydney's dad.

And if what I'm seeing is real, where the fuck is Silas?

I break away from all of them and roam to where Ophelia came from. "Silas!" I call out into the void. "Silas, are you out there?" I summon my power to help me locate him. Nothing comes.

"She's a persistent little bugger, isn't she?" Mammon pokes fun at my hysterical cries for the man I love. The man I sentenced to an eternity of what I thought was Hell.

"Silas, please answer me." The void in my chest only aches more with the awareness that I may have actually lost him forever.

Hands grip my shoulders, and I recoil them off.

"Willow, please, it's me." Sydney flinches at my rejection.

How can I go to him knowing he brought me here to a place where his parents are, and Silas is nowhere to be found?

It only adds to the painful gaping wound where my heart once was.

"Let's go home." Sydney takes my hand anyway.

"Going so soon?" Mammon creates a windstorm with a flick of his wrist and sends it out our direction. "How about a parting gift?" The ravaging force nearly crashes into us.

Sydney mumbles something I can't make out.

I close my eyes in anticipation for the impact that never comes. With the recognizable hard surface under my stiff body, I realize we're back in our home dimension. Tears roll down my cheeks, and I remain in place. Not wanting to move or speak or do anything other than mourn the loss of Silas.

"Willow," Sydney breathes. He wipes at my face. "I'm so sorry."

How is he still here? Didn't he want to go back to Hell and get his parents and bring them back to safety? Clearly, they had both been through a tormented time. Why isn't he rushing to their aid?

"We'll try again. I'm not giving up, and neither are you." Sydney's voice cracks with emotions I can't quite comprehend.

I finally open my soaked eyes to look at him. Really study him. I do the one thing I told myself I wouldn't do. I hate the lack of trust I have and the insane invasion of privacy, but I have to get the truth. I can't keep doing this without knowing for sure.

I cup my hand around Sydney's. "I'm sorry for this." I pop into his mind space.

He doesn't resist; if anything, he relaxes into my probe for information.

Why would he do that if he had something to hide?

Maybe that's just it. He hasn't.

"Are you really trying to help me find Silas, no ultimatums?"

A heavy sadness falls across him. *"Yes."*

I wait for any wandering thought that may give him away. The only thing that comes is his desire to take my pain from me. To give me a chance to be whole again.

I cry harder at having doubted him once more. I hate how quickly my mind reverts to assuming that he's betraying me. I guess that's what I get for dating the son of my archnemesis.

Sydney and I walk back to the school in silence.

Our hands intertwined but our minds separate. We give each other some space while staying right there. It's not only me who's suffering a loss, it's Sydney, too.

I can't imagine the heartache he experienced when he saw his parents. No matter how incredibly cruel and evil they are, they're still his flesh and blood and mean something to him. I absolutely hate them and yet still felt pity and sympathy for the unending damnation they have ahead of them. In a matter of weeks, they withered away to almost nothing.

What will the rest of eternity do?

I assume that Sydney feels responsible for letting me down, too. Not to mention, the sorrow of knowing how little I trust him at times.

He's done everything right. He really has. He's sacrificed so much, and yet I still have moments when I'm unsure of his loyalties. He consumed his glitch to show me he wasn't a threat. He's proven himself time and time again. He's given up his life and his family and traded it for what in return? A girl who is quick to give up on him when things get tough?

If anything, today proved more than any of his other acts that he really is who and what he claims to be. He left his dying parents in Hell to get me back to safety. He was there to help me find Silas and nothing more.

I have to do better. He deserves much more than I've given him. From this point forward, I will make a vow to treat him with the respect he's so rightfully earned.

"Sydney." I shut my bedroom door behind me and break the silence.

He turns slowly to face me. His eyes are red, and exhaustion weighs heavily on his shoulders. "Yeah?"

I lean up against the wall, giving him whatever distance he still needs. "I'm sorry."

Sydney sluggishly shakes and lowers his head. "No. I'm sorry."

I take a cautious step toward him. "You have nothing to apologize for."

"For disappointing you. For making you feel like you couldn't trust me." His voice cracks, and it breaks my heart.

"May I?" I want to touch him, but I don't want to overstep any boundaries.

Tears line his eyes when he glances up at me. "Please."

I close the gap and wrap my arms around him. I hold him and let whatever calming powers I have soak into his body.

We stay that way for minutes.

I pull back and grip his cheeks between my hands. I force him to meet my gaze. "I shouldn't have doubted you. I won't make that mistake again."

He reels me in and buries his face in my neck. "I love you."

I steadily walk him back and guide him down onto the mattress. "I love you, Sydney."

CHAPTER 28

We sleep most of Saturday away.

Sydney and I take turns being the big and little spoon and stay hidden away despite the sun coming up and threatening to break through the window coverings.

Which in the moment, is freaking glorious considering how exhausted we are, but totally sucks given the lack of birthday presents I have prepared for Deghan and Kyra.

I've been so focused on the finding Silas thing that I let it slip about getting them gifts.

At some point, someone dropped us off a bag of pastries and a steaming pot of java. Whoever it was didn't mess around with our usual individual cups, they brought a whole kettle full.

I pour us both a full mug.

He rubs at his eyes groggily and takes his, warming his hands on the sides. He breathes it in deeply and sighs. "I love the smell of coffee."

"Me, too." I take a sip of my own and swallow down the wonderful bitter taste. I grip the brown sack and dump it on the nightstand. "Apple or lemon?"

"Apple," Sydney confirms.

I hand him his and bite the corner off the other fancy thing that only Cameron is qualified enough to create. Don't get me wrong, the chefs at the school are *okay*. They've got nothing on Cam, though. On numerous occasions, they've asked him to help tweak certain recipes and come up with new dishes for our meals.

Cameron hasn't even stepped foot out of Harper Academy, and people are already recognizing his talent. It won't be long until he sees great success with his abilities.

I groan and sigh. "What am I going to get them? I'm the worst at picking out gifts."

Sydney ponders over his very late breakfast. "I have an idea." He hops up from the bed and reaches out for my hand. "Come on."

I glance down at my pajamas. One of Deghan's massive tees and a pair of undies. "Um, I need to change first."

"Throw some pants on." He drags his shirt over his head and ruffles his bedhead in the mirror.

"Let me at least brush my teeth."

With our coffee cups in hand, Sydney leads me out of my room and downstairs to the main floor of our school. He weaves me through the random crowd of students congregating in the foyer, and out the front door.

I bring my arms to my chest to cower from the fall chill that lingers in the air.

Sydney goes straight to the side of the building and points at a beautiful flowering bush.

"I don't understand. I should get her a shrub?" I study the bloomed hydrangea and its color variations. Light blues lead to pale purple and some that are even stark white. It's truly beautiful—one of my favorites.

"No, silly. You should make her a bouquet. Willow Oliver style." Sydney winks as if I should understand what he means. He rolls his eyes and points to the thing. "Pick a few. Trust me."

I hand Sydney my drink and go to work snapping off a few of the florets and holding them gently in my arms. Once I'm satisfied, I say, "What's next, boss?"

He sheepishly grins. "This way."

We head back into the building and make our way to the glorious garden posted in the center of the structure.

Sydney quickly locates the handle and opens the door to grant us access.

I shuffle my gaze to the group of our peers.

"Don't worry. They're more focused on themselves to notice us." Sydney pauses next to a gorgeous lavender plant.

They're more vibrant and livelier than any I've ever seen. Their aroma is gentle yet decadent.

"And some of those, too," he confirms.

I kneel and slowly cup my hand to the side of the long-stemmed beauty. Upon impact, a light drizzle of magic crackles. I crane my neck at Sydney. "I freaking knew it."

"How else did you think they stayed so pretty all the time?"

I shrug. "Good fertilizer?"

Sydney chuckles. "Go ahead. They'll grow back."

I examine the selection to make sure I pick the right ones. I stack them on top of my already decently full collection.

"Okay, now you head back to your room. I'll be there in a moment once I find one more thing." Sydney takes a long drink of his coffee.

I let him lead the way, considering I never can quite seem to find the way in and out of this conservatorium.

He heads toward the dining hall, and I go straight to the stairs across the way.

At the top, I'm stopped abruptly by Abigail. "Hey, Willow." She eyes my bounty and crinkles her brow in response. "Umm?"

"Birthday present for Kyra. I hope you don't mind." I fight down the panic at having possibly done something wrong. It's one thing to go against the school's orders and travel to other dimensions, but to have taken some flowers from the garden seems entirely criminal.

She laughs slightly. "Oh, no. By all means. What a wonderful idea, actually."

Whew.

Abigail's energy immediately shifts from calm to something else I can't pinpoint.

I brace for what's about to happen next, wishing like hell that Sydney was here.

"I've been meaning to talk to you." Abigail lowers her voice and looks out to the unsuspecting students going to and fro.

"You have? Is everything okay?" Could something be messed up with the shadow realm? Are we potentially about to be under another demon attack? Could this have anything to do with what Sydney and I did last night? A million questions pile up in my head.

"Yes. At least we think so. It's just...we've noticed a deviation in the power here. It's something we've been monitoring since the demon realm accident. I wanted to touch base and see if you've developed any additional sources. Things have been *unique* with you, to say the least. We suspected that's where the excess came from but want to verify prior to auditing the system. It's a rather lengthy process, manually combing through each supernatural being in attendance to account for the magic." Abigail tightens her ponytail and waits for my response.

My panic of thinking I did something bad has shifted into needing to come up with a reasonable excuse that she'll believe.

I'm sort of a terrible liar. This is absolutely not the way we planned on people finding out about Lillian's newfound magic.

"Oh. Um. Yeah." I clear my throat to try to regain my composure and buy some time to think properly. "After the whole curse-breaking thing, I keep unlocking new abilities. Who knows when I'll plateau, but for now, I'd attribute the variance to me."

She studies my answer carefully. "That much we suspected. Do let me know if things change, though. It'll help us keep our system more up-to-date and weed out any issues that may arise."

"Of course." I bob my head up and down like an idiot.

Abigail reaches forward and caresses the purple flower. "Anyway. I'll let you get to it." She smiles warmly and strolls away, leaving me behind with my deceit.

I rush down the corridor and into my room in a desperate attempt to get away from any prying eyes that might be able to see through my dishonesty. I lean my back against the door and let out a sigh of relief.

The knob unexpectedly turning against my hip nearly sends me bolting across the space.

"It's only me. What happened?" Sydney sets the large mason jar on the table and comes to my aid. "I leave for less than five minutes and something goes wrong?"

"I'm fine. I just hate lying." I lay the bountiful assortment next to the makeshift vase that Sydney found.

"About...?" He eyes me seriously.

Anything, really. I strongly dislike that slimy feeling of a lie, no matter what the reason.

"Abigail. She confronted me. Said they sensed some *new* magical powers at the school. That they were checking with me prior to doing a complete sweep of the supernatural students here to account for the difference." I watch the look of shock register on his face. "I told her it was me. I don't think she suspects it's Lillian."

Sydney glances to the floor, a very clear indicator that he's lost in thought.

"How much longer are we going to be able to keep this hush-hush?" I don't exactly want to out Lills and put her in any danger, but if they find out without us telling them, they'll definitely think we're being suspicious. "Maybe we should consider filling them in."

Sydney slowly nods. "You're probably right. I just need a little more time to figure it out, though. We can hold off longer. You bought us extra time today, Will. Here's to hoping we can determine where her powers came from."

If we didn't already have enough going on, now there's a rush order on the Lillian project. Right now, I have to focus on a task that is totally out of my comfort zone.

This surprise birthday party that's only hours away.

CHAPTER 29

Remi insists on dropping off an outfit for me to wear to the party. "I don't have time to do your hair and make-up." She tosses a bag into my bathroom. "Curling iron." She twirls her finger around my silver locks. "Do something with this. I believe in you."

"What about you?" I ask. "Do you have everything under control?"

She breaks into a smile. "Oh yeah, babe. I'm the queen of party planning, *especially* surprise ones."

I hold up the small fabric of the red shirt she brought. How the heck am I supposed to stay warm with next to nothing on?

"Meet us in the dining hall at seven sharp. I told Ky that we're going to have a bonfire before the movie. She totally bought it and thinks it's just us." Her eyes glisten with excitement. "Anyway,

Don't be late. And seriously..." She points to her hair and then at me.

When she's out the door, I fling the top on the bed and rummage through my own clothing selection. I don't have much, but I'd prefer not to freeze to death with what she chose for me.

In the far corner of my closet is a shiny black shirt that Brooke insisted I pack.

She bought it for me for Christmas last year in hopes I'd at least *try* to step out of my comfort zone a little.

I pull it out and hug it to my chest. With all of the chaos that has consumed me since being at Harper Academy, I've made pretty much minimal effort to keep in touch with her. Not that she's really done anything differently either. Although, not having any cell reception has really put a damper on our line of communication.

We were both afraid this kind of thing would happen when we went to college—growing apart and finding new friends and lives. Hopefully, when we're both home for the holidays, things will be the same as they once were. Despite everything being so incredibly different.

There was one point when we spent an entire summer apart because her parents insisted on sending her to camp. The second she got home, we basically tackled each other on her front lawn and spilled the beans about our months apart. It was like we hadn't skipped a beat and fell right back into our incredibly close friendship.

So much has changed since we last saw one another. Could things ever be the way they were? She was there for me when no one else was. My longest and closest confidant. I can't imagine it any other way. Even with the dramatic turn of events.

I throw the shirt over my head and decide on wearing the skintight leggings that Remi brought. Hopefully, she'll see it as a compromise and not a direct disobedience.

Remi and Brooke would get along well.

I go to the bathroom and dramatically sigh at the sight of the curling iron. Sure, I've used one in the past, but I dread the long and daunting process of the whole thing. If only I could snap my fingers and have it done without putting in the heated effort.

I stare into the mirror at my pale complexion.

My cheeks are slimmer based on the combination of being not totally great at remembering to eat and training with the guys. My long eyelashes make my hazel eyes stand out. I settle my gaze onto my arms where my biceps are somehow visibly more defined.

Thank you, Charles.

I snatch my very minimal makeup bag off the counter and decide on the bare essentials. Black mascara, a touch of pink blush, and a healthy coat of ChapStick.

I bite at the inside of my lip and gawk at my hair. I could throw it into a braid and call it a day. Remi will probably be pissed about that, especially since I didn't wear the sad excuse of a shirt she brought me.

I plug in the device and wait for it to heat up. I stare into the mirror and imagine the same curls she's capable of making. I try to come up with a plan. She usually puts it in sections, right?

Then, something strange happens.

The right side of my hair twists into perfectly elegant coils.

I run my hand through it and hold it out, not believing my eyes.

Did that really happen?

I grin and focus on the other half. It repeats the motions and forms something better than I ever could have come up with myself.

"Holy shit," I mutter.

Who needs expensive hair products when you have magic?

I joyfully unplug the thing and make my way to the small table where Deghan's present lies in wait. I tuck it carefully into my pocket and check the clock. With my enchanted get-ready-quickness, I'm going to make the most of the extra time.

I seize a sweater off of the back of the chair and head straight to the library.

"Hey." Sydney pops around the corner and leans against the doorframe.

I shut the text and shuffle the books around so he doesn't realize what I was studying.

"Hi." I fake a smile and examine his face. Here I am hating being a liar, and Sydney is holding out on the biggest piece of information ever.

"I thought I'd find you here." He cranes his neck to peek at my table. "Discover anything useful?"

I shake my head. "Nope." This lie comes much easier than the one I fed to Abigail earlier. This time, there's so much more on the line and there is no room for error in my admissions. "Same old stuff."

Sydney's face droops, and his energy saddens. "We'll figure it out. I promise."

And not for a second do I doubt that. Sydney would go to extreme measures to bring me any level of happiness, even if it involves sacrificing himself to bring Silas back to me. Too bad for his sneaky idea, though, I'll never let him go through with it.

What kind of person would I be if I allowed him to give up everything for me?

It's not his responsibility to clean up the mess I created.

I'm the one who caused this situation to happen, I have to fix it.

Even if I'm required to risk it all.

No more of my friends have to get hurt as a result of my failures. I won't allow that to happen—never again.

CHAPTER 30

We walk into the dining hall promptly at the requested time.

Kyra and Deghan seem none the wiser to what's really going on.

Remi scowls at my change of outfit. "At least I approve of the hair. You freaking nailed it." She nudges my arm and winks. Her makeup is flawless, and it looks like she spent the greater part of her day getting ready. She's in a long-sleeved dark-blue sweater that barely covers her midriff and a matching high-low skirt.

Everyone naturally pairs up—Lillian and Ethan, Remi and Kyra, Deghan and Cameron, and me and Sydney.

"Absolutely gorgeous." Cameron takes my hand and kisses the top in such an old-fashioned romantic way.

If we were alone, I'd probably jump his bones for it.

What if I never get the chance to be close to him again?

"Totally agree." Deghan drags me in for a big-ass Deghan embrace.

I relax into him and savor what could be the last time I get to feel his smothering touch.

"You two are ravishing as always." I fight away the heavy emotions that threaten to give away my cover.

I will be strong; I have to be.

I've done the impossible. What's one more thing?

We weave our way through the crowd of students congregating on the patio and head toward that familiar clearing in the woods for one final get-together.

Sydney's fingers flit to mine, but I pull away and cross my arms, playing it off like I didn't know he was trying to hold my hand.

He reacts by putting his palm against my lower back. His touch is comforting and exactly what I need in the moment.

The fire is already crackling when we approach. The smoke is filtering through the air and masking the scent of all the hidden bodies behind the trees. With only the flames lighting the area, Deghan and Kyra still have no clue what's about to happen.

"Aw, this is perfect," Kyra coos.

Remi tugs her toward the lone cooler that's situated next to a bale of hay. One of many that provide ample seating around the campfire. She locates one of Kyra's favorite fruity alcoholic beverages and gives it to her. Then she tosses me and Lillian bottles of water. She asks the guys what they want, and when everyone finally has a drink in hand, she raises her cocktail up. "A toast. To the greatest group of friends I've ever known. To a girl who always brings a smile to my face and never fails to blow my mind at what she's capable of. I adore you, Ky-bear. I am proud you chose me and I'm even more grateful to spend this day with you. Happy birthday, babe." She turns her glass to Deghan. "Happy birthday, Deg."

"Surprise!" Total chaos ensues.

People funnel out from various locations, and more coolers are toted out. A table appears with endless stacks of pizza boxes and another with two absolutely beautiful cakes. A portable DJ stand is carted out, and music starts blaring. Bodies jump up and down and swing to the beat, and everyone is laughing and smiling, and not a single person has any clue that tomorrow I'll be descending into the gates of Hell.

Deghan grabs me by the waist and spins me around. "Did you know about this?" He plants kisses all over my face.

"Maybe." I giggle. "I have something for you."

His eyebrows rise, and he grins. "You got me a present? How did you...?

I point at the shy, super-cute guy standing beside Sydney. "That one right there."

Cameron blushes and rubs at his neck.

Deghan slaps him on the shoulders and drags him in for a hug. "You're the best. Or the worst. I'm not really sure."

It warms my heart to witness those two growing so close in a short amount of time. I only wish Sydney had that same type of companionship to fall back on when I'm gone. I hate leaving him, but he's much better off than Silas, and Silas clearly needs me.

Deghan tickles my sides. "What did you get me?"

I weave my fingers around his and take him away from the loud group.

"Ohh, are we about to have a quickie in the woods? Because that might be the best present I've ever gotten." Deghan cocks his head to the side.

I shake my head. "Sorry to disappoint." I reach into my pocket and retrieve two palm-sized grey stones. "I'll explain. Give me your hand." I make sure the coast is clear and then place his on top of mine and mutter the spell I had memorized. The rocks warm to our touch and glow for a brief second until fading completely. "Here." I take a step a little away from him and hold on to the one in my grasp tightly. It lights up again.

"Whoa." Deghan grins from ear to ear. "What the?" He squeezes his, and it does the same thing.

This time it's me who smiles. "Pretty incredible, right?"

"It's like...you're giving me a hug." His eyes grow wide. "This is by far the most amazing thing on the entire planet. You guys have officially made this the best birthday ever." He yanks me into his arms and suffocates me with his appreciation.

"You two get over here," Remi calls out to us from her spot dancing beside Kyra.

We join them and swing our bodies to the rhythm. I even somehow convince Sydney to get involved. I've never really seen him let loose like this before. Maybe he's doing it for the same reasons I am.

"So, are you pissed?" I yell over the music to Kyra.

She smiles, and it lights up her golden eyes. "How could I ever stay mad at this one?" Kyra twirls Remi in a circle and brings her in to dance close. "I knew she was up to something. I'm just glad she didn't hire a clown. Those things freak me out."

Remi laughs and grabs Kyra's arm. "Let's do shots!"

The two of them run to the liquor station that I make sure to avoid. It's enough that people are slopping around their open solo cups, I don't need to go straight to the source. All of my guys have stayed diligent to notice when a drunken idiot was nearby with an overflowing drink. It's like I have my own little group of sexy bodyguards.

Lillian puts her hand around my ear and loud-whispers, "You doing okay?"

I nod and fake a smile. Leave it to my best friend to notice I'm off my game.

"Just checking. You seem...different." She studies my face and finally decides to get me alone. She turns to Ethan. "I'll be right back."

He goes along with it like an obedient puppy.

"What's up?" Genuine concern lines her energy.

I reach out and pump some of my calm into her skin. "Nothing. Well, the usual."

Her magic is a bit resistant at first but then grants me access. It's like it somehow understands I'm no threat to her.

"Are you sure?" She can read right through my bullshit façade.

I'm going to have to give her something or she'll keep prying. "Actually, Abigail came to me. Said they suspect a new *power* source at the school. I think they're onto us about you. I told her it was me, given the whole broken curse thing. We should be good. We need to be careful, though."

She brings her hand to her mouth. "Oh. Yeah. That is something to worry about. Wow. I'm sorry I put you in that position."

I grip her arms. "No, you're fine. Really. We'll get through this together."

The last word out of my mouth nearly sends me spiraling. What will happen to Lillian when I'm long gone? Will Sydney keep protecting her even when I'm not around? He's a good man, I have to put faith in his honor to keep her safe.

Lillian reels me in and puts her arm around me. "Thank you."

I clench my jaw and force away the tears that crave to rain down.

One night. That's all I ask for.

Then my soul will be the Devil's for the taking.

CHAPTER 31

"No, it's totally fine. I'm surprised, that's all." Sydney snatches his keys off his desk and grabs his sweatshirt. "Of course. I'm more than happy to help."

Sydney and I were supposed to spend the day studying in the library and training with Charles. Considering my rush order on getting to Hell prior to Sydney, I changed things up a bit. I've clearly been avoiding confronting my mom about what had happened, and now, with the looming potential eternal damnation, I thought I should make an effort.

I'm not really sure what scares me so much about going home, but something has made me hesitant to follow through. Is it fear? The unknown? The uncertainty of it all? I just haven't been ready. I'm not sure I am right now—I just don't really have any other choice.

I have to at least meet my father and give him a chance to explain the last eighteen years.

We are about to walk down the stairs when someone calls out.

"Willow!" Kyra runs across the upstairs common room area in her tank top and comfy pants. "Those flowers, they're absolutely gorgeous."

"Happy birthday, Ky. I'm glad you like them." I elbow Sydney. "Syd helped me pick them out."

"Whoa, I didn't know you had it in you." She winks at Sydney. "Seriously, I love them. Thank you. Both of you." She wraps her arms around us for a quick group hug and then jogs back the direction she came from.

"Told you." Sydney teases.

"Yeah, yeah. You're the best with gift ideas."

"If only you knew." A not-so-hidden message lingers in his words.

"Mm-hm."

"Do you want me to go inside with you?" Sydney puts his car in park.

I stare at my childhood home's front door and then at Syd. "Please." My eyes well with tears, and I have to dig my fingernail into my thumb to ground myself from losing it all right here.

It's not just saying hello for the first time, it's saying goodbye for the last, too.

Sydney wipes my hair from my face. "I'm ready whenever you are."

We step out, and the sound of the old creaky screen door rattles.

"Willow Victoria..." It's the sweet melody of my mother's voice.

Oh, how I've missed this woman.

The last time I heard my middle name it came from Silas's

mouth. I push that thought away for another time. I don't need another reason to break down.

"Mom." I close the space between us.

Her touch is electric, and that familiar sense of Oliver magic kisses my skin. She holds me for a while and pats my hair and coos into my ear. It's a strange feeling having your parent baby you when you've spent so long caring for them.

Finally, I break away. "This is Sydney."

He extends his hand. "Mrs. Oliver, it's a pleasure to meet you."

"Oh, a guy with manners. I think I like you already." She accepts his offering with a firm shake. "You can call me Anne, no need for the formalities."

"Thank you, ma'am."

"Come on in." She motions for us to step inside. "Your father's in the shower. I have to run him out in a bit, but if you want to stay and wait, you're more than welcome. I could make brunch."

I hadn't anticipated staying *that* long, nor did I expect them to be leaving so soon. I really should have put a little more thought into my farewell tour. I guess I'll take what I can get. I'm barely holding it together as it is; this forced shorter visit is probably a blessing in disguise.

Sydney and I sit side by side on the worn-in couch in the living room. The lemony scent of a burning candle floats around.

"No, it's okay. We're only stopping by. I thought it was a bit overdue." I cross one leg over the other and then swap it for the opposite direction. My nerves are taking control of me. Who would have expected me to be so uneasy about meeting the guy who played a pretty big role in my creation?

Mom nods and glances at the kitchen. "What can I get you to drink? Tea? Water? I think we have some lemonade." Her nervous go-to is to always boil a kettle full of some Earl Grey.

"Whatever you're having," I answer for me and Sydney. I can't imagine he's any thirstier than I am.

"Very well. Tea it is." Her footsteps funnel away and toward the sink.

Without being able to see her, I can imagine her path exactly.

Water runs, and the knob is clicked into place on the stovetop. The kitchen cupboard opens, and glasses clink together.

She pokes her head around the corner. "Do you take sugar?"

Sydney shakes his head. "No, thank you, ma'am."

She goes back to her busy work.

I say quietly to Syd, "This is terrible."

He scoots closer and puts his arm around my shoulder. "You're doing great. I'm proud of you."

A few minutes later, Mom brings a tray full of cups with a small plate of cookies.

"Where were you?" The question falls out of my mouth, and for a second, I don't recognize my own voice.

Mom takes in a deep breath and exhales dramatically. "Well, Willow. That day you came here, to tell me that you had broken the Oliver curse. Never in my wildest dreams would I have thought it was possible." She shakes her head. "I should have never doubted you. You've always been special from the start. Anyway, I had noticed my power coming back, which was the strangest sensation, having been gone for such a long time.

"When you told me, I recognized exactly what it meant. That your father...oh, how I had longed for him. It was the moment I knew I could finally get him back in our lives. I only had to find him. I didn't expect it to happen the way it did. I thought it would be quick, you know? A locator spell, a drive to wherever he was, and then bam. It wasn't that simple; I couldn't do it. I wasn't in control of my magic like I used to be. It was like I had to relearn how to use it all over again." She stirs the cup that sits on the saucer in her hand.

My palms moisten with the anticipation of what happens next in her story.

She continues. "Honey, do you remember Mommy's old friend Jenny?"

The tone of her voice and the use of 'Mommy' comes across more condescending than I think she intends. "Yes, Mother."

"I'm sure you may have gathered this by now, but we aren't the only *different* beings out there. Jenny, she's..."

"A vampire," I answer for her, clicking the pieces of the puzzle together.

She nods. "Yes. After her...death, we kept in contact here and there. I reached out to her to see if she could help me find a more powerful witch to help me with the location of your father. She was more than happy to help. Again, I thought it would be quick. I had no idea there would be forces in place to keep us away. Honestly, I'm not sure what it was or why it happened." She trails off like she's lost in thought, remembering a terrible memory. "The day I found him, it was an emotional reunion. Full of questions and loving embraces and running for our lives. Someone had come for us. They set fire to the house we were staying in. We thought it was a fluke until the next place was ravaged, too. We tried coming home, but there was this invisible barrier we couldn't break through. We stayed in hiding, bouncing around from place to place...we couldn't catch a break."

"Mom, I'm..." I have been so mad at her for abandoning me the way she did, when in reality, she was fighting a war I had no idea about. I went through phases of being concerned and straight-up pissed off at her lack of simply checking in to let us know she was okay.

She smiles weakly. "Each day that passed, I became familiar with my magic again. And eventually, we got through it. One day, it simply stopped. I couldn't sense the wall blocking us anymore, and no one came for us. That's when we rushed back home. Honey, I was worried something happened to you while I was gone. I'm so sorry I left you." Tears build up in her eyes. "I should have told you, and I'm terribly regretful for that. I should have taken you with me. You've been through so much, and I wish I could have been there for you."

In all my life, this is the most I've seen her motherly side.

She's genuinely upset about the role she's played in my abandonment.

The floorboards at the top of the stairs creak, and footsteps pitter-patter their way down.

I blink the moisture away from my eyes and hold my breath as the man I've never known walks down the steps.

Our eyes meet, and I suddenly feel like I'm staring in the mirror. Our eyes are nearly the same shape and color. His cheekbones are a hairier, more rigid version of my own. There's an uncanny resemblance that renders me speechless. He's the same handsome guy my mom told me about briefly when I was little, before it became too difficult for her to talk about.

He pauses at the edge of the room and parts his lips to speak.

I sit, completely spellbound and unsure what to do.

Should I stand? Stay sitting? Do I shake his hand? Hug him? What's the proper protocol for meeting your dad for the first time?

I chose to rise to my feet or, well, my body seemingly does on its own.

He cautiously comes closer. "Willow." His voice is just a whisper.

"Dad." I match his tone.

I'm not sure which one of us makes the first move, but in the next moment, our arms are wrapped around each other and we're both sobbing and laughing and holding on for dear life.

Who knew it would be this easy to love someone you've never met?

A little while passes, and my mom clears her throat. "Do you two want to take a seat? We don't have much longer until we have to leave."

My dad breaks away and holds me at arm's length. "Let me look at you." He studies my tear-streaked face. "I see so much of your mother." He sniffles and does one of those super-sad but incredibly happy smiles. "You have my eyes."

I take the spot next to Sydney on the couch, partially because I need his proximity to hold me together.

Sydney stands and nods at my dad. "Sir, Sydney LeBlanc."

They exchange a manly yet friendly shake.

"You can call me Luke." Dad glances at me. "Thank you for bringing my daughter."

"Of course." Sydney sits back down and reaches out to put his hand on my back, a silent and comforting gesture.

"I'm so sorry I wasn't there to see you grow up. To be the father you should have had in your life." The broken man in front of me sighs heavily. "You deserved much more."

"I don't blame you." My voice cracks. "Could you tell me what happened, though? What made you stay away?"

He shifts uncomfortably. "It wasn't long after your mom got pregnant. Something changed. A strange, invisible force that drove me mad. This rampant voice in my head that made me crazy. If I had to try to put it into words, it was like there was this fire burning inside my mind and the only way to not be consumed by the flames was to leave, to go far away. I didn't want to. I tried to resist it. Oh, how I tried. It got to a point where it was out of my control, I'd wake up in the middle of the night and be miles away, drenched in sweat on the side of the road. There was this uncontrollable thing that made me leave." He stares off into space and then meets my gaze. "I attempted to come back for years and years. I thought if I could get a little stronger, I could overpower whatever influence was stopping me from being with you and your mother. Nothing worked. I thought I'd never see either one of you again." He grabs my mom's hand. "I never once stopped loving you both."

I sit there and process what he's saying. All my life I've juggled the sadness of not being good enough, for thinking he left because he didn't care about us. About me. That I ruined his perfect relationship, and he wanted nothing but to get as far away as possible. That he didn't want me in his life. That I ruined it. I've always had this feeling of not being worthy, that I deserved to be left by the wayside.

Boy was I completely wrong about that.

This whole time, he's been waging an unbeatable battle. One that only I was capable of beating.

Mom glances at her watch. "We're going to be late if we don't get going." She focuses on me. "Your dad has a job interview at the local hardware store. Oh, how I hate to rush this. Are you sure you can't stay?"

I slowly shake my head and frown, glancing at Sydney out of the corner of my eye. "No. We have studying to catch up on. I fell behind with things when I took time off."

"I understand. I'm glad to see you prioritizing your education. With all these new witches, though, I'm curious to see what happens in our side of the world."

I whip my head around to Syd to verify he registered what she'd said. "What do you mean?"

"Oh, you haven't heard?" She stands and takes her pale-yellow sweater from the back of the couch. "There are random reports of unsuspected people finding their power. I swear it's like ever since you broke that final curse, you unleashed countless magical sources all throughout the world. And if I'm not mistaken, they're all tied to the Oliver bloodline."

Which would explain exactly what happened to Lillian.

How many more of them are there? Does that mean we are related? I guess that's something I'll have to put in the hands of someone else since I won't be around long enough to solve that mystery.

My dad's voice breaks my concentration. "Will you at least come back soon? I want to get a head start on making up for all those lost years. It's all I've ever dreamed of."

"Yeah," I lie, knowing damn well I'll probably never see him again. "Maybe next weekend."

A smile of relief washes across his aged face. "That would be wonderful."

It truly would be, but things don't always work out how you want them to. Sometimes you have to take what life hands you and appreciate it even though it's not what you had hoped for. And that's exactly what I'll do. Meeting my dad and hearing his truth was more than I ever could have imagined. It bandaged a long-formed wound I thought would never be remedied. If anything, at least I'll go head-on into the depths of Hell knowing I am loved.

That I am worth fighting for.

CHAPTER 32

The situation with Silas is similar to that of my parents. On both accounts, there are insurmountable hurdles.

With my mom and dad—an invisible force, aka the curse, that kept them from each other, and from me.

With Silas—the endless pit of Hell that stole him from this world.

But this time, I'm on the other side of the conflict, and I won't stop fighting until Silas knows I haven't given up on him. Nothing will stand in the way of making sure he never feels even a trace of what I have felt my entire life.

Self-doubt and insecurities are evil little bugs that can eat away at your confidence and give you trust issues not only with others, but yourself, too. Once you convince your mind that you aren't worthy of someone's love, or even their time, that you repulsed them so much they had to literally run away, you second-guess pretty much everything.

That's probably why I have had such a difficult time accepting the fact that the people in my life actually care about me. I was always waiting for the other shoe to drop and them realize I wasn't deserving. I kind of assumed they would eventually leave me, just like my dad had done, and eventually, what my mom would do, too.

After all the sacrifices I had made to care for her when no one else wanted to deal with her delusions, I couldn't fathom the fact that she wouldn't think twice about abandoning me. It was a difficult pill to swallow, and ultimately, it solidified my original beliefs that I didn't matter. That I never did.

I've spent my entire life battling those mental demons, and to have my own mother reignite them when I was finally starting to find my place in the world was a rude awakening.

But each time my guys proved they were there for me through thick and thin, that wall of doubt was knocked down just a little more. Every sacrifice and kind gesture led to the realization that sometimes things aren't really what you create them to be in your head. People aren't always there for some ulterior motive. In some cases, those around you really do care, unconditionally, without wanting a damn thing in return other than your own happiness.

That alone is why I will stop at nothing to make sure they understand I want that same exact thing. Them to be happy, to be safe, to know someone would do anything for them.

And when I tell Sydney I need some time to myself, it's not completely a lie.

"Are you sure?" His concern lines his lovely face.

I shut the book I was studying and push it alongside the others. "Yeah. The whole dad thing wore me out. I think I just want to call it a day."

"That's understandable. Is there anything I can do for you?" Sydney comes over and takes my bag from the back of my chair.

"No, I appreciate it, though."

"Let me at least walk you to your room." Sydney's energy is all over the place.

If I had to pin it down, I'd say he's feeling helplessness.

Here's to hoping I can make it through another five minutes without breaking down and telling him my plan, that I'll be taking the biggest risk of my life to save Silas.

But I know I can't speak the truth. Because if I did, Sydney would sacrifice himself, and I won't allow that to happen.

The walk to my dorm is quiet, filled with anxious sadness. I keep my arms crossed over my chest so Sydney can't hold my hand and enter my mind space. I'm far too vulnerable to grant him that kind of access.

We stop in front of my door, and he hands me my backpack.

"Syd." I meet his glorious green gaze for what might be the last time. "I might not say it very often, but...you're a wonderful man. Truly. Everything you've done for me; it hasn't gone unnoticed."

He goes to speak, and I place my index finger over his lips to shush him.

"I'll never be able to thank you enough." I let out a breath. "I hope you know how sorry I am for ever doubting you. Please understand that wasn't because of you, it was my own insecurities that made me think I couldn't trust you. You've done nothing but prove yourself, and I failed you time and time again. For that, I'll forever be in your debt."

I move my hand to his cheek and absorb his warmth. I run my thumb along his stubble and take in every freckle and imperfection.

He moves closer to me, until he's a breath away. "Why does this feel like goodbye?"

Because it is.

"I'll see you tomorrow." I spit out the words, knowing damn

well that tomorrow never comes. Maybe in another life, we'll be together again. But in this one, I have to save Silas.

Sydney lowers his face and trails his nose against mine. He lays the gentlest kiss along my lips and mutters, "I love you."

I close my eyes, and one rogue tear rolls down. "I love you."

My bedroom door latches shut behind me, and I slump to the floor. I allow myself this brief moment to weep before I regain my composure and follow through with my dodgy plan.

Silas's life for mine, that seems like a fair enough bargain.

Here's to hoping I choose the right Hell, otherwise, we're all royally fucked.

I tiptoe down the supernatural girls' dorm hallway and along the stairwell. I concentrate hard on not being noticed by anyone, so hard that when I glance down, I can't see my arm.

I'm fucking invisible.

My magic continues to surprise me with each insane thing it brings into fruition. Is it possible that *anything* I think will come true?

I pause, straining my mind to Silas, begging my powers to bring him back to me.

"Please, please, please," I mutter.

This would be *much* easier than traveling to the underworld.

Nothing happens. Of course, my powers lean more toward curling my hair and concealing me from prying eyes than rescuing a man I love.

I guess there are limits to what I can do, and bringing someone out of Hell definitely supersedes those abilities.

I quietly stroll through the foyer, stealing a peek at the beautiful garden one last time. I side-step an oncoming group of students and slip out of the front door right behind a tall blond-haired boy.

A piece of gravel crunches under my shoe, and the guy stops abruptly.

I go still, barely a few inches from his body. I hold my breath and wait for him to be done with his inspection of the area.

He shakes his head and takes off toward the parking lot.

I turn left and head around to the side of the school and into the forest, totally relieved that I somehow made myself unseen. That definitely made it easier to sneak out without any of my friends noticing.

It won't be long until I'm gone for good.

I become completely covered by the ever-changing trees and then think myself visible. Don't get me wrong, it was super helpful, it's also just super creepy not to be able to see your body.

I breathe in the cool night air and let it soak into my lungs. I can't imagine I'll get another taste of oxygen quite like this where I'm going.

Without allowing much more time for thinking, I pick up my pace and jog the rest of the way to the sacred witch building outside Harper Academy. There's no sense in prolonging the inevitable or risking someone figuring out I'm missing. I left a note for Sydney, and I'm hoping by the time he finds it, I'm already in another dimension. I can't risk him coming after me, so I have to act fast.

Once I'm tucked inside the old dusty building, I take a box of matches around the room and light candles of various sizes. Tall and skinny, short, stubby, and partially melted. I burn a bundle of sage and waft it around, cracking the window open like Sydney had done.

I find the few stones I need and wrap a long piece of leather around my biceps to secure them in place. It seems silly, but I could use any extra protection possible at this point if I don't want to be murdered on the spot.

I snatch the herbs and flowers necessary for the spell and sprinkle them into a neat pile where Sydney and I had drawn our outlines in chalk not too long ago. I dust away any remnants of our time here and seize the chalk to create a new design.

First, a large circle around myself and the ingredients. In one open area, I create a Leviathan cross, followed by another ring with three equally spaced loops along its body. The last symbol needed is the most detailed, with its gear-like intricacies and complex design.

I toss the white chunk across the floor and kneel in the remaining open area within the confines of my art. I take one last breath and come to terms with what I'm about to do.

"Oh braki nye wo runda...oh fallum unghur saintea prima brota makler vartal." The words roll off my tongue in a strangely familiar way. They share a striking resemblance to the ones I spoke when I had lost Silas. I clear my mind and let them flow through me, channeling my power forward and into the small space.

I allow my hands to naturally whisk the air and create a funnel of vibrantly pink magic.

An iron taste appears on my tongue, and a trickle rolls down my lip.

My nose is bleeding.

A deafening sound fills the room, making it hard to concentrate. My head pounds, and my eyes close from the brightness that consumes the void.

The door rattles with loud thuds that add to the chaos.

"Willow, please," Sydney screams from the outside.

I panic, doing everything I can to stay focused and on task.

I will not fuck this up. I cannot ruin my one chance.

I grit my teeth and concentrate. I desperately picture the place I need to go to.

Sydney blasts through the entry and sends the wooden thing flying.

The relief on his face tells me he thinks he's in time. But it doesn't matter, he's too late.

My body detaches from our plane and fades into nothing.

Sydney's expression shifting into panic is the last thing I see before everything goes black.

And like someone flipped on the lights, I'm blinded by the achingly recognizable flames that flicker up all sides of my newest reality.

I'm no longer in Harper County...

I'm in Hell.

I swallow down the fear that threatens to empty the contents of my stomach.

Fire all around. Bright glowing red and orange and yellow with tones of blue and black and even green. A thick smog fills the air. It's difficult to breathe through. A cough flits out of my mouth, and I clamp my hand over to suppress the sound. Sweat beads up and rolls down my forehead.

There is faint crying in the distance. Howling somewhere deep within. A laugh.

Someone is being tortured, and someone else seems to be enjoying it.

I get acquainted with the very real version of my nightmare that I've stepped into.

Gloomy pathways lead all over to the unknown.

I close my eyes and test my magic, confirming whether or not it's still intact. This is definitely not the ideal place to be without it.

A gentle light flickers inside my chest and reassures me I'm not totally alone.

I recall those endless dreams and my attempts to find Silas. Is that what I'm supposed to do now? Was my subconscious preparing me for what was to come?

Silas, where could you be?

My heart flutters. That memorable tether pulling the string to my soul.

He's here.

I take a few cautious steps, curious if my shoes will hold up in this inferno. Somehow, despite the intense heat, they do.

Shoes and magic, that's all I need to find Silas, right?

A creature that resembles a rat scurries out from the path I'm taking. It stops and locks its sights on me, hissing and spewing some tar-like sludge from its mouth.

I narrow my burning eyes at it, and it squeals and runs away before I get the chance to exterminate it.

Guess this Hell thing isn't so bad after all.

A shadow looms overhead.

My stomach turns, and my panic alarm seems to sound in my mind.

A dragon-shaped thing with massive wings and thick scales stands just a rock-throw away. It has long fangs protruding from its jaw, and sharp horns sticking out of its body. The same as the one from my training session with Charles.

Without putting too much effort into it, I create a sharp dagger that appears in my right hand. I grin, the satisfaction of such an easy target in front of me.

I quickly sprint around to the backside of the beast and throw rapid bursts of power at its hind in an attempt to get it to reveal its weakness. I run to its front and gasp in horror at the missing red spot.

It should be right here, a glowing ruby of defeat. But there's nothing other than more of the impenetrable covering coating the gigantic demon.

How could I have been so foolish to assume I knew what I was doing?

Another scream for help and a moan of agony. A whimper.

One too fucking close to the sound of someone I love.

I can't leave, the thing has blocked me into a corner with no clear shot of an exit. I do the only thing I can, I improvise.

I dash around the space, throwing balls of pink energy at the creature and checking to locate the weakness. I dodge the foggy acid that leaks from its mouth each time...until I don't. One tiny drop lands on my shoulder and singes my skin, melting down through the layers of flesh. I bite my lip to suppress the scream of pain.

Fuck, that hurts way worse in real life than it does in the simulation.

I grip at my arm and cower, trying to regain my composure. That's when I see it.

The small blip coming from between the creature's gangly toes.

I calm my breath and bring the handle of the blade up to my line of sight. I glance up to the beast and then at its foot, hoping it has no clue what I'm about to do.

With all of my might, I release the dagger, completing annihilating the demon with the flick of my wrist.

I take off in the direction of the sound, completely unsure of where I'm going but only having one thing on my mind.

I have to get to him.

Another cry whips me around the other way. The one opposite me. It's like the time all of those Silases kept spawning in the forest and I wasn't sure which was the real him. In reality, none of them were. Is this that same trick?

"Willow," his voice weakly calls out.

I run through flickering flames that nip at my arms. Hot and sharp pain flows through me. I grit my teeth and fight my way through the madness to find him.

A silhouette in the distance appears, only for it to vanish once I'm near.

"Silas," I answer. "Where are you?"

Coughing. "Willow, please. Don't."

I disobey and go straight to the sound of him.

He calls out from the opposite side.

I stop and focus. One of these *has* to be him. I just have to choose the right one.

A comforting sensation floats over my body like a hug. It takes me a second to realize, that's exactly what it is.

Deghan must be holding on to his stone.

I dig into my pocket and return the gesture. If I can't be *with* him, at least I can still bring him some level of peace.

I shove it in for safekeeping and use the newfound calm to locate the person I came here for.

A Silas sounds to my left, to my right. One in front and one behind.

Concentrate, Willow. Which one is him?

I smile, finally figuring it out.

It wasn't the sound of his voice I needed to determine, it was his soul. I let the wandering bits of mine float away until they settle onto his. Not a single Silas presented is the correct one.

I rush toward the silence and jump through the thick flames. They send a newfound ripple of pain across my skin but hold no candle to the sensation that consumes me upon landing my sights on Silas Jace Harlow.

It's equal parts heartbreaking and utter reprieve.

"Silas." I drop to my knees in front of him, rigidly sliding across the hot embers. I cup his frail face between my hands and examine his fragile state.

His skin is pale, much more than his typical vampire color. A shade of grey perhaps. His once effortlessly chiseled cheeks are sunken in. His silver eyes are red, and some of the blood vessels have burst around the purple.

"Willow," Silas's voice cracks.

I refuse to cry. Not here. Not when he needs me.

I reach a finger into his mouth to feel around for his fangs. I raise my wrist to his lips and press my flesh until it breaks. The blood trickles into his mouth, and his eyes close in response.

They were starving him. And for how long?

A low chuckle and slow clap floats in from behind me. "Oh, what a sweet reunion. I couldn't have imagined it better myself."

I continue to feed Silas but glance over my shoulder.

A strikingly handsome man stands to my rear. He appears a bit like Mammon, only older and more sophisticated. Dark hair like midnight and completely black eyes—no whites at all. A wicked smile lines his face. "You must be Willow."

I hold Silas's head while he drinks from my arm, regaining only a little of his color with each passing moment.

"Balial, I want to make a deal," I say the words confidently.

Silas peers through his thick lashes and furrows his brow. "What are you doing?" It's like he finally woke up from his stupor.

Another snicker. "She knows my name." He clutches his hand to his chest dramatically. "A deal...with the Devil himself? Oh, this ought to be interesting. Do tell." He seems to be growing annoyed.

I press my lips on Silas's forehead and whisper to him, "Silas, everything is going to be okay."

"No," is all he manages to get out.

I stand up and face the master of Hell.

He's taller than I imagined, coming in at probably seven-foot something. His shoulders are wide, strong, but not too bulky. These Princes of Darkness sure are attractive. The fire reflects in his eyes, reminding me of how badly I want to get Silas out of here.

"His life for mine. Even trade. Let him go, and you can have me." I meet his gaze, not daring to look away.

Silas sputters and reaches out for my ankle.

Balial blocks his contact and, with the slightest movement of his head, throws Silas onto the floor writhing in pain.

Anger from out of this world bubbles up inside me like nothing I've felt. I throw both of my hands at Balial and scream at the top of my lungs.

His eyes broaden, and he flicks his finger, creating an unseen shield that sends my magic pouring out in heaps around his completely unharmed body. He grins triumphantly. "No."

Well, my plan definitely backfired.

I expect to at least make a little scratch with throwing all of my magic at him or maybe intrigue him enough to consider my proposal. Instead, he turns me down and brushes off my bountiful energy like it's a pesky fly that won't leave him alone.

"To be fair, I applaud your efforts. I was curious how long it would take you to show up. I sort of anticipated it, really. But, unfortunately, your life means essentially nothing to me. I couldn't care less whether you live or die." Balial points to Silas, who is now trembling from the aftershock of his torment.

"Don't hurt him, please. Torture me if that's what you want." I block his path to Silas.

"I have something else in mind. Perhaps a better bargain, really." Balial winks in such a condescending manner.

"What do you want?" I spit out.

He pauses for dramatic effect. "A sacrifice."

"I don't understand. I have nothing to offer you." I peek behind me and toss Silas a ball of protective energy. Maybe it will help prevent Balial from his next pointless attack.

"Oh, Willow. Don't be so dumb, it really is quite boring. You know exactly what I have in mind."

What could I have that Balial could possibly want, other than my life or Silas's?

Balial locks his onyx gaze onto mine and steps forward. He

leans in right next to my face. His smoky scent is overpowering. He whispers into my ear precisely what he desires.

My eyes widen, and I freeze in place.

"Do think about it. You wouldn't want to waste any more of that poor sap's life away here, now would you?"

I process what he offers and consider the alternatives. "And if I refuse?"

Balial blinks, and Silas convulses.

My protection is nothing compared to what Balial is capable of.

"Okay!" I yell and throw out my arms in surrender. "I'll do it. Just please, stop hurting him."

"Willow, no," Silas whimpers. "You don't know what you're doing..." He coughs and drags himself to his knees.

I can't continue watching him like this for another second.

"Do you give me your word? You'll let him go?" I take a step toward the cruel master.

A wide grin settles on his face "Yes. I'd say that's a fair trade."

"Fine. I agree to your terms." I turn to Silas and lower myself to his level. I cup his face in my hands. "You're going home."

A single tear rolls down his dirty cheek. "No. Not without you."

That's when it happens, Silas vanishes before my eyes.

And I'm left here, alone with the Devil in Hell.

Join Willow in the fifth and final installment of the Harper Shadow Academy, Sacred Magic.

Acknowledgments

Ancient Magic was a wild adventure that I am so thrilled to have had the pleasure to create. These characters have completely taken over and are leading us all on an epic journey! This book did NOT want to end and if it weren't for strict deadlines, I'm not so sure it would have.

A few people that I have to give major thanks to: my tiny human, my parents, Victoria, Kelsey, Kate.

Those of you over on Patreon who support my author journey: Clayton, Dustin, James, Victoria, and Tyler Bunn.

My editor, Emmy, and my cover design team, Mibl Art. (This is probably my favorite cover so far.)

And always, to my enthusiastic readers. I'm sorry I left you hanging with the ending of Wicked Magic. Hopefully you hate me a little less with this one.

Also by Luna Pierce

The Harper Shadow Academy Series
(Paranormal academy reverse harem)

Hidden Magic

Cursed Magic

Wicked Magic

Ancient Magic

Sacred Magic

Harper Shadow Academy: Complete Box Set

Falling for the Enemy Series
(Paranormal reverse harem)

Stolen by Monsters

Fighting for Monsters

Fated to Monsters

Sinners and Angels Universe

Broken Like You (Standalone)

Untamed Vixen (Part One)

Villain Era (Part Two)

Wings of a Devil (Standalone novella)

Ruin My Life (Standalone)

London & Archer's Story (Standalone)

About the Author

Luna Pierce is a paranormal and contemporary romance author who loves getting lost in her stories. She brings you tough characters that love fiercely and fight for what's right. Luna loves all things gritty, and even supernatural, especially: witches, vampires, and werewolves.

Join Luna's newsletter to receive updates at:
 www.lunapierce.com/subscribe

If you enjoy my books, please consider leaving a review on Amazon, Goodreads, or Bookbub.

Want to chat about the book and tell me the things you liked and disliked about **Ancient Magic**? I'd love to hear from you!

Join the exclusive reader group — Luna Pierce's Gritty Romance Squad